Grace opened the door and two men walked in, the big galoot from last week and a wormy little guy. She let the phone hang at her side.

"I remember you. What can I do for you?"

"You can die," the little guy said, and struck her with a lead pipe one, two, three times. Grace screamed but couldn't fight back. "Mom! Mom!" Roberta yelled into the phone.

A thousand miles away, she frantically called the emergency number for the Oregon coast. The dispatcher alerted the state police and the rescue squad.

Her brother, Robbie, working that night as an emergency medical tech, responded to the dispatcher's call. He had to be restrained by his colleague from entering the house.

When they finally let him in, he was surprised to see his father there smoking a cigarette, something his mother would never let him do in the house. His mother was covered with a sheet, and the entrance foyer was splashed with her blood.

The rabbi said nothing.

Berkley Prime Crime titles by Alan Gold

TRUE CRIME
TRUE FAITH

TRUE FAITH

ALAN GOLD

BERKLEY PRIME CRIME, NEW YORK

THE BERKLEY PUBLISHING GROUP
Published by the Penguin Group
Penguin Group (USA) Inc.
375 Hudson Street, New York, New York 10014, USA
Penguin Group (Canada), 90 Eglinton Avenue East, Suite 700, Toronto, Ontario M4P 2Y3, Canada
(a division of Pearson Penguin Canada Inc.)
Penguin Books Ltd., 80 Strand, London WC2R 0RL, England
Penguin Group Ireland, 25 St. Stephen's Green, Dublin 2, Ireland (a division of Penguin Books Ltd.)
Penguin Group (Australia), 250 Camberwell Road, Camberwell, Victoria 3124, Australia
(a division of Pearson Australia Group Pty. Ltd.)
Penguin Books India Pvt. Ltd., 11 Community Centre, Panchsheel Park, New Delhi—110 017, India
Penguin Group (NZ), Cnr. Airborne and Rosedale Roads, Albany, Auckland 1310, New Zealand
(a division of Pearson New Zealand Ltd.)
Penguin Books (South Africa) (Pty.) Ltd., 24 Sturdee Avenue, Rosebank, Johannesburg 2196, South Africa

Penguin Books Ltd., Registered Offices: 80 Strand, London WC2R 0RL, England

This is a work of fiction. Names, characters, places, and incidents either are the product of the author's
imagination or are used fictitiously, and any resemblance to actual persons, living or dead, business es-
tablishments, events, or locales is entirely coincidental. The publisher does not have any control over
and does not assume any responsibility for author or third-party websites or their content.

TRUE FAITH

A Berkley Prime Crime Book / published by arrangement with the author

PRINTING HISTORY
Berkley Prime Crime mass-market edition / January 2007

Copyright © 2007 by The Berkley Publishing Group.
Cover art by Mark Tochette.
Cover design by Annette Fiore.
Interior text design by Stacy Irwin.

ISBN: 978-0-425-20856-4

BERKLEY® PRIME CRIME
Berkley Prime Crime Books are published by The Berkley Publishing Group,
a division of Penguin Group (USA) Inc.,
375 Hudson Street, New York, New York 10014.
The name BERKLEY PRIME CRIME and the BERKLEY PRIME CRIME design are trademarks be-
longing to Penguin Group (USA) Inc.

PRINTED IN THE UNITED STATES OF AMERICA

10 9 8 7 6 5 4 3 2 1

The Crime

The rain slashed the roads and struck the minivan's windows like handfuls of gravel. The underlit roads on the Oregon coast were never so dangerous as in the dark, wet, and windy winters. Streetlights were widely spaced when they were there at all.

This was a worse storm than usual, with steady winds above thirty-five miles an hour and gusts over sixty-five. Any time the wind gusted, the rain did not fall, it blew sideways. A few seconds out in this would soak someone.

The rabbi's wife was living dangerously, driving while talking on the phone and squinting to follow the cat's eyes in the pavement that were her only clue where the road led her. Trees came up to the shoulder on both sides of the road, and the west side of the road offered a drop to the beach or into the ocean many yards below.

The rabbi's wife was always amazed at how unfamiliar these roads became in heavy weather. Sighing with relief, she spotted the roadside mailbox encrusted with reflectors that announced her home and pulled the minivan into her driveway, trying to organize her various tasks.

"Roberta," she spoke into her cell phone, "let me call you back. I just got to the house and I have too much *chazerai* to deal with just to get in the door. And it's raining."

"So, what else is new?" her daughter asked. "Okay, call me back."

Grace Geller looked around at the proliferation of packages and bags, as well as an attaché case. She shrugged, and just loaded herself up. Taking a deep breath, she threw open the van door and jumped out, kicking it closed behind her. She ran to the house and opened the front door with a clumsy lunge at the key-hole.

Once inside, she locked the van with the remote, locked the house, and dumped her burdens on the nearest couch, sitting beside them. She sighed.

"Roberta," she thought out loud, and reached for her cell. "Hi, honey. I'm inside, and too pooped to pop."

Roberta laughed. Her mother had been using that silly phrase for as long as she could recall. "What's all the to-do?"

"Well, today's the day I collect the receipts from the bakery, I had to shop for dinner, and I had to stop at the hospital to do my weekly *mitzvah*."

"Where's Robbie?"

"He's working tonight."

"And Daddy?"

"I don't know," she sighed. "Something at the *shul*. He's usually home on Thursdays."

There was a knock at the door.

"I wonder who the hell that can be. Someone's at the door."

The rabbi's wife dragged herself up off the couch, still holding the phone to her ear.

"It's the bathroom guy," she said.

"What?" asked Roberta.

"That guy from last week who needed to use the bathroom. He's got someone with him."

"Be careful, Ma."

"I gotta let him in. It's miserable out there."

She opened the door and two men walked in, the big galoot from last week and a wormy little guy. Grace let the phone hang at her side.

"I remember you. What can I do for you?"

"You can die," the little guy said, and struck her with a lead pipe one, two, three times. Grace screamed but couldn't fight back. "Mom! Mom!" Roberta yelled into the phone.

The big guy smashed the phone with his heel. He turned to his friend. "Gimme that pipe. She's still alive."

He delivered a final two blows. Blood was everywhere. "Don't forget the purse."

The little guy went over to the couch and took a wallet from it.

"Let's get outta here."

* * *

A thousand miles away, Roberta frantically called the emergency number for the Oregon coast. The dispatcher alerted the state police and the rescue squad.

Her brother Robbie, working that night as an emergency medical tech, responded to the dispatcher's call. He had to be restrained by his colleagues from entering the house.

When they finally let him in, he was surprised to see his father there smoking a cigarette, something his mother would never let him do in the house. His mother was covered with a sheet, and the entrance foyer was splashed with her blood.

The rabbi said nothing.

1. Daddy's Little Girl

On Portland's east side, Lou Tedesco climbed the stairs to the offices of the *Oregon Weekly* with a spring in his step and a knot in his belly. He was greeted by his favorite pixie.

"Hi, Louie Louie," Patti chirped. "Your new knee is workin' great!"

"Yeah, thanks. I wish I'd done it years ago. Is Blanche in?"

"She came in about six this morning. She's only come out for coffee and to go to the ladies'. I heard Hilda is coming in from Seagirt."

Lou took off his baseball cap and shucked off his raincoat. "Yup. We are discussing the future direction of the paper, among other things."

Patti's eyes got big. "We're not gonna lose our jobs, are we?"

"No worries. We may be expanding, if anything.

Maybe an eastern edition. Wanna move to John Day or Umatilla?"

Patti hugged her shoulders. "No way. Too cold in the winter and too hot in the summer. I don't mind the rain here, and the summers are beautiful."

"I agree. Well, I'm going into my office to prepare for the meeting. Later."

Lou was still amazed by his new office furniture. The paper had come a long way in just a couple years, and much of the increased revenue had been plowed back into the offices. The paper now owned the loft building it was in. The whole office sported a paint job, carpeting, new phone system, and the latest computers and software. Real bathrooms and a real kitchen, too. Lou was still the unofficial coffee maker, as he was the first in most mornings.

He was getting paid more, his relationship with Hilda was odd but flourishing, and he had become a respected investigative reporter.

So he wondered why he was unhappy.

Hilda walked in through his open door, shaking rain from her newly cut hair and kvetching a mile a minute. The bottom ten inches of her jeans were soaked. Her eyes were wild and unfocused.

"We can send a damn robot to Mars, but we can't control traffic!"

"Good morning to you, too, Hilda. Nice haircut."

Hilda stopped and took a breath. "Sorry, babe. Good morning. I was just PO'ed that it took me longer to get the last fifteen miles than the first seventy-five. Damn!"

"Whoa, Nellie. Want some coffee?"

Hilda sat down in Lou's guest chair. "Yeah. No sugar, lots of milk or cream."

Lou stood up. "No sugar? New hairdo, new coffee order. Do I sense some sea change here?"

"Well, I have good reasons for both decisions, but I may be having an identity crisis."

Lou put on a sympathetic face. "I hate when that happens. With me, one day I wake up and realize that my self-image no longer jibes with my actual persona. Then I put off dealing with it until I can't stand the sight of myself in the mirror."

"Sounds about right. The hair, I just got tired of having wet hair for three hours after a shower. It dries much quicker now. The coffee, it's a general decline in my taste for sweets."

"Yikes! Does that mean I won't be able to go the easy route and buy you chocolates from now on?"

Hilda leaned forward. "Chocolate is not 'sweets.' It is a vitamin essential to existence."

"Check. I'll get the coffee."

Lou and Hilda made small talk for about a half hour before Blanche stuck her nose in the door. She was dressed in classic Blanche style: a lime-green vinyl minidress, pink fishnet stockings, white go-go boots, and hair dyed to match the stockings. She wore cat's-eye glasses, frames in a checkerboard pattern.

"Hello, you two. Cute haircut, Hilda."

Hilda took her in. "Blanche, I have no idea where to even look for clothes like that, although I hasten to assure you that I wore similar outfits . . . can it be thirty-five years ago?"

Hilda shuddered.

"Ah, well," Blanche shrugged, "if I had an actual social life I wouldn't have the time to shop like I do. Let's go to my office. If you need to pee or get coffee, do it now. I've arranged for lunch to be sent up, takeout from Fujin."

Roberta Mendelson sat in her silver SUV across from the *Oregon Weekly* offices. Am I an idiot? she asked herself. Is this necessary, or even helpful?

She opened the manila folder of press clippings going back four years. All stories by Lou Tedesco. All investigative pieces, many of which led to reopening cases, legal action against corrupt officials, or the downfall of the once mighty.

Roberta steeled herself and went into action.

"Hi," she said to Gillian the receptionist. "May I see Lou Tedesco?"

"Do you have an appointment?"

"Uh, no. Do I . . ." She shifted her feet.

"Oh, no, normally it's no problem. It's just that Lou is in a meeting. If he made an appointment and forgot about it . . ."

"No, no. Maybe I'll come back."

"Don't go yet. Have a seat. Maybe he'll want to speak with you. What's your name?"

"He won't know my name. Tell him that I'm Rabbi Geller's daughter."

Gillian gaped. "You're Roberta Geller?"

"Yes, only I'm married now. Mendelson."

"Sit down, I'll be right back."

They had been in deep discussion for two hours, the first of which was taken up with Blanche's vision for the paper. Upgrade Hilda's office in Seagirt, consider publishing twice-weekly, determine the feasibility of an eastern Oregon edition, and then, perhaps, a foray into southern Oregon.

Since there was little or no disagreement with the plans, it was smooth sailing.

Then Lou spoke up.

"Okay, I have something I'd like you to think about." Both women's antennae swung around. Lou never suggested anything.

"I've been doing investigative reporting for, what? Four years, now?" Blanche began to speak. Lou interrupted. "No, let me finish.

"Before that case in Seagirt, I was a food, movie, and music reviewer. I wouldn't even characterize it as 'criticism.' It wasn't that deep or thoughtful. I ate, I went to concerts, I saw movies. I was really happy. Now, I am, more often than not, involved with murder, sleazy politicians, and malfeasance of one kind or another. I get phone calls from whistle-blowers with unsolicited information, tough guys with threats, and outraged citizens who have somehow obtained my private number. None of these people seems to have a clock or a bedtime. They call me at 3 a.m. I might as well be selling methamphetamine."

Lou stopped for breath, and Blanche jumped in.

"Wait, Louie. Where is this going? Have you forgotten that your reporting put this paper on the map? That Hilda's little weekly was read for maybe a five-mile radius outside Seagirt, and now the whole coast gets covered? That she's hired four . . ."

"Five, now," Hilda interjected.

". . . five reporters, and other staff? That you've had pieces in the Sunday *Times Magazine*, and been interviewed on NPR and the *Today* show? Lou, you are a star! Your work is respected, your word is enough to get the DA's office off its can to look into a story. What do you want?"

Lou sat up straight and looked Blanche in the eye. "I want to be as happy as I was before this all started. I'm glad for you and the paper. I'm thrilled just to have met Hilda, to be in a relationship with her, much less to have helped her achieve her success. I'm humble and proud to have been published in the *New York Times*, between the recipes and the crossword puzzle . . ."

"Tough puzzle that day, too," Hilda said.

Lou smiled. Hilda knew just how to deflate his phony humility. "Okay, I know how this must sound. I'm not ungrateful, I'm just burnt-out, and a mope. This is the second stint I've done as an investigative reporter, and it took a lot out of me the first time, too. That's why I signed on here as a foodie."

Blanche wheeled the big guns around. "So, what you're telling me is that ten, twelve years ago, you were freshly widowed, a recovering drunk, and a mental basket case, and you have no greater internal resources now than you had then? You're no stronger as a person than you were then? This despite the support of two women who love and care for you?"

Lou's eyes narrowed. "Not fair, Blanche. I know you care about me, and that we were all each other had for years. I'd walk through hell in a gasoline suit for you. But how much of this is just panic that your recent success rests on my shoulders, that if I go back to movies and food that all this will come apart? I feel like Dumbo's feather. You don't really need me, you just think you do, and you want me to feel bad about my own needs."

It went quiet for a moment. Hilda looked at Blanche. "Guilt's in your court."

Before Blanche could respond, there was a soft knock on the door. Gillian stuck her head in.

"Sorry. Hi. Uh, Lou? Someone here to see you."

"Tell him to come back."

"Her, and I think you should see her."

"Gill, I don't think I can handle some city hall whistle-blower right now. We're in the middle of something."

"It's Roberta Geller. If I send her away, I don't think she'll come back."

Lou looked puzzled. "Who the hell is Roberta Geller?"

Blanche made an exasperated noise. "Where have you been living, under a rock? She's Rabbi Geller's daughter. See her."

"No, Blanche, not under a rock. I've been living in

the bubble you put me in. Is that the guy who was charged with killing his wife?"

"Yes, and there was just a mistrial declared." Blanche looked up at Gillian. "Offer her a cup of coffee or a soda, and tell her that Lou will be right there."

Gillian shut the door, and Lou gave Blanche a dirty look.

"Don't look at me that way, Lou. This could be important. I'll tell you what—if this pans out into a story, I'll put you back on the food and art-house circuit. Just do this one last one."

Lou appealed to Hilda with his eyes. She shook her head.

"Sorry, Lou. I think you might need to do this. Geller's is the only synagogue for miles out on the coast, and it was big news. Plus, it'll get you out to my neck of the woods for a while.

"Do it."

Lou made a gesture of helplessness. "Okay," he sighed, "I give up. I'm outnumbered, outgunned . . ."

"And out the door. Hilda and I will finish up, here. Thanks, Lou."

Lou walked past the reception desk. "She's in your office," Gillian said in a stage whisper.

Roberta stood up when Lou came in. "No, please sit," he said.

He looked her over for a moment. She was dark and petite, dressed with perfect taste in a navy pinstriped, tailored suit and blue silk shirt. Her hair was stylishly and carefully mussed and moussed. Her eyes were luminous and sorrowful. Lou thought of Edith Piaf.

As she sat, she seemed to withdraw into herself, as though in self-protection.

"What can I do for you, Ms. . . ."

"Roberta, please call me Roberta. I want you to look into my mother's murder."

"I hear that your father's trial was declared a mistrial. He'll probably not be retried. I don't know . . ."

"You don't understand. I think my father's guilty, I think he had my mother killed. I want you to make sure he gets what he deserves."

"Ms. . . . uh, Roberta, I'm reluctant to get involved here for a couple of reasons. First, it's really a police or a prosecutorial matter. If you have any information they can use, I'm sure Tom Knight would be glad to hear it. Plus"—Lou took a deep breath—"in family matters like this, things are seldom what they seem on the surface, buried issues tend to drive people's motivations . . ."

"Mr. Tedesco, I was on the phone with my mother when she was killed. I heard the men who were arrested for the crime beat her to death. My brother, who was working as an emergency medical technician at the time, responded to the call. My father was already there, and Robbie said that he was as cool as a cucumber."

Lou shrugged. "I don't know. People react to tragedy . . ."

"Mr. Tedesco, my parents' marriage was not an ideal one. There was some hint of divorce. My mother talked to me about it. I can't help feeling that her murder was entirely too convenient for him."

"Call me Lou. That's a remarkable comment about your father."

"My father's name is Robert Geller. I'm Roberta, and my brother is Robert, Jr., Robbie. I don't know if you know this, but eastern European Jews seldom name their children after themselves. Traditionally, children are named after a deceased relative. It's not a religious requirement or anything, just an old and well-established custom.

"Not only was I named after him, so was my kid brother. I love my father, but he's egocentric, vain, and selfish. And, I think he may be a killer."

Lou noticed that the sad, defeated look was gone. Roberta's eyes flashed determination. He decided to buy time.

"Roberta, let me think about this. I'm more sympathetic to your story now. But, I have to clear it with my editor." He looked her in the eyes. "If you go this route, you understand that I will be prying into everything, and publishing what I find. Can you handle that?"

"Lou, our lives have been turned over in the press for years. Did you know that it took four years for the case to come to trial? Four years of embarrassing revelations about our private affairs, and pointless recaps when nothing new came out for a while."

She reached into her large purse and withdrew a manila folder. "This is a file of your stories. I spent a few days in the public library looking them up and printing out the ones that impressed me the most. The thing about them is that you go out of your way to be fair, and you don't let details escape you. More often than not, you find something that helps exonerate the innocent. That's fine. I would like nothing more than to find out that my father, despite his failings, is innocent. I just don't think so."

Lou swam in familiar ambivalent feelings. These feelings had been his state of mind for four years. It didn't seem destined to end anytime soon.

"Okay, I'll get back to you by tomorrow."

Lou took her phone and e-mail addresses. It was a Portland number. He escorted her out under the gaze of Gillian and several other staffers who had contrived to be at the front desk. Patti smiled at him, firm in believing that Sir Galahad was off to the rescue one more time.

"Well?" Blanche asked as Lou returned to her office. Lou filled the women in.

"What do you think?" asked Hilda.

"She makes a pretty compelling case for our help. I don't know if we can live up to her expectations." Lou rubbed his chin.

"It sounds like she has a fairly solid grip on things, that we may come up with nothing, or that we get her father off the hook," Blanche said. "I say we go for it."

"You get to work with your old pal Tom Knight again," Hilda said, with exaggerated enthusiasm.

"Tom's okay. He doesn't automatically discount

your efforts because you're outside the law enforcement community."

"Yeah," said Blanche, "but he got that way from working with you. You've made him look good before."

"So," Lou said with resignation, "I guess it's a go."

"Will you be coming back to Seagirt with me?" Hilda asked.

"Let me check with the local paper's back issues first. Then, I'll talk to the *Weekly* reporter who covered the trial."

"That would be me." Hilda pointed to herself. "You never read those articles?"

"Sorry. I guess I was otherwise occupied."

"Hmph. Lucky for you I like you."

Roberta Mendelson got into her car and started it. She smiled to herself while the engine warmed up. When she drove away, she didn't notice the car parked a block away as it pulled away from the curb and followed her at a discreet distance.

2. Mr. Biggs

Lou climbed the front steps of the Central Library, the first time he could do it without pain thanks to his bionic knee. He smiled to himself.

Passing up the Starbucks on the first floor, he made for the elevator. The enormous marble interior staircase looked intimidating and he didn't want to push his luck.

The periodicals room held hard copy and/or microfilm for the local daily as well as more nationally known newspapers and magazines. He preferred the library to the daily's morgue, just a few blocks south.

Much of the verbiage on the arrest and trial was available online, but the newspaper image helped set the case into its place and time. He loaded a reel of microfilm into the clumsy viewer and fast-forwarded to the first story.

The murder occurred in early December, on the cliched "dark and stormy night." Oregon is notorious for its wet winters, but the coast catches most of the moisture and the raw energy of the storms roaring off the Pacific. There is plenty of both left for the Willamette Valley, and much less for the high desert east of the Cascade Mountains.

But that was a bad night even by Oregon coast standards. The reporter, one Lynda Melvyn, worked the grim weather for all of its metaphoric value. Lou wondered where the reporting standards he learned had gone to. The details of the crime didn't show up until the sixth graph.

"Everybody wants a damn Pulitzer," he muttered.

Melvyn was likely a stringer from the local area, since she had been able to get there quickly enough to witness the removal of the body and get the usual curt police replies to her questions. The state cops handled the crime scene, because there was no municipality close enough, or well-equipped enough, to deal with it.

Lou made a note to ask Gar Loober what he knew. Seagirt was too far away for him to have been called in, but Gar knew his stuff about processing a crime scene.

Next, Lou sought articles about the court case, delayed way past anything resembling the ideal speedy trial, written by Lainie Reiter. He made photocopies of all the relevant materials, including one of the later chronological recaps of the case, just to have an outline.

After a few hours of squealing tape reels and smudged photocopies, Lou called it a day. He noted from one article that Roberta Mendelson was living in northern California when her mother was murdered, but she had given Lou an Oregon phone number. She seemed determined enough to have put her married life in abeyance to work on him, but he decided to ask her what her status was.

He stretched, and left with his sheaf of papers. Maybe I'll call Blanche for dinner, he thought.

Just as Lou Tedesco was leaving the library, across the Willamette, Herman Brown poured himself a stiff single-malt Scotch. He looked around at the vast old house he shared with one other person. He wondered if he would get the opportunity to remain here, and whether he would if he got the offer.

The house had originally been built in the 1890s by a fur baron, and was set on an acre and a half. Now the house was set on a large lot in northeast Portland, in what was the closest thing to an African-American neighborhood. Most of the land had been sold off in parcels long before the current owner, Woodrow Wilson Biggs, bought it in the 1940s.

Brown sat in his favorite overstuffed chair and sipped the smooth and fiery liquid. Then, a bell rang, summoning him to Biggs's bedside. Without complaint, he set down his drink and walked upstairs.

Woody Biggs, once a strapping, glowering presence, was reduced by illness to a wraith, skin dull and gray. He lay in a vast bed, amid silk sheets and goosedown pillows and comforters, attached to various medical monitors, all of which gave off eerie electronic light and made the odd beep or whistle. A nurse hovered around him, keeping one eye on the machinery.

Brown entered the bedroom and said, "You ring, Boss?"

Biggs opened one eye. "That you, Kid?" The voice was weak and phlegmy.

"In the flesh."

Biggs touched the nurse's arm. "Honey, why don't you take five so the Kid and I can talk?"

"You sure, Mr. Biggs?" The nurse was none too sure about Herman Brown.

"Yeah. Don't go far."

She nodded, not quite reassured, and walked out. Biggs looked up at Brown.

"Help me up here, man." Biggs writhed, lurched forward and Brown quickly worked another pillow behind the old man's shoulders. "Thanks."

"What can I do for you?"

"First thing, blow some of that fine Scotch on your breath past me. I can't drink it no more, but I still love the smell."

Brown suppressed a smirk, and gently blew across Biggs's face.

"Mmmm-mm! I'm glad someone is enjoying that. Pull up a chair."

Brown looked around and grabbed the nurse's chair. He sat.

"Kid, I got a lot on my mind. I need to unburden."

Brown rubbed his chin. "You want me to get a minister?"

The old man shook his head. "Naw. I ain't been inside a church for fifty years, and that was to get married. Don't need none of that."

"Then, I'm not sure what you mean."

"I need to set the record straight about lots of things. The old days, mostly. Lots of BS been written about me. Some reporter just did that again. A whole bunch of stuff, not much he got right."

"Should I bring him in?" Brown knew that a local hotshot had just published a book about Portland's wilder days in the 1940s and 1950s, and Biggs had featured prominently in the narrative. He also knew that most of it was tricked-up nonsense, ranging from legend to lies.

"Naw, he's a lost cause. Got his head too far up his own butt. Gotta be somebody else in this burg can do the job."

Brown thought a second. "Maybe this guy on the *Oregon Weekly*. Lou something. He's got a rep as a straight shooter."

"Okay. Check him out. Oh, and is that other thing taken care of?"

"Yeah, Boss. Got it covered."

"You my main man, Kid. Send the nurse back in. I need to give her a hard time. Only fun I got, anymore."

Brown smiled, stood up, moved the chair back and left the room.

He knocked on the nurse's door. "The Boss is callin'. Get it in gear."

The nurse opened the door and threw him an offended look. Brown went back to his Scotch, and made a note to call the *Oregon Weekly*.

* * *

Roberta pulled into the garage of her residence hotel. It was a good thing I married a wealthy man, she thought. I never could have financed my Portland trip on my own. She decided to be extra nice to her husband Gary.

When she got to her room, she called Gary and gave him an update. Then she asked about her brother.

"Have you heard from Robbie?" she asked.

"Nope. Should I have?"

"I guess not," she sighed, "I was just hoping."

"Hey, he's doing his internship. He's a busy boy."

"Yeah, I know. But I'd think he'd be a little more interested in what I'm doing."

"Baby, everybody deals with this in their own way. He's more or less come to terms with it. You, well . . ."

"Are out of my mind. Speaking of that, have you heard from Stevie?"

Gary laughed. "You got that right. No, no one's heard from that *meshugganeh* since he ran out of the courtroom. You think he's okay?"

"Who knows? He really hasn't been okay for years. This can't be making it any better."

"I'll tell you what. If I hear from Stevie, I'll tell him to call you. If you want to speak to your brother, you should just call him."

"Well, duh! Why didn't I think of that?"

"You're being sarcastic again, right?"

"I love you, Gary. Even the fact that sarcasm goes right over your head. Talk to you soon." They hung up.

Roberta changed into a pair of old jeans and sneakers and threw on a sweatshirt. She borrowed an umbrella from the concierge and went for a walk in the Pearl District. The clouds hung heavy over the city, but no rain was falling. The Pearl was slowly losing its industrial past and becoming a playground for the urban upwardly mobile.

She remembered the sprawling old Henry Weinhard brewery, now dismantled or renovated out of existence, replaced by shops and restaurants. The smell of beer brewing, a yeasty perfume not unlike baking bread, had been one of her favorite things about the area. It and the brewery were long gone, a victim of take-no-prisoners urban development. Referring to the development as the Brewery Blocks struck her as an insult.

Roberta popped into a trendy faux-funky restaurant. There were dozens of beers on draft. She ordered something that sounded exotic and indulged in a cheeseburger and fries.

After eating, she took out a notebook and pen, ordered another beer, and started listing information she thought might be important for Lou Tedesco.

Let's see, she thought: Robert Geller, born in Brooklyn, raised in New Jersey, mostly Newark. Father, Bernard, called Barney, deceased about 1957. Mother, Mildred, deceased about 1993, estranged for many years.

She listed her father's high school, Weequahic, and year of graduation. She knew he attended Rutgers for a while, but did not know when or why he dropped out. She did not know what he did before he went to rabbinical seminary, or when he settled in Oregon.

In fact, her knowledge of her father's life before he met her mother, Grace, was spotty at best. He seldom spoke about it, and she had never asked her mother. She wondered if Robbie knew anything.

Well, she thought, Tedesco is an investigative reporter. Let him investigate.

She wrote down phone numbers for everyone she thought important on both sides of the family. She made little notes about each person, and when she came to her uncle Steven, she hesitated. With a little shrug, she wrote, "Mom's youngest brother, more like her son. Loose cannon."

"Well," she said out loud, "that ain't the half of it."

Roberta paid her check, and headed back to her hotel happy for her borrowed umbrella.

Rural New Jersey, 1950

Bobby Geller and his father sat on their little concrete patio in beach chairs listening to *The Lone Ranger*. The staticky kitchen radio was plugged in inside the house, and several extension cords connected it. The summer evening was slowly edging toward dusk, and the crickets were rehearsing their songs.

The little house was set off the road on a small plot of land. It was a labor of love for Barney Geller, a fixer-upper in an area that would explode with suburban growth in just a few years. Now, it was just a cabin in the woods. The patio was the latest project, less than a week dry enough to use. The barbecue pit would be next.

Bobby was only five, but his attention was focused on the radio play, and he knew by the sound of the voices who was a bad guy. The Ranger's nasal baritone and Tonto's monosyllabic grunts were as familiar to him as the voices of his parents.

Barney sipped a bottle of Rheingold beer and answered his son's questions.

"Why does the bad man want to hurt the lady?"

"For money. He wants her father's money, so he kidnapped her."

"What's 'kidnapped?' "

"That's when you steal someone away from their house and family for money."

"Will I get kidnapped?"

Barney put down the beer and hugged his son. "No, sweetheart. Your mommy and I won't let that happen."

The sliding glass doors opened and Mildred Geller poked her head out. "Why do you let him listen to that junk? There's classical music on, you'll both be better off with that."

"Millie!" Barney answered, with a slight mocking tone. "This is the Lone Ranger, Robin Hood of the Old West. He goes around righting wrongs and making the world safe."

"Ha! The idealist. The war didn't cure you of that?"

"Yes, it nearly did. Thank heaven I managed to salvage it."

"A lot of good it ever did you. Dinner's ready."

"Five minutes. The show's almost over."

"Eat it cold for all I care!" She slammed the door closed.

"Is Mommy mad?"

"No, Bobby. She just wants us to enjoy the nice dinner she's made for us."

"Should we go in?"

"We can listen to the end. Here comes the Ranger and Tonto!"

Barney looked over his shoulder at the patio door, and wondered where the girl he married had gone.

Later that night, after Bobby was in bed, Mildred confronted Barney.

"I want you to stop filling our son's head with fairy tales." She stood with her hands on her hips, her mouth set in the grim line she showed when she expected no back talk.

"Millie, he's five years old! When, then, should he get fairy tales?"

"Never! It's not what he needs to hear. The world doesn't like dreamers, and you're living proof."

"Has it been so bad with me? Haven't you had a minute's happiness in all these years?"

"What happiness? We get married, and a month later is Pearl Harbor. Four years struggling, never knowing if you were alive or dead. I'd get a package of letters, maybe three month's worth. I didn't know if you were already dead and I was reading letters from a ghost."

Barney looked at his wife. "Why did you marry me? Wasn't I always like this?"

She waved her arms, frustrated with his questions. "I thought you were smart and could make a living. I thought you would grow up when you had responsibilities. I don't know what I thought."

Barney sighed. "Come on, let's sit down on the couch and talk."

She made a face, but she sat.

"Millie, you can't blame me for the war. A lot of people had it worse than us. At least I came back, and with all my arms and legs. Mushie Birnbaum left half his body in the South Pacific, and Mickey Flaster never came back from Europe. All I got was a scratch, and it got me home early. It's been five years. We have a smart, beautiful son. What's bothering you?"

"Yeah, you're home two days and I'm pregnant!"

Mildred burst into tears. Barney tried to comfort her, but she pulled away.

"You don't have any sympathy for me. I never get a break. My father was a bum, a drunk. My mother barely supported us. I had to work from the time I was six years old. I had to wear those home relief clothes, all the dresses the same . . . At least I had a little job during the war, but I had to quit because of the baby."

Barney had heard all this before. It was Millie's Standard Speech Number One. Standard Speech Number Two featured the anxiety she felt since the war, but she seldom trotted it out anymore.

When she ran out of energy, Barney took her in his arms.

"Millie, I can't promise there won't be another depression, or another war. Right now, knock wood, it isn't so bad. I'm going to school on the GI Bill, we were able to get a loan to buy this house, which we could never afford without the breaks I get for being a veteran. It got us out of Brooklyn and into the country.

"I hated the war. I saw things that changed me forever. It's been hard. But right now we're doing okay, and I'll get a better job after I graduate. Try to have a little hope."

She pulled away. "Hope? Every time I start to hope, I get kicked in the teeth. I don't hope anymore. I hope only that it won't get worse."

He made his voice as gentle as he could. "Millie, don't you want your son to have a real childhood, the kind you never got? Don't you want . . ."

"I want him to be a tough guy. I want him to scare people. Not a pushover, not a sissy."

Barney considered the things she left unsaid and sighed. "Let's go to bed. I have a big day at the factory tomorrow and I have to study for a test on Thursday."

"You go. I want to sit here for a while."

He shrugged. "Fine. Don't stay up too late."

After he was gone, Millie sobbed into her apron and asked God why he hated her.

3. Mistrial

It was late enough in the afternoon for Lou to skip going back to the office. He walked over to the MAX tracks, and took the light-rail train back across the river. Since the knee replacement, he made an effort to walk more, and the rain was just a drizzle. No rain at all by Oregon standards.

Not that it was without some discomfort. His old knee's damaged joint had been a fair gauge of barometric pressure, but the metal-and-plastic appliance was even more sensitive. Lou wondered if it would ever go away, or if he was fated to be a walking weather station for the rest of his life.

As the train crossed the bridge, Lou gazed at the west-side skyline noting that the sun was peeking through the clouds above the hills even as the rain fell. Portland was good for what he called "sun showers" back east.

He got off at the Rose Garden stop. The Rose Garden was the basketball arena and a venue for other large public events. The city was making noises about developing the old industrial area which included his neighborhood. He hoped that either it took a long time to come to pass, or that it was done with more thought than the city gave to the Pearl District. The Pearl was one of the hottest real estate parcels in the country, and most Portlanders couldn't afford to live there.

Lou made the ten-block walk south and east to his loft building without much rain.

He took the elevator. No sense pushing his luck.

After brewing himself a decaf espresso, and putting a Horace Silver CD on the stereo, he settled on the couch with the news articles he had gleaned from the library. Luckily, the *Oregonian* supplied e-mail addresses for the reporters who wrote the articles. He noted the address for Lynda Melvyn, not one of the staff addresses, and for Lainie Reiter, who was on staff.

Before he went online, he called Blanche.

"Hey, wanna have dinner tonight?"

"It's the best offer I've had today. Actually, the only offer. Where?"

Lou ran a list of possibilities, knowing that Blanche would work the list over and over. It saved time to include several of her favorites. They settled on a Vietnamese noodle joint short on ambience and long on flavor, and set a time to meet.

Next, Lou logged on to the Web using his dial-up connection, the source of many jokes among his younger colleagues. ("Hey, Lou, why don't you get into the current century and get a high-speed connection?" "What, to make the dirty pictures load faster?")

He accessed his e-mails, deleting the spam and assigning a priority to the remaining ones. Nothing very important. Checking the stack of articles, he composed an e-mail to Lynda Melvyn:

Ms. Melvyn,

I am doing some back-checking on the Geller murder case and I would appreciate some of your time. I hope you can respond to these questions.

He asked her how she learned of the crime, when she arrived at the scene, and what she was able to see that didn't make it into her piece. Then he asked if he could meet with her on his upcoming trip to the coast.

Next was an e-mail to the staff reporter requesting a face-to-face and offering to buy her lunch. He included his phone number.

His mail program indicated a new message. Lynda Melvyn was online and had responded to him.

Dear Mr. Tedesco,

Thanks for your inquiry. I haven't thought about this case in years.

I am a stringer for the Portland paper out here a few miles south of Seagirt, so it didn't take me much time to get to the scene, despite the horrible weather. I took the call off a police scanner and called the night editor, who assigned me.

The police were there, and the crime scene unit

and rescue squad got there just ahead of me. The rabbi was already there, although I was told that and did not see him for myself. I was too timid to interfere with the EMTs, but I knew one of the state cops. After things settled down, he gave me what details I used in the article.

I was able to catch a quick look inside the door as I drove away. Blood was everywhere and the corpse was covered with a sheet. I couldn't see any further into the house than the entrance hall.

I wanted to do a follow-up piece, but the editors had assigned a regular staffer to the case by that time. The life of a stringer, you know.

By all means, give me a call when you get out here. Your reputation precedes you, and I read the North Coast Edition every week.

Lynda

Lou responded with thanks. Nothing yet from Ms. Reiter, so he logged off, opened his word processing program, and began taking notes as he read the articles about the trial. It was a mess.

Sloppy work by the prosecution, untracked leads by the police, grandstanding by the defense, and recanted confessions. Most amazing were the cast of characters. A private investigator named Laurence Gottbaum, who was in the Inflated Resume Hall of Fame, claiming at one time or another to have been a CIA operative, a Mossad agent, and capable of killing a man twenty-three different ways. He was alleged to have been and had even admitted to having been hired to kill Grace Geller by her husband.

His partner, a strange little man named Arnie Plisskin, who was currently residing in a state mental hospital, had argued in court over who had struck the fatal blows, changing his own position at least once, yelling at his alleged accomplice, and annoying the judge.

And Robert Geller, sphinxlike, enigmatic, terse, unyielding. All these adjectives were brought to bear to describe his courtroom demeanor.

None of the prosecution's tactics or machinations could hang a plausible motive on the rabbi, and Gottbaum's dramatic jailhouse recantation resulted in a mistrial.

Lou considered calling Tom Knight in Waldorf. It had been his case as Klaskanine County DA, and Lou was betting he'd get some rich unpublished detail about the mistrial.

He placed the call. It took him a minute or so to get past the DA's iron-pants receptionist who'd maintained a vigorous grudge against him from their first meeting years before. Lou believed she put him on hold as a matter of course to cool his heels, even if Knight was free to talk.

"Tom Knight," the DA barked.

"Hi, Tom. Lou Tedesco."

"You're not calling about the Anselmo case, are you? I can't discuss that."

"No, I'm calling about Rabbi Geller."

Knight uncorked a burst of invective, remarkable not so much for its originality or creativity as for its contempt and vileness. When he wound down, Lou asked, "So, you weren't happy with the outcome?"

Knight laughed in spite of himself. "I guess you could say. I gave it to an assistant DA, Shirley Downes, because it was a slam dunk and she's a rising star in our sky. Give her a little profile, you know?"

"Aha, so you're grooming your successor for when you run for governor?"

Silence for a moment. "This is where I usually utter my 'no comment.' But, because it's you, I'll speak— off the record, of course."

"Of course," Lou acceded.

"I'm not getting any younger, and I really don't want to be governor. But I don't want to croak at my desk here, either. So, I'm lightening my load by bringing new talent along.

"Now, I won't say 'never' about the governorship, but, frankly, I don't need the grief of fundraising. Rubber chicken dinners, endless meet-and-greets, taking advice from people I have no respect for . . . I'd rather deal with rapists and killers. They're less trouble."

"Okay. Send me a yard sign when you accept your party's draft. Now, about Geller?"

"Yeah. What a pain in the ass! First we have nothing. Then a possible robbery motive. The vic was known to carry large sums of money from her business. There were a couple of local B&E specialists, burglars we looked at. They were just stoners looking for some weed money, never violent, and they were not in the area at all that night."

"How do you know that?" Lou asked.

"They were seen at a bar watching basketball on the night in question. Besides, one has night blindness, can't see to drive in the dark, and the other is deathly afraid to drive in the rain. Seems like he's in the wrong state."

"Nothing beyond that?"

"Nothing credible."

"Okay, so what next?"

"We're running out of leads, and *voila*! This Gottbaum guy comes outta nowhere and confesses to the murder, him and his little buddy Plisskin."

"Plisskin, funny. Like Snake Plissken in the movie."

"Search me. Anyway, Gottbaum says that Geller hired him to kill his wife, he hired Plisskin, and they did it. Gottbaum did it as a favor, because he and the rabbi were such good friends. And, of course, for a few grand, which he claims the rabbi stiffed him on. Most of it, anyway.

"So we arrest the bunch. Geller gets out on bail, and the thugs are remanded. Geller is as cool as you please. Denies everything, professes deep sorrow, but I couldn't see it. Meanwhile, the state cops are spinning their wheels. There's no physical evidence connecting Geller, no checks made out to Gottbaum, no record of phone contacts, no witnesses to any but the most public of meetings.

"Geller's attorneys are hitting us with motion after motion, and time is ticking away. All we got is rumors, innuendo, nothing we can substantiate."

"What was the nature of the rumors?"

"Oh, that Geller was having affairs with women in the congregation, and had his wife killed to be rid of her. But really, if he was having his cake and eating it too, it was hard to make the case."

Lou cleared his throat. "Eating his cake and having it too."

"What?"

"Tom, it's no trick to have your cake and eat it. The trick is eating your cake and still having it. Sorry, a pet peeve."

"Hmph! Yeah, whatever. Geller, by the way, is a walking pet peeve. I've never seen a guy so torqued out of shape by little things.

"Finally, we get to trial. It's not going well. We don't have much more than Gottbaum's word. His pal Plisskin has slipped over the edge and is now in the state laughing academy. We're having midnight oil sessions discussing how to nail this guy. The state cops are still beating the bushes.

"Then, the excrement hits the air supply. Some mook of an inmate comes forward to say that Gottbaum told him in jail that he killed the rabbi's wife all on his own, because he and the rabbi used to be friends, and the rabbi was now giving him the cold shoulder. The rabbi's lawyers jump all over this, accuse us of suppressing evidence, blah blah blah.

"The mook testifies, we can't shake him off his story, the jury deadlocks, mistrial. Truthfully, I'm amazed that any of the jurors bought our case."

Lou whistled softly into the phone.

"You said it," said Knight.

"So," Lou asked, "what's the latest?"

"Well, unless we can develop some new evidence, Geller is home free. Gottbaum is poisoned as a witness, Plisskin is howling at the moon, and we are left holding the well-known end of the stick."

"Anything new on the rabbi's alleged motive?"

"The women, if there were any, have failed to come forward. You'd think that if he dumped someone for a new model she might harbor a grudge. Even the rumors were nonspecific in terms of names. It was always, 'Well, we heard things, but I have no personal knowledge, yadda yadda yadda.'"

"Have you tried priming the pump?" Lou asked.

"What? You mean floating the rumor in the papers? Been there, done that. No bites."

"Any options?"

"We can always retry with the same case, but frankly, the defense team will put Gottbaum's lunch companion on the stand and we have an eight-hundred-pound reasonable doubt. I'm not willing to waste the taxpayer's money on another comic opera."

"So Geller walks?"

"For the time being, at least. Gottbaum and Plisskin will do time, because they admitted the killing. And, even if the motive has changed, the crime remains the same."

"Tom, I wouldn't want your job. I have enough frustration just reporting on it."

Knight sighed. "Yeah, but you know, I've nailed a lot of miscreants to the barn door. I can sleep at night."

Lou thought a second. "Can I get in to see Gottbaum?"

"Strictly up to him. I'd go through his lawyers if I were you. They'll want to be there." Knight gave him the names and phone numbers of the defense team. Lou thanked him and hung up.

Lou checked his voice mail messages, and heard Lainie Reiter's voice agreeing to speak with him. He called back at once.

"Ms. Reiter? Lou Tedesco. Do you have a moment?"

"Sure. Call me Lainie. I like your stuff in the *Stump*."

"Thanks. Call me Lou. And, it's the *Oregon Weekly*, now. My editor would insist. You covered the Geller trial?"

"Yeah. I've been covering the crime beat and the resulting trials for a long time. They're mostly cut-and-dried, dull even. Murder trials get buried in forensic detail until the weight of it just overwhelms the defense. All that TV drama is a bunch of crap. Sure, you get the occasional titillation, the rare surprise, but not like this one. It was like one of those avant-garde plays."

"Meaning?"

"You know, reality as Silly Putty, what you see is not necessarily what is. First, Geller's lawyers, two middle-aged suits with chiseled profiles and an Ally McBeal type in a micro-skirt. I think she was there just to cross her legs and distract the men."

"Nice work on that, by the way. You described them as a commando operation: dropped behind the lines to disrupt or otherwise neutralize the enemy while performing their mission."

"Thanks. I argued with my editor for two hours, and bought him several drinks to keep that in. But it was true. Like that old TV show where these secret agents each have some skill that they get to show off. One was the law guy. He was the inside man. He objected to the prosecutor's work. He wrote notes and passed them to his colleagues as the ADA made her case. The other was the actor, hitting poses, big gestures, grandstanding while he did the active questioning. Stopped just short of pissing off the judge.

"And Ally sat closest to the jury box being visible, shuffling papers, writing furiously, leaning over to talk to the law guy and airing out her panty hose. I'm surprised she wasn't wearing a garter belt and hooker fishnets."

Lou laughed. "That's great. You should write a novel."

"Yeah, in my copious spare time."

"Were you there when Gottbaum's jail buddy dropped the bombshell? What was his name?"

"Laughton? You bet. What a day in court that was. Laughton is this small-time crook, weaselly little bug. Been in and out of jail since he was a kid. Got two felonies now, so he's looking at life if he goes down for a third." She cleared her throat. Lou thought he heard her drag on a cigarette.

"So," she went on, "he gets called by the defense. The ADA, Downes, makes a big show of objecting to his appearance, and the whole defense questioning lasts maybe five minutes. 'Did you hear Gottbaum say something at lunch on the twenty-fourth? What did he say? Was there another witness?' Bang, bang, bang. 'No further questions.'"

"There was another witness, right?"

"Yeah, Laughton's cell-mate. I don't remember his name right now. He never got to testify. The courtroom went numb."

"What did Downes do?"

Lou heard a sigh. "She went at his throat, but she couldn't rattle him. I felt bad for her. She made all the usual charges about coming forward with a story to get his sentence reduced, et cetera. He just sat there and defied her attempts. Guy like that's been questioned so many times, he could handle her before breakfast."

Lou switched gears. "Did you ever talk to Geller?"

"Ah, the rabbi. I thought it was just TV evangelists who were that slick. What a piece of work. He had two modes of response to my questions, reticence and overkill. Most questions got one-word answers, not much more than grunts. When he felt like it, the words rolled like the mighty Mississip': copious and muddy. A total line of crap."

"You certainly have a nice way of describing things. You should write for our paper. Did you ever ask him about the rumors?"

Reiter was quiet for a moment. "First, I doubt that my paper would allow me to moonlight, and second, in my copious et cetera? I asked him about the rumors. He dismissed it as vicious gossip which appeared only after the charges were made. Mind you, I would have no problem believing that he's an opportunistic seducer. He came on to me, subtly.

"Also, mind you, the prosecution was unable to find a woman willing to testify. I only heard rumors, and I'm pretty good at ferret work. As an afterthought, the rabbi took the high road on the matter. You know, 'I did nothing wrong in this area, and I would not reveal a woman's name even if I had.' A real gent." She coughed.

"It sure would be nice to find one of his conquests," Lou mused.

"Alleged conquests. But it was blank-wall city. If anyone had a name, they weren't telling.

"Okay, let me check my notes," she went on. "Geller's son testified that as an EMT he was called to the scene of his mother's murder and was physically restrained from entering by his colleagues. When he managed to get by them, he was appalled at the gruesome sight, and shocked by his father's apparent calm."

"Yeah," said Lou, "I heard that. I'd love to ask him about that. Do you think he'd talk to me?"

"Won't know if you don't try. I think he might be a bit full of himself right now because of the mistrial, which he probably sees as a vindication. What else have I got? Aha, the victim's whole family attended the trial, but her younger brother walked out in a rage during the private eye's testimony and never returned. And there was a difference of opinion on the witness stand between Gottbaum and Plisskin about who actually did the murder and what happened to the evidence."

"Did anyone ever try to exploit the rift between them?"

"Well, neither one has much of a firm grip on reality and their responses are suspect in any case."

"Okay. Anything else?"

"One other thing," Reiter said. "Grace Geller was heavily involved with the homeless issue. Once Gottbaum confessed, we just dropped the thread. You might think about that."

"Why?"

Reiter made shocked noises. "Lou! Snap out of it! How many killings have there been in the last few years among homeless people? It's not out of the question that she might have been offed by one of her social work projects. If I had the time, I'd go after this one myself."

"Lainie, you're a peach. I can't thank you enough."

"You can buy me a beer."

"Well, I don't drink, but I often hang out in bars with my tosspot friends. Permanent designated driver. You're on."

"Better a designated driver than a designated hitter."

"I couldn't agree more. But, what do you do with aging sluggers who can't field their position any more? One excuses Paul Molitor, of course."

"Spoken like a true sage. It was good talking to you."

"Wait!" Lou yelled, struck by a sudden thought.

"Yeah?"

"This took forever to come to trial. Wasn't there more to the case than this?"

Another cough. "Well, yes, but not on my watch. There was another girl, uh, woman reporter covering the thing from the time the crime was committed to the arrests. Jodie Coram. She did several articles on the progress, or lack thereof."

"Can I talk to her?"

"She took off for California, which I believe is where she was originally from. I knew her slightly, but I don't have an address or phone number. I could ask around."

"I would appreciate that."

They rang off. Lou noted that Knight had never mentioned the homeless angle, and he had not found any articles by Ms. Coram. A quick Google search on her name yielded nothing since her tenure at the local daily.

Lou looked through his notes for Rabbi Geller's phone numbers. It was time to go to the source.

But first, he had a dinner date with Blanche Perry.

Rural New Jersey, 1955

Mildred Geller was beside herself with rage.

"You got fired? What are we gonna do?"

Barney waved his hands, searching for words. "Millie, I'll get another job. There's plenty of work out there."

"My God, how can we pay the mortgage?" Mildred looked around. "This place is no palace, but it's ours, or at least I thought so until now."

Her eyes narrowed. "What happened? I thought you were the fair-haired boy."

"Bill Goolsby. He's been treated badly since he got there. I had to say something."

"Goolsby? The *schwarze*? What did you need to stick your nose in there for?"

"Hey, Millie, he's a vet. He was in the war, too. He deserves some respect. The boss treated him like crap, and fired him for no reason. All I did was stick up for him."

"And you got fired, too. What are you, a communist? Mind your own business. You'll never learn, will you? The goddamn idealist without a job!"

She turned and walked to the bedroom with a violent slamming of the door. Barney sighed and dropped onto the couch. He tried to think about what his options were for work, but his emotional upset clouded his mind.

Bobby Geller walked in the front door at that moment, home from school. He wore his uniform: striped T-shirt, grubby dungarees with rolled bottoms and PF Flyers sneakers, the white pair.

"Daddy, what are you doing home?" He put his books on the coffee table.

"Hiya, Bobby." Barney's mind worked for something to say to his son. Sighing, he said, "Sit down, son. I have to talk to you."

Bobby shivered, as from a cold chill. He knew something bad had happened. His father looked older, and very tired. "Is Mommy okay?"

"Yeah, yeah sure. She's fine. She's in the bedroom. Bobby, I lost my job today."

"Are we poor? Will we lose our house?"

"No, we're not poor, and I don't think we'll need to move. But, I have to find a new job, so we'll need to be careful with our money for a while."

"I'll get a job. I'll deliver papers."

Barney nodded. "Thanks, Bobby. That might be a good idea. Even if we don't need it, you can start a bank account for college."

"Why did you lose your job?"

Barney cleared his throat. "Do you remember Mr. Goolsby? We went to a Newark Bears game with him."

"The Negro man?"

"Yes, that's him. Well, Mr. Gould, our boss, treated him very badly, and yesterday he fired him. I stuck up for him and argued with the boss. Today, the boss fired me."

"Just because you stuck up for him?"

"Uh-huh, but it's more complicated than that."

"What's 'complicated'?"

"That means it's more than it looks like, that there are reasons you don't see right away."

"So, what reasons?" Bobby's forehead wrinkled.

Barney turned to look at his son. "Bobby, people have been treating Negroes very badly for years."

"We learned that they used to be slaves. Was Mr. Goolsby a slave?"

"No, he's much too young. But his grandparents were."

"But Abraham Lincoln freed the slaves, right?"

"Yes, but that doesn't mean that their troubles ended there."

Barney gave his son a capsule history of the status of the former slaves and their descendants. Bobby indicated that he understood, and Barney was proud of his son.

"So, Daddy, what does this have to do with Mr. Goolsby?"

"I think that the boss was very unfair, and that he was prejudiced against Bill. Bill did his job well, and it was just unfair. I got mad, and told Gould off."

"Mommy always tells me to mind my own business and fight my own battles."

"Yeah," Barney sighed, "she always tells me that, too. She's very upset."

"Daddy, was this the right thing to do? What you did?"

"I think so. Sometimes you have to stand up and be counted, and there may be a price for it. I'm paying that price."

Bobby understood that his father had told him something important. "I'm proud of you, Daddy."

Barney hugged his son, tears forming in his eyes.

Bobby remembered, years later, that his father seemed physically smaller after that day.

4. Coffee with the Kid

A dry wind was streaming in from the east, down the Columbia Gorge, and the skies over Portland were blue and streaked with high clouds. Lou felt the change in the barometer.

"But," he said aloud, "I'll take this beautiful day."

He was just finishing breakfast and about to head off for the office. He had to make a bunch of calls to set up meetings with Geller and Gottbaum. And there was some more research to be done on the case.

Lou recalled the past evening's pleasant dinner with his editor and closest, dearest friend. He worried about Blanche sometimes, hoping she would find a man who would appreciate her. She claimed to be too busy with the *Oregon Weekly* to care, but he knew better.

A quick check of an open window indicated a warm enough temperature to walk to work without a coat. Lou remembered the first day in spring he could walk to school without a jacket, and what a big deal it was.

All his friends would begin to get that summer-is-coming faraway look in their eyes. If only life were that basic now.

He checked his voice mail. No messages. He'd check e-mails at work.

Lou walked briskly to the office. When he got there, he set up the coffee and got online. When he walked back to the kitchen to get a cup, he found a stranger, a black man of indeterminate age, sitting in the waiting room.

"Can I help you?"

The man stood up, fit and trim in his well-cut suit. The pattern was a bit flashy for Lou's taste, but it looked fine on the visitor.

"If you could find Lou Tedesco for me, it's all the help I need."

"Well, I'm Lou. And you are . . . ?"

"Herman Brown. Pleased to make your acquaintance." The man reached out to shake Lou's hand. Lou responded.

"Mr. Brown, that's quite a grip. You take good care of yourself."

Brown gave a modest shrug.

"Herman Brown. Not the lightweight boxer, Kid Cocoa?"

"The same," spoken with a slight bow.

"Want some coffee?"

"I wouldn't mind. Got cream?"

"Yup. The real thing. Follow me."

Lou walked Brown to the kitchen, where they

poured coffee, Brown doctoring his with cream and three sugars.

He gave a sheepish grin. "I lost my sweet tooth, except for my coffee. Got to have my sugar."

Lou spoke as they walked to his office. "I saw you fight on television when I was a kid. It was an undercard for a middleweight championship fight. Man, the middleweights were a couple of brawlers, and you were an artist. Do you remember that?"

"Yes sir, I do. Fought Anthony Calluzzi. They called him 'The Assassin.' Didn't live up to his name."

They entered the office, and Lou directed Brown to a chair and sat behind his desk.

"Didn't live up to his name? You took him apart like a jigsaw puzzle. Worked on the body until he could barely move, then KO'd him with a nice right cross. Scientific."

Another slight bow. "I thank you. Yes, all these kids now are head-hunters. They go for the kill from jump street. And not many have any real skills, just punchers, like bar fighters."

"How did Calluzzi get a match with you? He wasn't near your class."

Brown shifted in his seat and crossed his legs, carefully arranging his pants leg to spare the crease. "Tony was a mob fighter. You may know that the fight game is not the most honest of sports. He got hand-picked opponents until he met me, and he had to get past me to advance. His people approached me to, what shall I say? To get out of his way.

"I refused. My manager almost had a heart attack. He begged me to reconsider, but I wasn't having any."

Lou leaned forward across his desk. "What happened?"

Brown shrugged. "Not much, really. I had two, three more fights, suddenly the good opponents dried up. I couldn't get the matches I needed to fight for the championship. I was gonna go to the boxing commission, but my manager told me that it might be injurious to my health.

"I got tired of dancing with third-rate pugs, but I didn't have no choice. Then, Mr. Biggs bought my contract, brought me out here to the coast."

"Mr. Biggs?" Lou rubbed his chin. "Why does that sound familiar?"

Brown sipped his coffee. "How long you been out here, Lou?"

"Maybe ten years."

"Woody Biggs, Woodrow Wilson Biggs. His time was in the forties and fifties. He pretty much retired thirty years ago."

"Retired from what?"

Brown cleared his throat. "Put delicately, rackets. He was one of the kingpins in the black community for more than twenty years. Gambling, girls, after-hours clubs, a little street tax. Never no dope. He hated that stuff, thought it was gonna be the new slavery, the death of the black man."

Lou sighed. "Looks like he may have been right. At least for a while."

Brown nodded. "Things a little better now, no doubt. Get rid of that damn hip-hop, we be in good shape."

Lou laughed. "What do you do for him?"

"I used to fight for him. Got me maybe a dozen matches out here, we made some money, then we got the attention of the boys back east. Biggs decided it would be best if I retired from further prize fighting and be his bodyguard. I been his chief cook and bottle-washer ever since. Outlasted two of his marriages."

"I guess that leads to the question of what you need me for."

Brown nodded, sipped his sweet coffee.

"Mr. Biggs wants to talk. I don't know about what, really. It may be he thinks he needs to get his side of the story out there before he croaks. Maybe something else. He wants you to come out to the house."

Lou held up his hands. "Well, I've got a pretty full plate right now. Any chance it can wait a month or two?"

Brown shook his head. "Naw. He hooked up to machines, got a full-time nurse. He may be dead while I'm sittin' here."

Lou drummed on the desk with his fingers. "Okay, maybe. I need to make a bunch of phone calls, but I can probably come out this afternoon. That work?"

"I guess. If he don't last until then, it wasn't meant to be. You won't be sorry, I can tell you that. I'll come back around two o'clock, okay?"

"Yes, all right."

The men rose and shook hands.

"Thanks for the coffee," Brown said, and walked out.

Newark, New Jersey, 1957

Twelve-year-old Bobby Geller looked around at the dreary little apartment in a run-down section of Newark. He missed his house, his friends, and his old neighborhood. Mostly, he missed his father. He sighed.

The flat had one bedroom, which his mother had insisted that he take. She slept on a sofa bed in the small living room. The windows in both rooms overlooked an airshaft, a vertical space between buildings to provide something like open space for the interior apartments.

It was about thirty feet square, the ground at the bottom was overgrown with weeds, and ugly trash collected in the corners. Light entered, if ever, only at midday. It's main feature was that it provided glimpses into the lives of your neighbors, particularly if they were careless about drawing the blinds.

When they moved in, the paint was peeling off the walls, and was dirty where it clung. The floor was worn linoleum, or stained and gouged wood. In the small, dank bathroom the tile floor was chipped and gruesome-looking. His mother told him he was lucky they had a bathroom. In her miserable childhood flat on the Lower East Side, the tub was in the kitchen and the toilet down the hall, and shared by everyone on the floor. When it worked.

Bobby had seen his first cockroach in this place. It made him puke. Now he was used to them. He smelled the strange smells of cooking and lives lived with different standards of cleanliness. He heard noises, both titillating and embarrassing, the price of living so close to others. He never realized that other people had different ways until they moved from their little house.

Mildred and Bobby spent the first month cleaning the place up, and painting. It made a difference to him, but his mother said, "*Nu?* A gift-wrapped turd."

Mildred, never a ray of sunshine, had become bitter and silent since his father's death. In the last few months, a never-ending bad dream, Barney Geller died of a heart attack, and Mildred Geller learned that her husband had cashed in his insurance policies to finance the failing business he started with Bill Goolsby.

With no money, and only their house as an asset, the course was clear. Mildred sold the house, making a small profit, and moved to this apartment in Newark, where she got a job as a file clerk in an office. The money they cleared from the house was their only nest egg, and Mildred guarded it fiercely. They got a little from his father's Social Security, but lived close to the bone. Her salary alone would not have supported them.

Bobby swept up and delivered orders for the corner grocery for spending money and to add to their income. He had made no new friends in his weeks at the new school, and despaired of ever finding any.

The worst thing was, when his mother said anything at all, it was most likely to be an angry condemnation of his father. Sometimes, he just wanted to hit her. He couldn't stand the way she ran her dead husband down, and the flat was too small to escape her diatribes.

Once, he locked himself in the bathroom to get away, and she bellowed at him through the door. The neighbors thought she was a little crazy, and so did he. He felt very guilty about that.

Worse were the arguments, the latest being just the day before. Bobby had asked his mother about his bar mitzvah.

Mildred looked at him with something between contempt and annoyance.

"So, all of a sudden you're Jewish? Why, may I inquire, do you care about this?"

"Because, Mom, Daddy would have wanted it. We used to talk about it before . . ."

"Before he dropped dead and left us high and dry? Well, if he wanted it, let him pay for it. We don't have the money, his relatives are not speaking to me, and I'm not speaking to mine. Who's going to come? It's not like you have many friends."

Bobby cringed, not yet hardened to his mother's casual cruelty. That would come later.

"Please, Mom. Don't you care about this? Isn't this important?"

Mildred held up a hand, and rolled her eyes. "Spare me. If there is a God, I'm not speaking to him, either. He's worse than my relatives." She exited the kitchen with her nose in the air.

The next day after school, Bobby walked to the local temple and spoke to the rabbi. After he had told his story, the old man sat silent for a full minute.

"Robert, you will come for classes with the other boys. Don't worry about paying, we'll squeeze you in. When the day of your bar mitzvah comes, you will read the Torah like all the other boys. I can't promise you a party like all the other boys will get, but you will be accepted as a Jewish man in this congregation."

Bobby nodded. "Thank you, Rabbi."

A few months later, Bobby spoke to his mother over breakfast.

"Mom, in two weeks I'm being bar mitzvahed. I want you to come."

Mildred started. "Where did you get the money for lessons?"

"The rabbi let me take the class for free."

"Hmph, a charity case."

"No, Mom, he said it was a *mitzvah* for the congregation. Can I get a suit for the service?"

"A suit? What else does Bonnie Prince Charlie want, a reception at the Ritz? No, you can't get a suit. When I die, you can get a suit for my funeral."

Two weeks later, Bobby Geller, dressed in clean school clothes, stood before the congregation and sang and recited to perfection. He smiled afterward. He knew he had done well.

After the service, he walked home alone.

When he got home, his mother said nothing. She said almost nothing to him for a long time. Her silences, long and deep, were welcome.

At thirteen, the boy had no way out. He would always remember this as the low point of his life.

5. Knocking on Heaven's Door

"This is Rabbi Robert Geller. I am unavailable to speak with you right now, so please leave me a message at the beep."

Beep.

"Hello, my name is Lou Tedesco, and I'm with the *Oregon Weekly*. I would really appreciate a face-to-face interview concerning your recent, uh, experience at trial. I am coming into this with no preconceived notions, and what I want is your take on the matter. Thanks."

Lou hung up and called Roberta Geller's cell.

"Hi, Lou. What's up?" It sounded like she was on the street somewhere.

"Hi. I spoke with DA Tom Knight, and with two reporters who filed stories on the case. I just called your father's home phone and got his machine."

Roberta made a noise. "He won't call back. He uses

that phone to screen calls. If he didn't pick up, you didn't make the cut. Let me give you his cell number."

More than one level of meaning there, Lou thought as he jotted the number down.

"You can tell him I gave you the number," she went on, "and it may buy you some time with him. He's been playing it cagey since the trial."

"Doesn't he know that you're suspicious of him?"

"No, and don't blow it. I'm hoping you find something that clears him. You know, my heart says that, but my brain says 'guilty.' That sort of thing."

Lou heard horns honking. "Where are you?"

"On Hawthorne. I'm looking for a used clothing shop I heard about."

"Oh, it's on Thirty-seventh, just a half-block north of Hawthorne."

"Now, how would you know that?"

"My editor won't wear anything produced later than 1970. I think her underwear is new, but I may be wrong."

"Somehow I feel better that you don't know that."

Lou chuckled. "Yeah, so does my girlfriend. Thanks for the help. Oh, one more thing. Does the name Jodie Coram ring a bell?"

"Nothing immediate. Male or female?"

"Female. She was the reporter of record directly following the crime."

"I wasn't in Oregon when my mother was murdered. Once I got there, there were so many press people . . . Do you know what she looked like?"

"Actually not. It may not be important. I'd kinda like to speak with her."

"Sorry. Can't help on this one."

Lou said good-bye, leaned back in his chair, and drank cold coffee. Making a face, he dialed the rabbi's cell phone.

"Rabbi Geller."

"Rabbi, my name is Lou Tedesco. I'm a reporter with the *Oregon Weekly*. I just called your home phone . . ."

"How did you get this number?" The rabbi sounded miffed.

"From your daughter, Roberta."

Silence. Then, "Okay, what do you want?"

"Just a few minutes of your time to talk about . . ."

"I know what you want to talk about. Unless you want to talk about fly-fishing?"

"Sorry, I don't indulge. Is tomorrow okay? I'll be coming out to stay in Seagirt for a while."

"Yeah, I don't fly-fish either. Do you want to come to my home, or to a neutral setting?"

Lou wanted to see the house. "Your home works for me. I understand you're a few miles south of Seagirt?"

Geller gave him directions, they set a time after lunch, and rang off.

Lou called Hilda and told her he'd be arriving that night. He had one more stop to make before he took off.

*   *   *

Lou pulled up in front of the palatial home of Woodrow Wilson Biggs. Doing well by doing good. Lou chuckled at his own ironic thought.

He made the long walk up to the front steps and banged the elaborate brass knocker in the shape of a coho salmon. Herman Brown answered the door.

"Glad you could make it, Lou. Mr. Biggs is in a good frame of mind. Anxious to talk."

Lou stepped in and gasped. Brown laughed.

"I did the same thing, first time I was here. Couldn't take it all in."

Lou looked around. It was out of a movie, or one of those TV shows about the rich and famous. Intricate parquet floors in forest designs replete with birds. A grand entrance hall dominated by an enormous sweeping staircase. The entrance hall itself was bigger than his high-school gym.

Tapestries on the walls and velvet drapes, thrown open to let in the summer light. On one wall were nearly life-size paintings of Joe Louis, Willie Mays, Paul Robeson, Wilma Rudolph, and other African-American sports heroes in action. Louis standing over a white opponent. Mays making his trademark basket catch on the run, cap flying off his head. Rudolph smashing a serve. Robeson in his college uniform breaking across the goal line.

A more modest portrait of Kid Cocoa hung off to the side with a pair of bronzed boxing gloves hanging from one corner. Lou walked over to it.

"Nice," he said.

Brown ambled over. "Thanks. Painter took it from

a wire photo after my last fight. You wouldn't believe how much it cost to bronze them gloves."

"What's going to happen to all this when Mr. Biggs passes on?"

Brown shrugged. "You got me. The Boss left me a bunch of envelopes and instructions. I guess I'll know then. He won't forget me.

"Let me take you to him."

Brown directed Lou to a bookshelf. He jiggled a copy of *Uncle Tom's Cabin* and the bookcase slid left to reveal an elevator. "Boss's little joke," he smirked.

"I like it."

One flight up, the door opened on a narrow hallway lined with what must have been California redwood. Lou gawked.

There were four doors on the corridor. They walked to the one at the end of the hall, and Brown knocked with a light touch. The door was opened by a young, attractive black woman in a nurse's uniform. "Mr. Brown," she said, with no real greeting in her voice.

"Miss DuBois. This here's Lou Tedesco."

She nodded in Lou's direction. "Come in, then. Mr. Biggs has been expecting you."

"Do I detect New Orleans in your voice, Ms. DuBois?" Lou asked.

"Right across Lake Pontchartrain, in Slidell," she said with a slight smile. "Good guess. Come this way."

Lou saw the bed at the far end of the big and well-lit room. The windows looked out on what looked like a patch of old-growth trees, huge Douglas firs. He doubted that the old man lying in bed had seen them lately.

He was hooked up to several machines, monitoring his vital signs or providing oxygen, nourishment, and relief through tubes. Still as massive as a football player, Woody Biggs must have been an imposing presence in his day. Now, his cheeks were sunken in and his skin had a curious lifeless, almost artificial quality.

"Mr. Biggs?" the nurse whispered. "You have visitors." She gestured Lou to a bedside chair, and he sat down.

Biggs opened his eyes.

"Kid? That you?"

"Yeah, Boss. Got Lou Tedesco."

Biggs focused. "Mr. Tedesco, good of you to come." His voice was rough.

"Call me Lou. I'm happy to be meeting you. You're a bit of a legend in these parts."

"What'd the Kid tell you?" he rasped.

"Mr. Brown? Not much."

"You a writer?"

"I like to think so."

Biggs cleared his throat, restoring some of the old rumble to his voice. "You know that Shakespeare fella? Mighty smart for a white boy." He turned his head toward Lou. "No offense."

"None taken. I agree."

"That funeral speech for Caesar? 'The evil that men do lives after them. The good is oft interred with their bones.' That one?"

"Yes, sir. I know it."

"I don't want my good work buried with this body. Someone need to set the record straight." He panted, and the nurse made an adjustment to his oxygen flow. "There's plenty of the other stuff. Most people would call me a criminal, and I wouldn't argue. I like to think I just gave people what they wanted that they couldn't get at their local Fred Meyer supermarket."

He coughed, and the nurse put her hand on his brow.

"Girl got some cool hands. I give her a hard time, but she a blessing. I never sold no dope. Poison to my people."

"Not so good for anyone else, either."

"That's the gospel. I want you to tell my story. I won't be here to read it. Hell, I might not be here for the dinner comin' through that tube. Will you do it?"

"Mr. Biggs, sir . . ." Lou shuffled from foot to foot. "I have kind of a full plate right now . . ."

"Whatever you got, I will make it worth your while to add another helping."

"I don't know how much time I can spend on research. I'm working on a very complicated matter right now, the murder of that rabbi's wife. It's taking . . ."

Lou hesitated, noticing a glance pass from Biggs to Brown.

"Nurse, could you crank my bed up a couple notches? I need to look this man in the eye."

The nurse touched a button, and the top half of the bed rose. When Biggs was almost level with Lou's eyes, he nodded. The bed stopped.

"You tell me you workin' on the Geller case?"

Surprised, Lou answered, "Uh, yes."

Biggs shifted his gaze. "Kid, you know where that file is? The one . . ."

"Yes, Boss. Want me to fetch it?"

Biggs nodded, and Brown left the room.

"Lou, son, this could be your lucky day."

"I, uh, I don't understand. You have something to do with that case?"

"Seek and you shall find, Lou. Bible say that. When the Kid come back, we'll talk."

Biggs closed his eyes. Ms. DuBois leaned over to whisper to Lou.

"He doesn't have much strength. He may not last the day. Or, he may be here next week. I hope you can take on the job. It'd do him good to hear that."

Lou sighed. A few moments later, Brown returned with a fat manila envelope and a small white one. He handed both to Lou. The name on the manila envelope was William H. Goolsby.

"Boss?" Brown spoke.

Biggs opened his eyes. "Check out that file, Lou. I know you will find it interesting. The envelope, too. Do you want to look it over before you decide?"

Ms. DuBois flashed Lou a look.

"Mr. Biggs, I'll be happy to write your story. I'll get on it after I finish up with the Geller case."

"Good man, good man. Don't spare me now. You call 'em the way you sees 'em."

"Yes, sir. Willie Mays and Paul Robeson are heroes

of mine, too. I take my view of personal integrity from them."

Biggs raised up a hand, and Lou took it giving it a small shake.

"I'm gonna rest, now, and give my nurse a hard time. Kid'll show you out. And thank you."

"Yes, sir."

Lou arose, said good-bye to a smiling Ms. DuBois, and followed Brown out the door and down the elevator.

Lou took in the immense entrance hall once again.

"Lou, over in that corner there?" He pointed to a space under the windows. "Dizzy Gillespie and his quintet played here more than once. The whole damn Count Basie band was here, too. Ella Fitzgerald, Anita O'Day, and Roy Eldridge . . . This place was somethin' else when the Boss was in his prime.

"You made him very happy today. Thanks."

"Glad to do it. Do you know what's in this file?"

Brown shrugged. "Only bits and pieces. Read it for yourself."

Lou gave Brown Hilda's phone number in Seagirt and walked out to his car. A peek into the folder showed a fat trove of information. The white envelope contained a check for $25,000. The memo read "Deposit for personal services."

The last traces of sunset were consumed by the inky dark as Hilda served drinks on the front porch of her house. Fresh-made lemonade for Lou, with a bottle of Idaho potato vodka on the side for Hilda to spike hers with.

"Nice dinner." Lou patted his stomach.

"I don't cook much unless you're here, so I'm happy to do it. Besides, I can usually convince you to whip up a couple of meals to justify your existence."

Hilda poured a generous dollop of vodka into her iced drink and stirred it with her finger. Lou had learned not to say anything about Hilda's alcohol consumption, because it always led to a fight and an accusation that he was a zealot reformed drunk. He couldn't raise a good argument to that charge.

"Now," Hilda asked, settling down with her drink, "what's all this about some old black man and the rabbi?"

"I don't know, yet. I got a big, fat file I haven't had a chance to go over. I was just amazed that Woody Biggs had even heard of Rabbi Geller, much less that he'd provide information."

"Portland's a big, overgrown small town now. It must have been even more so all those years ago. Besides, who knows what Geller was into in the time he spent in Portland?"

Lou leaned forward. "You knew he lived in Portland?"

"Lou, when Geller started that synagogue it was the only one on the coast, at least until you got to Brookings, and I'm not sure there was one there. Portland, Eugene, maybe Waldorf, Corvallis, and Ashland, but the coast was pretty wild and primitive forty years ago."

"Think there's anything in your father's files about Geller?" Lou asked. The files of Carroll Truax, Hilda's father and the editor-publisher of the erstwhile *North*

Coast Clarion, had been helpful more than once in the past. They were complete, accurate, and enhanced by the insights scribbled in as marginalia.

"If it happened on the north coast, Daddy wrote about it. This would have been big news."

"Wanna take a look?"

"It can wait. I'd rather spend time with you than some dusty paper."

Lou raised his lemonade. "I'll drink to that."

Newark, New Jersey, 1960

Mildred and Bobby sat in their flat eating lunch and listening to the Metropolitan Opera on the radio. Saturday lunch and Sunday breakfast were the only things Mildred splurged on. They ate corned beef, pastrami, rye bread, and knishes from the deli a half-hour bus ride away. On Sunday, it was lox, or smoked whitefish, on bagels and bialys, pickled herring for an occasional treat.

And, the *New York Times*. Mildred insisted that Bobby get to read a real newspaper at least on weekends.

Bobby was happiest at home on these days. His mother sang along with the operas, the food was great, and he lost himself in the voluminous text of the *Times*. When Mildred was really content, they would do the Sunday crossword together.

At fifteen, he was medium height and slender, with unruly hair he refused to glue down with the hair tonics his mother bought him. His dark eyes and good looks, and his quiet, deep demeanor, were a frequent topic among the girls in his school. He was vaguely aware of this, but he had no time to hang out or explore his popularity.

Things had improved for them since the low period following his father's death, and the trauma of his bar mitzvah. Mildred earned more money, and had been promoted from the tedious filing job that had been her start. Bobby worked at the modest neighborhood supermarket afternoons and some evenings, and was the unofficial assistant manager. The owner promised him a manager's job when he graduated from high school, but Mildred insisted that Bobby go to college. His grades were good, and he could go to a state school for low tuition while living at home and commuting.

Mildred had decided that Bobby would be a certified public accountant. They were always in demand, and could make extra money during tax season. Bobby assented by not refusing. He was hoping to get to school and look for something that really interested him.

Meanwhile, to preserve the peace, he kept his feelings about accountancy to himself. He had three years before graduation, and a lot could happen in three years.

A commotion arose outside in the hallway. "My God," Mildred growled, "it sounds like a herd of elephants coming up the stairs."

The noise stopped at their door, and a frantic knocking made them jump.

"I'll get that!" Mildred said, her voice edged with disapproval.

She unlocked the three locks to disclose three young men clad in jeans and surplus Army jackets. One asked with breathless urgency, "Mrs. Geller, is Bobby . . ." he peered around her to see Bobby sitting at the table.

"Hey, Geller, get your tush in gear. We gotta go."

"Just a minute, young man, who do you think you are?" Mildred was offended by his boorish behavior.

Bobby got up. "It's okay, Mom, it's my friends."

"No, it's not okay. I don't care how they act at home, but in my house they'll have some respect." She turned to look at her son. Bobby noticed eyes rolling at the door.

"Come in, guys. Mom, this is Heshey Nadler, Davey Gottlieb, and Paul Greenberg. Guys, this is my mom." They nodded in turn, muttering greetings.

Heshey put on his best ashamed look. "Sorry, Mrs. Geller, but this is important."

"So, what's so important that you have to act like Cossacks?" Mildred had that look on her face.

"Geller," Heshey addressed her son, "the Nazi is speaking in the Village, in Washington Square Park. We're gonna go throw eggs at him."

Mildred looked at him like he had suggested jumping into a volcano. "What are you saying?"

"It's right here in the *Times*, Mom. George Lincoln Rockwell is having a rally in Washington Square. Look." He held up the front page.

Mildred looked at Heshey. "And what business is this of yours? Or my son's?"

"Mrs. Geller," Heshey whined, "he's the head of the American Nazi Party. We gotta go bust his, uh, give him a hard time."

"Have a good time. My son has no use for this *mishigass*. Now go, and be more quiet on the way out."

"Wait a sec. I'll be right with you." Bobby headed toward his room.

"Over my dead body."

"Come on, Mom. This needs to be done," he said over his shoulder.

"Oh yeah? And what if you wind up in jail, or in the hospital, or one of those thugs kills you? You're still a child, and these hoodlums won't take care of you." She turned to face Heshey. "And tell me, please, how are you getting into the city?"

Heshey squirmed. "My cousin Sheldon has a car. He's waiting downstairs."

Mildred turned to see Bobby emerging from his room with a New York Giants baseball jacket on. He refused to acknowledge their elopement to San Francisco.

"I'll be careful, Mom, I promise."

Mildred's body went rigid. She bit off her words.

"Robert Geller, if you leave this house, don't come back. Your stuff will be packed and left outside the door. Go live with Heshey. His mother obviously doesn't care what he does."

Bobby stared at his shoes for a second, as though considering the possibilities.

"Sometimes you have to stand up and be counted, even though there may be a price for it. I'll see you tonight, Mom. I won't be late." He headed for the door.

"Tonight? You'll see me in a coffin tonight. Don't you dare leave this house!"

Bobby closed the door slowly. Mildred tore her clothing and wailed like a woman in mourning.

The young men traded wise-guy comments and insults on the drive into Manhattan. Sheldon found a place to park on West Broadway, a few blocks from Washington Square Park. They got out and walked north.

Washington Square is an urban park graced with a magnificent arch at one entrance, at the foot of Fifth Avenue. It was, and still is, the navel of the bohemian Greenwich Village, a combination of village green, town hall, and primary hang-out spot, especially on weekends. Young people would gather around the central fountain, laden with guitars, harmonicas, and banjos for a hootenanny, your basic open-ended folk music extravaganza.

On an early spring afternoon like the one American Führer Rockwell chose to make his case for Nazi philosophy, there was a guaranteed crowd, mostly young, overwhelmingly liberal, and largely Jewish. In later years, this confluence of factors would be known as a "perfect storm."

Bobby and his friends were in a transport of ecstasy

just being in the Village, the Mecca of cool. They tried not to look like tourists. Sheldon, who attended NYU, was a regular in the area. They passed a grocery, owned and operated by an old Italian man. Sheldon walked in.

"Excuse me, sir."

"Yeah, young fella?"

"Do you have any eggs?"

"Nice and fresh. Thirty-five cents a dozen, from Jersey."

"Um," Sheldon lowered his voice, "do you have any that are not so fresh?"

"Whaddaya gonna do wit' rotten eggs?"

"Well, sir, you know that Nazi that's gonna talk in the park?"

"Sonomabitch! Nazi bastard! You gonna trow dem eggs at him?"

"Yes, sir."

"Wait here." The old man went through a curtain to the back of the store. A moment later, he emerged with a brown paper bag.

"I was gonna put inna garbage. But, you can have 'em. Hit him one time for me."

"Thank you, sir."

"Nazi bastard!" The old man spat.

Sheldon thanked the old man again, and stepped out of the store. The faces of the boys were raised to him, as eager as baby birds waiting to be fed.

"Hey." Sheldon held up the bag. "Look what I got."

He opened the bag. "Phew," said Heshey, "you can smell 'em right through the shell."

"Let's go," said Paul.

They walked into the park and saw a chaotic scene. Hundreds of young people, a sea of denim and khaki and suede, were gathered around a raised platform. There was nothing yet to see, but chants ran through the crowd, mostly of the basic "Kill the Nazi scum" variety.

There were also signs held by union men and women and veterans of the war, many wearing the caps of veterans' organizations. Some of the union guys and younger vets were anxious for trouble. They clenched their fists and waited.

Cops surrounded the whole circus, warily sweeping the crowd with their eyes, and slapping their billy clubs into their palms. The singers gathered at the fountain sang union and anti-fascist songs. The balmy air wafted music and tension.

Bobby's group hovered around the edge of the crowd. Sheldon waved to people he knew. Bobby surveyed the scene. He tingled, like he had just discovered that there was life beyond Newark. He couldn't believe the raw realness of the place. He saw a dozen girls he could fall in love with.

"Hey, whaddaya think?" Heshey asked him.

"This is cool!"

"Better than listenin' to opera with your old lady?"

"Yeah, wise guy, better than that."

"Hey, Bobby," Davey said, "we come down here most Saturdays. If you can escape the apron strings, come along."

"Thanks, man," Bobby replied. "That'd be cool."

"Yeah, well, he just feels sorry for you, 'cause you're such a pathetic mama's boy." Heshey's voice dripped with sarcasm.

"Hey, up yours, Nadler." Bobby got into the spirit of the moment.

Just then, there was a commotion. Entering from one corner of the park came the flower of Aryan America, in brown shirts and carrying swastika flags. An obscene roar of disapproval rose from the crowd, and the cops held back the surging masses wielding their billy clubs at chest height. Rockwell and his boys ascended a platform.

The brownshirts threw the Nazi salute and yelled, *"Sieg heil!"* This was answered by a thousand-throated scream of rage from the assemblage, and a forest of upraised middle fingers. The cops were hard pressed by the crowd, straining to reach the platform.

Rockwell began to speak. His words were drowned in a wave of loathing and shouted insults.

"What's he saying?" Bobby asked.

"Who gives a goddamn. Take an egg."

The boys picked eggs out of the bag with exaggerated care.

"Now?"

"Whaddaya want, an engraved invitation?"

They launched their missiles. Bobby watched his egg arc over the heads of the crowd and hit Rockwell in the chest. Two more eggs found their mark, and the other smashed on the stage. Rockwell looked up with a peculiar bewildered look on his face. Something about that look disturbed Bobby deeply.

Soon, the air was filled with thrown objects, not all as harmless as the eggs. Rockwell carried on until the hail of debris drew blood from him and his cohorts.

"Nazi blood. Looks the same as ours, don't it?" Paul snickered.

"Like Shylock says," replied the college boy.

The brownshirts left the stage and retreated to lick their wounds. The barrage of trash and the vileness of the insults hurled was undiminished until they were out of sight. Someone began to sing "*Le Marseillaise.*" Those that knew the words sang along, and the rest hummed the tune. Bobby's hair stood on end. It was like the scene in *Casablanca* where the Germans were drowned out by the patrons of Rick's Café Americaine.

Yet, something ate at him. His joy couldn't be as glorious and absolute as the people around him.

He was quiet all the way home.

They dropped him off at nine o'clock, after stopping for a burger and a soda. He thanked them all, disguising his disquiet, and walked up the stairs to his flat.

It was empty. He had no idea where his mother would be at this time on a Saturday night. He turned on the tiny second-hand television, but payed no attention to what was on. He was deep into his own thoughts, and worried about his mom.

When the news came on at 11 p.m., Mildred walked in.

"Mom, where have you been? I was worried."

"What's good for the goose is good for the gander. If you can go out, so can I. Now, get out of my bedroom. I'm tired."

The next morning, it was bagels and lox and the Sunday *Times*. Mildred said nothing, but the look on her face was the same as it had been when his father lost his job.

Sometimes you have to stand up and be counted, and there may be a price for it, Bobby thought. I'm paying that price.

They did not do the crossword together.

Bobby never found out where she had gone, and she never mentioned his trip to the Village again, even though it was not to be his last.

6. Relationships

Roberta Geller admired herself in the full-length hotel mirror. She was wearing the maxicoat and Frye boots she had purchased in that second-hand store off Hawthorne. The coat had a tear in the lining, fixable, but the boots seemed to be brand new. She had heard that the boots were coming back into style.

Her cell phone rang.

"Hello."

"Who the hell is Lou Tedesco and why did you give him my private number?"

"Hi, Daddy. Nice to hear from you."

"Don't get smart with me. I don't have enough problems?"

"Look, this guy is very well thought of. I felt that he might turn up something to help you . . ."

"I don't need any help from a reporter. Reporters have been a pain in my ass for years now. Besides, Jason says that the DA probably won't retry this case.

They have nothing since that *meshugganeh* Gottbaum shot himself in the foot."

"Jason? Ugh. That guy gives me the creeps. I feel like taking a shower every time I have to see him."

"Yeah? Well, I didn't hire him to give you a thrill. He got me through this and it feels like I'm a free man."

"Daddy, did it ever occur to you that you're not really a free man? You lost your job, and there will always be a cloud over you because of this. You weren't found guilty, but that doesn't make you innocent. Lou might be able . . ."

"All right, already. I'm talking to him tomorrow. But don't do anything like this again without asking me first."

"Thank you, Daddy."

"How long are you gonna be in Portland?"

"Not sure. A few more days, maybe."

"So, Gary can dress himself without you?"

"He managed to earn several million dollars before he met me, which is more than any of the *zhlubs* you fixed me up with can claim. He's good to me and he loves me, and he's not . . ."

"A bastard like your old man?"

"I never said that."

"So, do you think you can wander out here to the coast and visit me?"

A chill shook her. She hesitated a second to calm her voice. "Yeah, sure. Maybe in a day or so."

"Good. You're still my little girl, kiddo."

"Bye, Daddy."

Roberta turned off her cell phone and fell on the bed. She cried herself into an uneasy sleep.

"Wakey, wakey!"

Hilda stood at the foot of the bed with a cup of coffee in her hand. Lou rolled over, stretched, and smiled. "That coffee for me?"

"Hell no. No coffee for you until you get your sorry behind out of bed and down to the kitchen."

With a theatrical groan, Lou lurched out of the big, old bed and washed up. He pulled on some sweats, after the ritual checking of the fading scar on his repaired knee, and walked barefoot to the kitchen.

The huge old place was warmed by sun streaming in the window. The early summer had been particularly mild and dry, and the usual morning clouds had burned off already.

Hilda poured Lou a cup of coffee, and they sat at the table. She had set out fresh fruit and a couple kinds of cold cereal. Lou fixed himself a bowl, and ladled in some peaches.

"So," he asked, "how is your day shaping up?"

"You know, I finally have some trustworthy help at the paper, so all I need to do is show up there for an hour or so, and then we can play with Daddy's files."

"Do my ears deceive me? Has the Control Queen learned to delegate?"

"Don't be snotty. I ran that paper alone for more than twenty years, and if you and Blanche hadn't quadrupled the workload, I could do it still. I was lucky to find these kids, or I would be there twenty-two hours a day."

"Okay, okay." Lou held up one hand in surrender as he spooned cereal into his mouth with the other. "What say I shower and consolidate my notes, look through the Biggs file, and we can strategize when you get back?"

"Yup."

"By the way, what do you know about Woody Biggs?"

Hilda shrugged. "Just the minimum, what was in the news over the years. Remember that his real heyday was before I was born, or when I was a very little kid."

"What about William H. Goolsby?"

"Never heard of him."

"Maybe I'll Google him later . . ."

Lou chewed his breakfast and spaced out. Hilda leafed through the newspaper and sipped coffee.

"Are we getting boring?" Hilda asked.

Snapping out of his reverie, Lou said, "Huh?"

"Are we getting boring? Are we like some old married couple who never talk?"

Lou resisted rolling his eyes. He cleared his throat and rummaged through his mind for the proper response.

"Ahem. Well, no. We're just getting comfortable with each other, and we don't feel the need to fill every second with talk. It's the difference between the courting phase and the development of the relationship."

Hilda looked at him. "Where'd you get that, from Dr. Phil?"

"Ouch! That was uncalled for. Were you expecting

some brilliant insight about what is a common human experience?"

She stretched, yawned. "Yeah, yeah. On the road to dangling conversations and superficial sighs. I'm getting dressed."

Lou allowed himself an eye roll, if she was going to quote Paul Simon.

"I'll tell you what. When you get home from the office, I'll greet you at the door wearing only Saran wrap."

With a shrug, Hilda said, "We'll just have to take another shower. Forget it."

Lou finished his breakfast, wondering whether this moment came to all relationships.

Brooklyn, New York, 1962

Bobby Geller sat on a couch in a living room in the Flatbush section of Brooklyn. Lindy Peress lived there, a girl he had met on a Sunday afternoon in Washington Square Park. She was petite and pretty, with wavy black hair that hung long down her back, and luminous gray eyes.

The room was nicely furnished. Wall-to-wall carpets, stylish furniture that matched and art on the walls, including colorful posters advertising Polish theater productions. It was far beyond anything he and his mother could afford, and he was always worried that he might be soiling something. Lindy's parents were going out for the afternoon, and had made Bobby feel welcome in their home.

"Now, you two have fun. We'll be back around six. Bobby, do you want to stay for dinner?"

"Thanks, Mrs. Peress, but I'd better get back to Jersey. It's a long trip on the train from here."

She smiled and put on her coat. "Well, it's an open invitation. I have a feeling we'll be seeing more of you." Mr. Peress had a wry look on his face. Lindy cringed with embarrassment as they left.

Recovering, she asked, "Do you want to listen to some music?"

"Sure. What do you have?"

Lindy walked over to the massive console record player and flipped through a stack of LPs on the floor. "Joan Baez? Dave Van Ronk? Pete Seeger? There's this weird kid named Dylan . . ."

"Lindy, who are these people? I thought maybe you had Bobby Dam or The Shirelles, or . . ."

"This is the kind of music you hear at the hootenannies in the park. Folk music. Don't you have any of this stuff?"

"Oh, man, I didn't even know this was on records. I thought, you know, folk music is just . . ."

"Made by folks?" She laughed.

Bobby looked hurt.

"Don't look so crushed. I'm only kidding. If you've never been exposed to these records, there's no way you could know about them. I learned about them from older kids. And my parents."

"Your parents listen to folk music? The only thing my mom listens to is the opera on Saturdays."

"Folk music's been around for a long time. Pete Seeger has been singing since the thirties. Woody Guthrie, Leadbelly . . ."

"Leadbelly? You're making fun of me again."

"No, he's a Negro singer who was discovered in jail. Do you remember 'Rock Island Line'?"

"Yeah, that was cool. Lonnie Donegan."

"Well, that was Leadbelly's song. I have it by him on a record somewhere. " She looked through cabinets and cupboards. She pulled out a ten-inch LP. "I'll put on some Woody Guthrie in the meantime."

She turned on the record player and slipped the disc over the spindle. Guthrie's ironic, nasal voice and insistent guitar sound filled the room. Like most kids his age, Bobby's musical roots were early rock 'n' roll. He loved Elvis and Chuck Berry and Brenda Lee. He listened to whatever came on the radio, as long as his mother wasn't home. She thought of rock 'n' roll as "garbage."

But, this was another thing. Acoustic guitar and words not only about love, but also about the struggles of the poor and the working people, sometimes funny, sometimes bitter and accusatory.

Bobby studied the record cover, a photo of Guthrie, eyes closed, head back, cigarette dangling from his lips, strumming a guitar. The guitar had a hand-lettered sign taped to it, reading: "This Machine Kills Fascists." He gave himself over to the music.

Lindy provided the occasional explanation. " 'Do Re

Mi' is about the poor people during the Depression who lost their farms and took off out west to go to California. They got turned away at the border if they were broke."

He listened, rapt, to both sides of the record. Lindy put on Pete Seeger.

"Pete was blacklisted because of his political beliefs," she told him.

"What's 'blacklisted'?"

Lindy launched into a quick history of the blacklist, the remnants of which were still affecting the entertainment industry. Bobby got a look into a world he didn't know existed. He heard songs about history not taught in schools. "Strange Fruit" sung by Josh White made him cry.

"You should hear Billie Holiday sing it," Lindy said.

She was about to put on another record, when he realized that it was getting late.

"I'd better go. It's an hour at least back to Newark." Bobby rose and put on his coat.

"Lindy, I can't thank you enough. I never heard any of this before."

"You may have heard one or two of these songs in the Village, but I'll bet you were more interested in the girls than the music."

"Well, it's how I met you."

She stood on her toes and kissed him. "Call me."

"When I get home."

Back in Newark, he realized how small and gray his world was. He greeted his mother, whose expression indicated that she was unhappy with his all-day absence.

He called Lindy to tell her he got home safely, and she told him she wished they could live closer. Bobby thought he might be in love.

"Who was that on the phone?" Mildred asked.

"Just a friend."

"It sounded like you were talking to a girl."

"Yes. Her name is Melinda. Lindy."

"A shiksa?"

"Mom!"

"Answer me. Melinda is not a Jewish name."

"They're Sephardic. Her last name is Peress."

"Humph! Those Spanish Jews are stuck up, almost as bad as the Germans."

"Actually, they're from Egypt," he said, his voice weary.

"Don't be a snotnose. You seem to know an awful lot about them."

"We've talked a lot. I told her about you."

"So, now she hates me, too?"

"Come on, Mom. She's nice, her parents are nice. They live in a nice apartment."

"Ooh, isn't that nice!" She oozed sarcasm.

"Look, I'm tired. I'm going to bed."

"So you can dream of your little baby doll? So you can forget about this crummy flat?"

"Good night, Mom."

Bobby went to his room, thinking that it wouldn't be so bad to dream about his little baby doll.

7. Back to the Beginning

Showered and dressed, Lou logged on to Hilda's computer in her spacious home office and sipped the dregs of his cold coffee. Ah, he thought, just like the real office.

After dealing with his e-mail he Googled William Goolsby. Hundreds of articles kicked out, and it was quickly established that Goolsby was a successful New Jersey businessman dealing in construction and facilities management, with a custom software division headquartered in northern Virginia.

He was also the former or current chair, president, or general secretary of several African-American political or educational associations, head of a foundation to improve relations between races and religions, and former candidate for the governorship of New Jersey.

There were pictures of him with presidents from Eisenhower to Clinton, senators of both parties, and black leaders from Jesse Jackson to Bishop Desmond

Tutu. A short bio described his financial and moral support of the Freedom Riders in the early '60s, and his efforts to ease the violence of the Newark Riots, at great risk to his personal safety.

"Thoroughly admirable guy," Lou said out loud. "I wonder what he has to do with Geller?"

He printed off a few of the items and pictures, and a bio. Then he turned to the file he received from Biggs. It was full of official correspondence from various civil rights groups, both local in Oregon and national, with the majority from Goolsby's BGF Foundation.

Biggs had donated thousands over the years to BGF, and the file contained effusive letters of thanks and embossed certificates of appreciation. Filed latest date first, the correspondence went back to the 1970s. Lou skimmed them for anything he could use.

A few minutes later, he heard Hilda come in.

"Hey, Louie, whaddaya know?" Hilda dropped her briefcase on the desk and kissed Lou.

"A little more than this morning. William Goolsby has quite a personal history."

Hilda sat down next to him as Lou filled her in about Goolsby's life and good works. Hilda made impressed noises and scribbled a note or two on a yellow pad.

"So, from what you tell me, this guy is golden. Do we know what connection he has to Geller?"

"You know, I asked myself that same question, and I was just looking through the file I got from Biggs. So far, all I know is that Woody Biggs made generous contributions to Goolsby's BGF Foundation, and got many letters of appreciation. This goes back thirty years, or more. Some of the letters are just friendly banter, some official thanks, but I haven't made any more than a cursory look, and no mention of Geller."

"Let me get a cup of coffee, and I'll grab half the file."

"Maybe you better make some fresh. This is tasting kinda bitter."

"Lou, why do you drink old, cold coffee?"

"Reminds me of home."

Hilda gave him an exasperated look, but stood up. "Men. Be right back."

While Hilda was gone, Lou dove back into the file. He found a carbon copy of a letter on yellow tissue from Biggs to Goolsby. It was dated May 1976, and two sentences stood out. They said only: "Bobby Geller is engaged, I hear. Good for him, because he hasn't been the same since losing the girlfriend."

Lou noted the nickname and the reference to the girlfriend. He looked some more.

The very first letter in the file, last in the folder, was from Goolsby to Biggs and dated September 1974. Lou read it.

Dear Mr. Biggs,

I am Bill Goolsby of Newark, New Jersey, and I am a businessman and a supporter of black improvement organizations and causes. I can supply references, if you wish.

I am writing to you in behalf of my young friend

Robert Geller. I call him Bobby, since I have known him from his childhood. He is currently in a rabbinical academy in Vancouver, British Columbia, and I hear that he may well be settling in your area.

You may wish to know why I have an interest in this boy. He is the son of my best friend, now deceased. I have never known a finer, less prejudiced man than his father, and Bobby is very much like him.

Bobby was severely injured in Mississippi in 1964 while setting up a freedom school. He was beaten by peckerwood thugs so badly he nearly died. His girlfriend was killed, and two young black men with them have never been found.

He has led an uninspired life since then, but has recently found a calling to the clergy. Should he settle near you, I would appreciate your keeping an eye on him and seeing that he is safe and sound. It is his nature to become involved in matters that put him in harm's way, usually in service to the black community.

I have heard many things said about you, and I choose to believe the stories of strength and integrity. We both know what it takes for a black man to succeed in this society.

I know you are the person for the job. Please do not approach him directly, because he is too proud to accept help knowingly. If it ever comes to a matter of funds, don't hesitate to contact me. I owe him much because of his father.

I consider this a personal favor of the highest

*level, and I am beholden to you if you accept.
Thank you for your consideration.*

Lou whistled. "Man," he said aloud, "you just never know."

"You never know what?" said Hilda, returning with two cups of coffee. Lou jumped.

"Scare you, did I?" she asked.

"You always scare me. Read this."

Hilda sipped coffee, put down the cup, and took the letter. She whistled.

"See what I mean?"

"Yup," she said. "Let's go find my father's files on this guy."

The files of Carroll Truax, editor and publisher of the *North Coast Clarion*, lately merged with the *Stumptown Weekly*, had served Lou well in the years since he met Hilda, Truax's daughter and heir in every way. The articles in the microfilm images of the newspaper often told less than half the story, absent Truax's commentary, insights, and observations. He never left out anything he thought his readers should know, but never pandered to the hunger for gossip or scandal, unless scandal was the topic of the article. Then, he resisted the half truth or the unprovable, and never printed a blind item or uncredited allegation. His reputation was solid.

And, the unprinted commentary gave a background and depth to the printed story that was a chronicle of a rural Oregon beach town in the throes of twentieth-century change. Plus, he was very funny.

Hilda and Lou noted the dates on the Biggs correspondence, and pulled files from the overstuffed metal cabinets. They riffled through the paper looking for references to Geller.

"Got something," Hilda said. "Looks like the engagement announcement. Blah, blah, daughter of Melville and Shirley Goldstein of Waldorf and Seagirt, blah, blah, rabbi of new temple under construction, to be completed and dedicated in the spring."

"Just the facts, ma'am?"

"You got it. Maybe a little more space given because it's a clergyman, and the first temple on the north coast."

"Did the paper cover the event?" Lou asked.

"Let's see." Hilda moved some more paper. "Oh, yeah. Whoa! The governor attended, the mayor of Waldorf, um, various mucky-mucks from the business world . . ."

"Any asides from your dad?" Lou sat down.

"You bet. Listen to this. 'Groom looked like he ate something bad. Beyond normal cold feet? Bride a take-charge type, looks and talks like her father. Mel doing the room like he was running for office. Is he? Great food, band flown in from NYC. Sprained my ankle doing the hora, a circle dance of sorts. Eased the pain with vintage champagne.'"

"Was your father able to read people that well?"

Hilda smiled. "He fancied himself as real perceptive, but I don't think he was any more intuitive about people than anyone else. I will say that he observed very closely, and might have picked up clues that most of us would miss. How well he processed that information is an unknown."

"He's seldom been wrong with his notes in my experience." Lou straightened papers.

"Yeah, but with facts, and speculation based on facts. He was winging it here."

Lou sat back and tented his fingers, quiet for a moment. Hilda made notes in the silence.

"You know what? I think we need to start at the beginning. We have no idea where the original reporter covering the case has disappeared to. Lainie Reiter has a good, solid view of the trial, but came in later. Tom Knight is ready to give Geller a walk because he has no credible witnesses any longer.

"I'm thinking that something has been lost in the shuffle. Either there's a witness we might find, or an angle they didn't explore . . . or Geller is guilty as hell and will get away with murder."

Hilda nodded. "His daughter thinks he may be guilty. There's no proof that extramarital affairs were a motive, because no one has come forward to say so. Ever wonder why?"

"Just the obvious three conclusions. He never had them. He had them and the witnesses are scared, or otherwise reluctant. Or it doesn't have any bearing on the crime.

"Do you think Knight subpoenaed his appointment book?"

Hilda shrugged. "Knight's pretty thorough, but the question really is whether Geller would record his conquests in his date book, no pun intended."

"Yeah, but his conquests, should they exist, may have come from his counseling sessions. If you're gonna prey on women, the emotionally vulnerable make a good hunting ground."

"I like the way you think. Let's draw up a battle plan for this, and take tasks to perform. We'll use the newspaper files, both here and in Portland, my father's notes, and whatever we can get from Knight in the way of evidence.

"Then we might get a fresh perspective."

Lou thought for a moment.

"What about Gar? Think he'll help?"

"Our esteemed police chief? I think he'd go to the moon for you. You know about Connie, right?" Hilda smiled with a choice piece of gossip to reveal.

"Connie? From the Dunes Café?"

"The same. A waitress no longer. She's been taking courses at the community college and acing them. She just quit the café and now works as a civilian employee in the chief's office."

Lou brightened. "That is so cool! Her mother must be thrilled."

"Not as much as Gar. They were dating, and I don't think it will quit now that she works for him. He likes having her around."

"Well, that's not necessarily a good idea . . ."

"Lou, a mom-and-pop cop shop!"

"Yeah, but outside of the doggerel potential . . ."

"Hey, Gar tells me that she's a budding genius in crime-scene work. She can secure and preprocess a scene with the best of them. It's a gift. The state crime scene unit loves her. Half their work is done when they walk in."

"I thought crime scene techs had to be sworn officers here." Lou looked puzzled.

"They do, but no CST is gonna kick if their work load is lightened a little."

"Let's hope she doesn't screw up a case. Wait! Did she respond to the Geller killing?"

"I wouldn't think so. It was too long ago. But, she might help us evaluate the reports."

"Okay. I haven't seen Gar in a while. I'll get a kick out of Loober in love."

One fresh cup of coffee later, Lou and Hilda planned their strategy.

Newark, New Jersey, 1963

They sat in front of the television set, numbed and horrified by the worst event in modern American history, a weekend of horror. Mildred had been sent home from work early on Friday with news of the death of the president. Bobby's school had been closed about the same time.

The stark, grainy black-and-white pictures were the perfect medium for the aftermath. The hushed tones of the reporters, the pictures of men and women crying on the streets of American cities, the widow in her blood-stained clothing, and in a moment that formalized the status of television as the national medium, the murder of the alleged assassin, live and as immediate as a home run or a touchdown.

Mildred wept, sighed, cried some more. Bobby sat and wondered where it would end. Jack Ruby, who shot the man who they thought shot the president, was a Jew. Mildred despaired that the blame for the whole thing would be hung around Jewish necks, and told Bobby so. For once he did not dismiss her fears as paranoia.

By Sunday, they were trying to make sense of it.

"Did he need this?" Mildred asked. "A young man. This is the first president younger than me. Was, was younger." She sobbed, "My God, he has small children. This will haunt them all their lives."

"It was the right-wingers, Mom. Mr. Peress says . . ."

"Please, spare me the opinions of your professor. Isn't it bad enough that Kennedy was killed?"

Bobby looked his mother in the eye; she turned away. "He's not a professor, he's just very interested in current events. And, yes, it's bad enough. But, it wasn't like a car crash, or like he choked on a bone. Someone pulled the trigger . . ."

"And he was killed by that Jewish bum, Ruby."

"We don't know that. We don't know if that Oswald guy did it. We saw Ruby kill him, but all that does is shut him up permanently."

Mildred's eyes narrowed and focused. "It's like hearing your father talk. There's no hope for you." She turned to look at the television.

Bobby felt a rush of pride, as warm as a summer

breeze. Her worst criticism was his greatest source of self-worth.

"Mr. Brown!" Miss DuBois shrieked. "Call 911!"

Herman Brown dropped the legal papers he was reading and called the emergency number. Then he ran up the stairs.

Woodrow Wilson Biggs was gasping, and his complexion was a scary gray. His eyes rolled in terror.

"Have you tried anything?" he asked the nurse.

"Everything I can do here. He needs to go to the hospital."

Brown nodded. "I'll go downstairs to let them in."

An hour later, the emergency room nurse took Brown aside.

"Are you a relative?"

"As close to one as he got. I got power of attorney, and written instructions from him."

"Does he wish to be resuscitated?"

"He don't want to live like a vegetable, all tubes and wires. He had enough of that. If he ready to go, let him go."

"We'll want to see if he responds, but I don't want to give you any false hopes."

"Nurse, if anyone was ever ready to go, it's the Boss. You need for me to bring in those papers?"

"By the time you come back, it may be over."

Brown sighed. "You got a chapel here? I guess I owe him a prayer."

Newark, New Jersey, 1964

"Robert Geller, if you do this I'm through with you."

Bobby looked up at his mother from his battered suitcase. The argument had gone on for days, and he was tired of it. Even Mildred was going through the motions, the fire long-since spent.

"Sit down, Mom." He cleared a place on his bed. She sat with reluctance, like it was a threat to her health.

"All we've been doing for the last week is arguing, and my feelings are the same as they were when I first told you where I was going. I have to do this."

"Bobby, what happened to you? You were such a good boy. After your father died I was scared you'd become a delinquent, a bum, hanging around in Greenwich Village . . . God knows what." She twisted a handkerchief in her hands.

Bobby looked at her hands, noticed the wrinkled skin mottled with age spots. His mother's hair was probably gray, although she had bleached it blonde years before and permed it into a succession of bouffant styles. She looked like everyone else's mom, and like the businesswoman she had become.

He also picked up the change in her tone. Rather than the usual routine, complete with trite phrases of disapproval, Mildred seemed like she wanted to talk.

"I'm not a bum, Mom." He sat next to her. "I'm in the top five percent of my class, and I won a scholarship to Rutgers. I work after school and you get most of what I make. I try to be respectful, and to do things around the house. Why would you say that I'm not a good boy?"

Mildred looked deep into his eyes for the first time in years. What she saw surprised her. No longer the fatherless boy, Bobby had become a young man. What she feared was that he would be like Barney, idealistic, vulnerable, selfless to a fault.

"Bobby, when Barney died he left us nothing. He had cashed in his insurance policies to invest in a bad deal, that business with Goolsby. I told him to get a real job, that I had no faith in this deal. He ignored me, and threw good money after bad.

"Why? I'll tell you why. He put his idealistic principles before his family. He let us down. I don't want you to be like that. I always tried to teach you to think of yourself first, but . . ." She heaved a dramatic sigh. "I guess it all fell on deaf ears.

"Please, baby, for me, don't go to Mississippi. I don't want you coming home in a box."

Bobby thought a moment and chose his words.

"Mom, I understand what you're saying. But first of all, Bill Goolsby is doing very well now. If dad hadn't died, we might be living in one of those big new houses in Teaneck. It was just bad luck.

"And I appreciate that you don't think this is my battle down south. I know it can be dangerous down there. Truthfully, I'm scared. But, sometimes you have to stand up and be counted, even though there may be a price for it."

A look passed over Mildred's face, and Bobby knew the magic moment had passed with it. His mother's face now had that hard, bitter cast he knew as her daily reality. He wondered if he would ever get close to his mother again.

"Okay, my son the idealist. Go. If you get killed they can always give your scholarship to a Negro.

"It's that girl, isn't it?" Mildred spat. "That little communist from Brooklyn? She talked you into this."

"She has a name, mom. Lindy."

"Not to me. To me she's the thief who stole my son. I wouldn't say the other names I have for her."

"She stole nothing. I was happy to give her whatever I could. She's done more for me than I can ever repay. And yes, she's going down south, too."

"Go with your tramp. Get killed. See if I care." She rose and swept out his bedroom door, like a tragic heroine in one of her operas.

He resumed packing, knowing that whatever he brought with him, the heaviest load would be borne in his heart.

8. The Lion's Den

"Lou?"

Lou had hesitated, thought for a second before answering the phone. He wondered who knew where he was, outside of the office staff. "Yes. Who is this?"

"Herman Brown. Mr. Biggs passed last night."

"Mr. Brown. Oh, I wasn't expecting to hear from you . . . so soon. I'm so sorry."

"You can call me Kid. The Boss used to. I got your number from your editor, because of the circumstances."

"Yes, of course. Don't need to explain. When will the funeral be? I'd like to come."

"Well, I was left instructions that the Boss was to lie in state in the house before they bury him, and then a big wake and party. If I was you, I'd make that, too."

"I wouldn't miss it, Kid. Can I bring somebody?"

"Anyone you want. Boss was busy when I wasn't around. I got envelopes here with my name on 'em, in number order. I open 'em as I'm instructed to. You're mentioned in some. We got some things to talk about."

"I'm sure we do. Right now I'm out in Seagirt. I have an appointment with Rabbi Geller later today, but I can be back in Portland tomorrow."

"No hurry. Boss gonna be laid out day after tomorrow, party start that same night. I hear you not a drinkin' man."

Lou laughed. "Right. All that is behind me. I can have a good time without alcohol."

"Later, then."

They rang off and Lou stared at the wall for a while. Then he left for the Seagirt Police Station for a visit to Chief Loober.

It had been a while since Lou had seen Gar Loober. The young deputy had assisted Lou in his first case as an investigative reporter for the then *Stumptown Weekly*, saving his life and Hilda's when they were cornered by a murderer and his henchman. The same case took down the former chief, who was involved in a cover-up. By default, Loober became chief, and had grown into the office.

Always smart and ambitious, Loober acquired gravitas and respect, first in contrast to the old chief, and then for his skill and compassion as a cop. The town was well served by the man.

Lou drove up to the cinder-block police station and jail, now nearly twice the size it had been and sporting a recent coat of light blue paint. There were two full-time deputies, each with academic training in police work and a service orientation. And now, there was Connie.

Once a waitress in a local café, Connie was a young woman with few prospects and a glum outlook. She saw a chance when Loober found himself the only cop in town, and asked to work in the police station as a civilian employee.

Perhaps motivated by more than practical considerations, Gar Loober hired her. He had always been a little sweet on her. In the years since then, Connie took classes in police science, CPR and first aid, and office administration at the local community college. At his urging and recommendation, Connie also attended every seminar and took every correspondence course available from the county and state police.

Still a civilian employee rather than a sworn officer, she was at least as valuable as any of the young cops on the Seagirt force, and more so to Loober, who relied on her good sense and emotional support. Their relationship enjoyed an inevitable deepening, and they were soon to be married.

Lou had not seen Gar Loober for more than a year, spending less time in Seagirt as his investigative duties consumed him, and most of that time was taken up as he grew closer to Hilda.

Lou checked the sky. The clouds seemed to be breaking up, and there was the threat of sunshine. He walked into the office and looked around, disoriented for a moment by the new set-up.

"Lou!" a voice came from his left, and Connie stood up from behind a desk. A tall young woman, she wore a neat khaki uniform that flattered her fit body. Lou noticed that she had lost the withdrawn and mopey attitude he remembered.

Two young cops looked up at Connie's greeting but quickly resumed what they were doing. Lou knew neither of them by sight.

"Connie, wow, you look great."

She blushed and walked over to Lou, throwing her arms around him.

"Oof," Lou uttered, surprised at the strength of the bear hug. "You've been working out."

Connie laughed, but blushed deeper. "And you aren't limping. Did I hear that you got that bad knee replaced?"

"Yes, ma'am, and I wish I had done it years ago."

Connie released him from her grip. "My mom just had both knees done. All those years as a waitress . . . How's Hilda?"

She gestured him to a chair.

"Oh, Lou, this is Officer Jim Willsie," a blond, dimpled cop waved at him, "and Mike Uhl." A wave from a serious-looking young cop. "Lou Tedesco is a reporter and an old friend of Chief Loober's and mine. Treat him like family."

"Thanks, Connie." Lou nodded to the men. "Good to meet you two." More waves. The cops were too involved in their work to get up.

"Will one of you guys handle the phones? Lou, let me buy you a cup of coffee."

"Well, sure, but there's a pot right there."

Connie wrinkled her nose, then spoke in a whisper.

"Maybe it was all those years drinking good coffee at the Dunes, but I can't handle that stuff. Don't tell Gar."

They left the station and walked toward a Starbucks. They purchased a couple of cups of overpriced coffee, and took a table looking out at the street.

Lou began to get the idea that Connie had something on her mind. "How's Gar?" he opened.

She gnawed her lower lip for a moment, then said, "That's kinda what I wanted to talk about."

Lou leaned forward. "Everything okay between you two?"

She waved her hands for assurance. "Oh, it's nothing like that. I think Gar is bored. He used to be out on the street working as a cop, and now, well, he's more like a manager. I try to take some of the paperwork load off him, but it isn't enough.

"It hasn't affected our relationship yet, but . . ."

Lou nodded.

"So," she went on, "I'm really happy to see you. Is there something you're working on that he could help you with? He still talks about that beach murder, the one where you two met."

"I might be able to use him, but the thing itself is out of his jurisdiction. The Geller killing."

Connie's eyes got big. "What the heck are you doing with that?"

Lou filled her in on the details, the edited version, then mentioned the peculiar possibility of the connection to Woody Biggs. Then he had to explain Biggs.

"Way before my time," she said.

"True enough. I'll tell you what. I'd love to see the

police reports on the murder and the forensics. I might be able to get my hands on them anyway, but maybe Gar can shorten the process, and then I wouldn't have to beg Tom Knight."

"Okay, that might be a start. He'll want to do more than you ask."

"Yeah, and maybe I'll need more. He can provide insights I'll need to evaluate the information."

Connie smiled. "Okay, okay. Be sure you tell him that you value his insights."

"Did it ever occur to him that the reason police work in this burg has gotten boring is because he's such a good chief?"

"I guess he knows that in his brain, but it doesn't help on a day-to-day basis."

Lou moved the conversation to local gossip about Seagirt, the women at the Dunes Café, and how the city had changed. Then, he excused himself.

"I have to go talk with Rabbi Geller."

"Whoa! That'll be an experience. I spoke to him about two years ago concerning vandalism at the temple. He's got an interesting relationship with authority figures. Good luck getting anything important out of him."

"I'll want to ask you about that sometime soon. Do you know where his house is, exactly?"

Connie drew a map on a napkin, although it wasn't that complicated. Lou had Geller's directions, but figured to play it safe and have the map as a backup. He had about a six or seven mile drive south, and just off the main drag. He walked Connie back to the station, and she gave him another bone-crushing hug.

Lou pulled up to a '70s-vintage house just off of Highway 101. He recalled that it was built for Geller and his late wife Grace by her father, Mel Goldstein, a developer and housing mogul. The style was rustic, not quite a log cabin. It was close enough to the Pacific that the on-shore breeze stirred the trees around the entrance.

Lou got out of his car and looked at the house, trying to picture it on a rainy night. The driveway was visible from the front door only for the last few feet out to the road, the two-car garage not at all. To the right of the door, the house projected out enough to block a view from inside. The trees restricted visibility even more.

A fine design for a development, Lou thought, not so good for an isolated house out here in the boonies. He guessed that daddy was willing to spring for the house, constructed with superior materials, but not for a new architectural design.

Squinting, he tried to imagine the killers parking, perhaps on the shoulder of the highway to hide their car, making their way to the house, and climbing the stairs. His gaze strayed up the stairs and then he jumped. There was a face peering out from the small round window in the door.

The door opened, and Rabbi Robert Geller called out, "Are you gonna come in, or are you just casing the joint?"

Taking a deep breath to calm himself, Lou answered, "Sure. I'm coming. Rabbi Geller, I presume?"

Geller waved him in without reply, a cigarette clenched between the fingers of his right hand. Lou walked up the six steps of the stoop, using the wrought-iron railing out of habit. The door opened wider and Lou stepped in, then gasped.

The walls were still stained with blood, dried and turned brown. Lou looked up. There was blood spray on the ceiling. Lou looked down.

"I had to get rid of the carpet," Geller said, "it started to smell."

"Um, uh . . . ," Lou stammered, "I'm sorry . . ."

"Yeah, I know. It's a bit of a shock. My daughter won't even come to the house anymore. Come to think of it, no one does. Can't imagine why, can you?" Geller smirked.

The rabbi gestured toward the couch, and Lou walked over to sit down. The living room was furnished in expensive, but old and worn, furniture.

The rabbi walked over to the couch. He was thinner and grayer than his pictures in the paper, and his beard had been shaved to a stylish goatee. He was dressed in chinos and a flannel shirt, open at the neck. Nike basketball shoes with argyle socks. Lou tried to get a sense of the man, a first impression, but Geller was closed and wary.

Geller sat at the far end of the couch, and pulled an ashtray over. "My daughter thinks you can save the family by finding the truth. Cute, isn't she?"

Lou, like most journalists, considered himself

something of a cynic. But, he sensed that he was now in the presence of the real thing. Geller flicked an ash and crushed out the smoke. Reaching behind him, he grabbed a pack of Camels and lit another one.

"Mind if I smoke?"

Lou shrugged. "It's your house. I can deal with it."

"My late wife wouldn't let me smoke in the house. We have a deck with a roof out back, so I used to go out there. Now, it's just me and my bad habits."

"I'm sorry."

Geller leaned forward, smoke trailing out of his mouth. "Sure you are. Who wouldn't be? Terrible thing like that." His voice was flat, emotionless.

Lou was determined not to squirm, but this guy was giving him the creeps. Geller's face was set in a fixed, insincere smile.

"Rabbi Geller . . . ," Lou began.

"A rabbi without a congregation. I was, ah, relieved of my post after the indictment. Still, I am entitled to the label."

"Yes. What happened the night of your wife's death?"

Geller's eyes opened wide. "No foreplay? I guess it's better like this." He took a drag on the cigarette. "I came home from the temple and found my wife lying in the entranceway. The door was ajar. The blood was nice and fresh then, bright red. I called 911 and waited. I had my first cigarette ever in my own house. The cops came, then the medical techs, then the crime scene unit.

"I'm just sorry that my son was on duty."

"You're not sorry your wife was murdered?"

Geller grinned, but his eyes were cold. "Cheap shot. One more and this tea party is over."

Lou shifted on the couch. "Look, I'm not trying to score points on you. Your phraseology was a bit odd."

"Yeah, well, chalk it up to grief."

One thing Lou didn't see was grief. "What did you think might be the cause? It didn't seem random, did it?"

Geller thought for a moment. "You know, no one has ever asked me that. No, it didn't seem random. My wife was a successful businesswoman, and she brought home cash receipts once a week for counting and deposit. We have one of those money-counting machines in her office, the kind the casinos use. It could have been someone from her office.

"Also, she worked with the homeless. Very admirable, but some of those people were mentally ill or had substance abuse problems, or both. It could well have been one of them."

"Did she bring home any money the night of the incident?"

"You can say 'killing' or 'murder' or whatever. I've come to terms with it."

At the very least, thought Lou. "Did she bring money home that night?"

Geller looked amused. "Yeah, she did. The killers didn't take it, though. It was right there in her purse."

Geller sat back, removed a bit of tobacco from his tongue with a fingernail, his expression blank. Then, he smiled.

"But we know it was that maniac Larry Gottbaum. He admitted it. He tried to pin the whole idea on me, but it was him. He's in jail, I'm sitting here entertaining you, case closed."

"How do you know Gottbaum? Do you mind if I take notes?"

"That's two questions."

Lou suppressed a remark. "Okay, do you mind if I take notes?"

Geller shrugged. "Suit yourself."

Lou opened a reporter's notebook and clicked a pen. "Now, how did you know Gottbaum?"

"He came to me with a bunch of problems. He was a drunk, and was starting to get a nasty little pill habit. His marriage was sliding into the crapper. His children avoided him. He was a marginal guy with a crummy life, so he lied to build himself up. He became a private investigator because there was no licensing requirement in Oregon in those days. And, he had this fantasy life as a Mossad or CIA agent. It depended which day you asked him."

Geller extinguished the cigarette, reached for the pack, thought a second, and put the pack down. "Want a drink? I got some really expensive vodka on ice."

"I don't drink alcohol. You have a soda?"

"I can find one. You're not from here. You didn't call it 'pop.'"

"That's right. I came here from California, but grew up back east."

"I'm from Jersey, Newark mostly."

Lou nodded. "My father was a craftsman. He followed the work. Whenever he got a semipermanent job, like with a construction company or a restorer, we moved. Lived in Boston, Trenton, Baltimore, Queens. He helped refurbish a lot of the colonial-era buildings in Boston."

"You don't have a Boston accent."

"Nope. Spent more time in New York than anywhere else, but I don't really sound like that either. A puzzlement."

"Mind if I get a drink?"

Lou shrugged. "Suit yourself."

Geller chuckled. "A wise guy."

He left the room, and Lou heard noises from another room. Looking around, he noticed pictures of the kids, pictures of Grace Geller with the kids, and the rabbi with the kids. No pictures of the happy couple together.

Ah, well, Lou thought, someone has to take the picture.

Geller came back with a cordial glass of clear liquid, icy on the outside, and a 7-Up.

"This do?" Geller asked. Lou nodded and Geller handed him the bottle.

"*L'chaim!*" said the rabbi.

"*Salud!*" said Lou.

They clicked drinks and sipped.

"Ah. Love this stuff. Grace said it tasted like something you pour on a wound. Say, how'd you end up doing this?"

Taking the opportunity to shmooze the rabbi, possibly get to him, Lou launched into the condensed version of his life. Geller nodded, smiled, and shook his head in all the right places. Lou talked for about ten minutes.

Then Lou sipped his drink and waited.

After a time, and one refill on the vodka, the rabbi began to reminisce. Lou paid attention, but wasn't interested in the direction the conversation was taking.

"Rabbi Geller, who's William Goolsby?"

The phrase "taken aback" had never meant much to Lou before, but Geller's body appeared to have been yanked backwards. His face showed shock.

"Where in the hell did you get his name from?"

"It came up in my investigations," Lou said with cool unconcern. "He seems to have a real interest in you."

"He has nothing to do with this, or really with me anymore. He's from the long-gone Newark part of my life."

"Does the name Woody Biggs mean anything to you?"

Geller seemed genuinely unfamiliar with the name.

"Biggs? Nope. Where are you getting this stuff from?"

"Here and there. One more thing, and I'll call it a day."

Geller nodded, relieved.

"There were persistent, if unproven, rumors about you and women besides your wife. Any truth to them?"

The rabbi went back into defensive mode. "Pure crap. I counseled women all the time in my work.

They were in all kinds of distress. Their husbands were dead or dying, or screwing a girl at the office. The women were cancer survivors, or had just been diagnosed. Or, they were just lonely and desperate. If I had wanted to, I could have gathered a harem. More than one of these women threw themselves at me."

Geller paused to light another cigarette.

"Can you tell me about Mrs. Geller's outside interests?" Lou asked.

The rabbi shrugged. "What's to tell? She was Mel's daughter. Everything she touched generated cash. The bakery she bought from some old hippie who was eking out enough for pot money baking organic bread and stuff like that. She tore out everything but the ovens, which were first-class, expanded the space, and started turning out baguettes, specialty loaves, killer cookies . . . and good bagels. You had a good bagel since you moved out here?"

Lou shook his head.

"Yeah," Geller went on, "even the gentiles can tell the difference. You should stop at the bakery and get some. I kept it open, and gave the employees seventy-five percent ownership."

"What about the homeless work?"

"I thought you said you were calling it a day."

"Promise, after this."

Geller nodded. "Okay. Eight, ten years ago, we started to have a homeless problem here. We've always had transients, hobos I guess, but some began to stick around, look for empty beach houses, or some of the abandoned logging buildings in the area. Squatters, I guess.

"Well, naturally there was a reaction. Families worried about their children, business types were offended by appropriation of private property, blah blah blah. Grace shamed the local Rotarians into donating an old chip mill and some bucks to renovate and maintain it."

Geller drew on his cigarette. "Next thing you know, Grace is getting local chefs to teach classes in restaurant work, food prep, catering, what-have-you. The homeless who couldn't get it together for work were housed and fed as long as they stayed around, mostly in the winter.

"A lot of these people are just rolling stones, no ability to stay put. Some, the ones who learned cooking and baking, are working locally or have gone on to jobs in Tacoma or Bend, wherever. Some cook for the shelter and make a stipend over their room and board."

"It sounds like a complete success," Lou said.

"About as close as can be. I have nothing to do with the shelter, but it's running under its own power and is self-sufficient. Grace was so good that she left a legacy of success in everything."

"You sound like you really admired her."

"I did. I do. I'm a screw-up compared to her." Geller's face darkened.

"Something?" Lou asked.

"Look, it's no secret that our marriage was rocky. I'm sure Roberta mentioned that. We even talked about divorce. All her energy and emotional resources went into her work. My mother-in-law knows what

I'm talking about, she had the same kind of problems with Mel. Grace used to joke that they had four kids, so she knew they did it four times."

"Were you getting close to a divorce?"

"Hey, I don't know. Things have a funny way of working out once a problem can be defined. No telling."

"How do you think a divorce would have played with your congregation?"

"It's the twenty-first century. Everybody's been divorced, or someone close to them has. It's not like some Orthodox community a hundred years ago. You know that story of the old Jewish couple? They'd been married for seventy-five years. One day, the wife asks for a divorce. The husband wants to know how come. 'Because,' the old lady says, 'enough is enough.' "

Geller stubbed out the cigarette. "We hadn't reached that point quite yet."

"Thanks for your time, Rabbi." Lou got up and extended his hand, which the rabbi shook.

"Do you mind if I call again?"

"Maybe. Call and I'll let you know. I'm still not sure about you and this whole thing with Roberta."

"Yes, sir."

Later on, as Lou returned to Hilda's house, he tried to come to some conclusion about Rabbi Robert Geller. He could not.

9. Rage

The next morning, Lou sat, coffee in hand, on Hilda's back porch and watched the sun come up over the coast range. Hilda, already dressed, had run out for pastries and newspapers.

The session with Rabbi Geller was yet undigested in Lou's mind. It sat there, defying him to make sense of it.

Hilda arrived, white bakery bag and newspapers from Portland, Waldorf, and Seattle. She dropped the whole load on a wrought iron table in front of Lou.

"Penny for your thoughts?" She leaned over and kissed his cheek.

"Bad deal."

"You hardly said a word after you got home yesterday. Wanna talk about it now? I have to go to the office for a couple of hours, but I can spare some time now. Besides," she gestured to the bag, adorned with translucent grease spots, "I want one of those cream horns."

Lou watched her go into the house and organized his thoughts. Hilda emerged with three plates, a knife, and some napkins. She opened the bag and arranged the pastry on one plate.

"Okay, Lou. It's time to emerge from your death-like trance and talk. Maybe it'll help put things in perspective."

He nodded and snagged half a cinnamon bun. Sitting back in his chair, he nibbled on the bun for a while.

After swallowing, he looked Hilda in the eye. "He never cleaned up the blood. The walls of the entrance foyer are still painted with his wife's blood."

Hilda shuddered. "Now, *that's* creepy. Maybe it put you off your game. By the way, these came from her bakery," she brandished a cream-filled pastry. "Her bakery was the best for miles around the day it opened. Better than anything in Waldorf."

Lou shook his head. "Nix on creeping me out. Did you ever have a conversation with someone who speaks no English, and yet makes himself understood by gestures and body language, stuff like that?"

"Yup. At least once each in France and Germany."

"Well, this was kind of the opposite. I sat talking to a man who communicated in English, and when I finished, I felt like I hadn't understood most of it. Geller would make a perfect con man. Or a politician."

Hilda sighed. "Look, Lou, he's just a man with an agenda. You've run into tough interviews before where practiced liars withheld the truth. Why is he throwing you like this?"

Lou managed another bite and a sip of coffee. "Fair question. I think that he's learned better than most from his experience talking to both prosecutors and his defense attorneys. He gives you a lot of what you ask him for, but I always get the feeling there's more."

"Tell me about it."

Lou went over the notes he had taken the day before and recounted the conversation in as much detail as he could. Hilda's attention never strayed.

"I didn't like that answer about his alleged affairs," she said. "He never really denied it, just discounted the rumors. Cagey."

"That's it exactly. Cagey and evasive, even when the answer seems adequate. And his eyes, like a shark's, nothing behind them."

"What was he like when you sprang that Goolsby thing on him?"

"Wow, that was the most human reaction I got. Whoever Goolsby is, beyond his bio, he has the power to shake Geller up. I should try to call him."

"What do you hear from the daughter?"

"Nothing for a day, or so. I'll call her, too."

"You know what? I think it's time for me to get involved. We have this neat plan, and we should implement it. When I get back from the paper I'll start lining up interviews with women from his temple. If there's something out there, it can't stay hidden forever. Juicy gossip will out."

"Deal. I'll call Roberta."

*   *   *

Roberta Geller sat in a coffee shop in northwest Portland watching the world go by. Twenty-third Avenue, dubbed "Trendy-third" by local wags, was a curious mix of old and new Portland, with the balance definitely tipping toward the hipper shops and restaurants. Still catering as much to the large student/youth population as to the wealthy matrons, the parade of humanity was constant and amusing.

She had been steeling herself for this moment and, now fueled by two double-shot soy lattes, Roberta was ready to call her mother's youngest brother.

"Steven?"

"Yeah?"

"It's Roberta, honey. Where have you been?"

There was a pause on the other end, and Roberta could hear her uncle's mouth-breathing rale.

"Stevie?"

"Yeah, yeah. Whaddaya want?"

"Where the hell have you been? No one's heard from you since . . ."

"Since your goddamn old man got away with murder?"

Roberta sighed. "Look, Steve, I know how bad that made you feel. The state couldn't make its case once that slob pulled that weird . . ."

"Is it true?"

"Is what true?"

"Is it true that you hired a detective to prove Bob innocent?"

"Boy, it's amazing how things get distorted. I . . ."

"Just say yes or no."

"No!" Roberta made it as emphatic as she could.

"Jeff told me . . ."

"Jeff is wrong." Jeff was her uncle, his older brother.

"So what's right?"

"Okay, I approached an investigative reporter to see what he could find."

"Yeah? So, what's the difference?"

"This guy has a proven record of finding the truth. I think the truth is that my father is guilty."

"What if he can't find anything?"

"It's possible," she said. "He may even find something to exonerate Daddy from . . ."

"This is worse! You could pay off a private eye to keep his mouth shut. This friggin' reporter will make a big story out of it. Jesus, Roberta, what were you thinking?"

Roberta's phone buzzed.

"Steve, I have another call. Can you hold?"

There was a grunt on the other end. Roberta switched over.

"Hello?"

"Roberta? This is Lou."

"Can you hang on? I got another call."

"You bet."

She switched back. "Stevie? Hello?"

The line was dead; he had hung up. She punched the button.

"Lou?"

"Hiya. I spoke to your father yesterday."

"Yeah, he told me you were gonna pay a visit. How did it go?"

Lou searched his mind for a diplomatic answer.

"Well, it was, um, interesting."

Roberta laughed. "Welcome to the land of the mystified. My father has been an enigma for as long as I remember."

"He said you won't visit him in his house. True?"

"Has he cleaned and painted the entranceway?"

"Not yet. That was freaky."

"Just the right word. He can't even explain why not. I wish I were a shrink, maybe I could figure it out. You got any ideas?"

"Nothing worth discussing. He's very smart, and seemingly forthcoming about most things. Every now and then the defenses go up."

"Like when?"

"Uh, well, when I asked him about the stories of other women. He got his back up."

"Yeah, well, that was a sore point with him. There was no shortage of *fartootst* women ready to move in on him, even knowing he was married."

"Boy, I haven't heard that word in a long time. Do you know who any of them were?"

"I could come up with a list, I guess. It was all strictly gossip, really, but where there's smoke . . ."

"I need to see that side of him, whether it really exists or not. Did his secretary make counseling appointments for him?"

Roberta sipped her latte. "You know, he never had a secretary. He never hired one because he learned to live without one at his previous temple. Said it streamlined things."

"What about an appointment book? If he's anything like me, he needs to write stuff down or it's gone."

"Yeah, yeah, he had one. Red leather. Got a new one every year for Chanukah. Us kids would buy it for him."

"Do you know where it is?"

"Might be in his bottom desk drawer. He used to hold on to them for a few years, then destroy them. I don't know if he kept it."

"Can you look?"

"I'll have to go to the house to look. I haven't been there . . . You know why."

"Can you handle it?"

"If I must. He'll like that I came to the house."

"Don't do it if you think it'll be too disturbing, or dangerous."

"I'll think of something."

"Thanks, kiddo."

Roberta shuddered. "Ooh. He calls me that."

"Okay, that's the last time you'll hear it from me. Talk to you later."

Roberta tried to call Stevie again, but his phone was turned off.

Chauncey Zerby looked out his window at the two young men shooting baskets in the clearing. The ground was wet enough to make small splashes and muddy up the ball when they dribbled, but it didn't bother them.

Zerby sighed and poured himself another cup of strong, bitter coffee. The two kids symbolized how his world had collapsed in the last few years. Once, the group had the cream of young men to work with. Strong, mostly smart, dedicated.

Now, he had Frick and Frack. Getting tattooed and shaving your head didn't make you dedicated. And they sure weren't smart. The worst part was that they talked like ghetto trash to each other. So far, they had spared him that hip-hop crap.

But, they were strong, and obeyed his commands without much lip. He had to settle.

In the glory days, the kids were readers; now, they just listened to that nasty music, the message simplified and driven home with a rivet-gun beat. They used to have some sense of history and mission; now, they were just angry losers looking to shift blame.

In his kinder moments, he allowed that this wasn't much of a life for a young man, off in the boonies with no TV, in rat-trap housing and not much money.

The two, Billy Wayne Cummings and Curt Himmler (what a chuckle the boys would've gotten out of that name in the old days), were standing around smoking and spitting. As if the ground wasn't wet enough.

They went off into their shack, probably to smoke pot and listen to that nasty music.

Zerby shook his head. "Ain't got the sense of a good dog between 'em," he said aloud, then sipped his coffee.

Twenty years ago, it was different, and not just because he was a young man then himself. They had 120 acres of ground, real buildings, dormitories, good food. The Boss taught classes about race pride, history, tactics, and strategy. They had guest speakers from other groups around the country: Klansmen from Alabama, survivalists from Montana, Nazis from everywhere, brothers. And sisters. And kids.

Every summer they hosted the White Pride Conclave, a week of seminars, concerts, rallies, games, and a nightly burning of the cross, courtesy of the southern boys. They knew how to do that stuff better than anyone.

The flames danced and shone in the faces of the crowds. The kids loved it, cute as hell in their tiny Klan or storm trooper outfits.

Zerby shook his head again. He'd been doing that a lot, lately. Especially when he remembered how it all ended.

Those kids who went into Portland and killed that jungle bunny on the bus. A real ape, too, from Africa. In front of witnesses yet.

At the trial, the Jew lawyer convinced the jury that the Boss had put that idea into their heads, that he'd sent them out to do the killing. The Boss had to go to jail, too. He was still there, dying of lung cancer in a prison ward, a shell of his manly self.

Then, the worst of it. The civil case, where the Boss got sued for damages by the spear-chucker's family. They got awarded the whole shootin' match: grounds, buildings, everything. First thing they did was to bulldoze and burn the compound. Jews, hippie faggots, and other mud people came from miles around to have a party at the expense of the white race.

When the fire went out, the dead coon's family sold the land to some enviro group, who let it go back to a natural state. It looked like a jungle, now. Somehow fitting.

The group drifted apart without the Boss to keep them together or a place to hang out. The dream was dead. The dream of a white homeland in the Pacific Northwest, no Jews or undesirables allowed. Zerby guessed that most of them found other white pride organizations to join, or just went back to some little job. The only one with a college education was the Boss. Hell, he was a professor until he got fired for his ideas. Wrote that book and got canned. The only steady source of income for Zerby and the boys was the sale of those books, and that was tapering off. Zerby wished he knew something about computers, because he heard that the Internet was the place to sell stuff like the Boss's book.

He shrugged. The Internet was probably a government trap anyway.

Now, he just waited in his pathetic house, hoping that jerk would call him with some more work in Portland. It gave them all an excuse to leave their depressing little piece of the world.

Newark, New Jersey, 1964

A few days after the attack in Mississippi, Mildred sat red-eyed in the waiting room of a Newark hospital, drinking cold, bitter coffee that matched her mood. She was waiting for news of her son.

Bobby Geller had been badly hurt in that hot, dusty Mississippi town. His bones had been broken and he had a head injury inflicted by night riders. He was lucky to be alive. Lindy Peress had been left bleeding and unconscious. The two young black men, local kids, working there had been taken.

The carnage was interrupted by a pickup truckload of local men, black and white, who had volunteered to provide protection. The hooded thugs managed to escape with their human cargo, who were still missing after the raid.

Mildred took time out from cursing God to curse her dead husband, his ideas, and all those who shared them. She saved her vilest curses for Lindy, who had seduced her boy into a suicidal adventure. That girl got exactly what she deserved. What else was she expecting? Brass bands? Ice cream socials?

She wished the girl dead.

"Mrs. Geller?"

Mildred jumped, startled by the mention of her name. She looked up to see a well-dressed Negro with a familiar face.

"What do you want?" she asked coldly. "I don't have any money to give you."

"Actually, it's just the opposite. May I sit down?"

"Suit yourself." She was now curious.

"I don't know if you remember me. My name is Bill Goolsby."

Recognition shown on Mildred's face. "Yes, of course. This is not a good time . . ."

"I know. That's why I'm here. It's on behalf of the local chapter of the NAACP. Do you know what that is?"

"The troublemakers who do all those sit-ins, right?"

Goolsby smiled. "Guilty as charged, and proud of it. We were very interested that your son would risk his life to go south to register Negro voters. I told my colleagues that Bobby was indeed his father's son."

"A fat lot of good it did him. I'm sitting here waiting to find out if he's ever going to walk again, or even recover. Just like his father, sticking his nose where it doesn't belong."

Goolsby frowned. "Mrs. Geller, this is not the time for me to argue politics, or even attempt to justify our cause. Suffice it to say that the Newark Negro community, and I personally, are deeply grateful to Bobby."

He reached into this pocket and withdrew an envelope.

"Please take this. It's more than enough to cover whatever medical bills you've gotten so far. And I have instructed the hospital office to forward any further bills to my office."

Mildred bristled. "I don't want your charity."

"No." He shook his head. "It's nothing like charity. Consider it a repayment of the money Barney gave me to start my company, with interest. If he had lived, you would all be doing well, as I have. If either of you ever need employment, I wish you would call." He offered a business card.

"After all these years? It's about time." She grabbed the envelope, ignored the card. Goolsby fought to control his feelings.

"Mrs. Geller, I phoned you several times and sent you more than one registered letter. All you needed to do was respond."

"Will that be all? I need to go check on my son." She rose from the bench.

"Yes, of course. Good luck, and give my best to Bobby."

Mildred walked away from Bill Goolsby.

10. The Quest

"Lou? I'm home!"

"In the office, Hilda," Lou called back. He was glancing through all the information he had accumulated thus far, trying to see something he hadn't seen before.

Hilda walked in, a glass of wine in her hand and a fizzy water for Lou.

"Thanks," he said, taking the bottle, "I'm a bit parched from trekking through the information jungle."

Hilda rolled her eyes. "Don't tell me. You're doing your swami thing again, right?"

"What the hell are you talking about?"

"You know, where you run through pages of stuff glassy-eyed and hope the meaning emerges like a vision in a crystal ball."

Lou furrowed his brow. "Do I do that?"

"Yeah. It usually comes before you actually do

some legwork on the case. That's what we're gonna do this afternoon"—she checked her watch—"uh, evening. The rain has begun again, and we're staying home to create a schedule of interviews. And you know what? I just got an idea. I'm calling Gar and Connie and asking them over for dinner."

"Know what? That's a great idea."

Two hours later, the four sat around the table in Hilda's large kitchen, licking the last of the barbecue sauce from their fingers, and catching up since their last meeting. Gar Loober, tall and still youthful, had lost his gangly manner and actually acquired a bit of a belly. Lou decided Gar was a happy man.

"Gar, has Connie filled you in on what we're doing?" Lou asked.

Gar sipped his beer. "Yup. What can I do to help?"

Connie winked at Lou.

"Well, first and foremost, I don't want to take you away from real police work. You have an important job."

"Lou, I'm a paper pusher these days. My deputies take care of the day-to-day stuff, Connie handles most of the administrative duties, and I sign requisitions for toilet paper and coffee service. Real police work? Haven't seen much of that lately."

Hilda began to clear the table, and Connie rose to help her. "Anyone want some coffee?" Hilda asked.

"Decaf for me," Lou said. Connie raised her hand.

"Yeah, okay, thanks," Gar added. The women went off together.

"Gar," Lou began, "Rabbi Geller is a mystery. I've

spoken to some slick operators, but this guy is the best. His manner is so suspicious, yet he has an answer for everything."

"Lou, this man has seen his wife murdered, been accused of adultery and murder-for-hire, lost his congregation, and been tried in a court by an, um, aggressive DA. It's no surprise that he might be a bit bent out of shape."

Lou sighed. "Yeah, you're right. I sure don't know how I would have handled that kind of a burden."

"So, what do you want to do here?"

"Okay, Hilda and I decided to work this case like it never came to trial, like fresh material. His daughter asked me to look into it, come what may. She wants to erase doubt. So, we are going to interview witnesses and people of interest.

"What we need from you is access to things like police reports, ME reports, trial transcripts, that kind of stuff."

Gar nodded. "Okay, the trial is a matter of public record. You can purchase transcripts from the court. The rest of the stuff you can get from Tom Knight."

"Okay, we'll handle the transcripts. I'm not sure Knight would be so willing to give us police reports and such. This case was a black eye for him and I think he wants to forget it. Plus, what we can't get from him is a working cop's perspective. I want that from you."

Lou watched Gar's face for a few seconds. Only a slight narrowing of his eyes indicated that anything might be going on in his mind.

"Remind me never to play poker with you," Lou said.

Gar laughed. "Cagey, am I? Okay, give me a list of what you want on this case. I'll see what I can do."

Lou bit his lower lip and drummed his fingers.

"Okay, Lou, just ask."

"See," Lou leaned forward, "that's why I don't play poker. Can you do a trace on a person?"

Gar shifted in his chair. "This is getting close to the line, Lou."

"Okay, I'll do a Google search first. I haven't tried that yet."

Hilda and Connie returned bearing coffee mugs, sugar, a cake box, and other paraphernalia.

"Connie and Gar brought this nice cake," Hilda said, "from Grace Geller's bakery. Somehow fitting, no? Coffee's a-brewing."

The rest of the evening went more socially, and the Geller case was put away for the time.

Earlier that afternoon, Robert Geller's phone rang. He grabbed the receiver.

"Yeah," he barked, irritable at the intrusion.

"Daddy?"

"Oh hi, honey. Sorry to be such a grouch. Where're you calling from?"

"I'm still in Portland. Can I come and visit?"

"Heck, yeah! When do you want to come?"

"How about tonight? I can be there in a couple of hours."

"What'll we do for dinner? Wanna drive up to Melly's?"

"Yuck! I'd rather go to the Dunes."

Geller sighed. "I don't know what you see in that shlocky place. But what the heck. I'll wait for you here. Drive carefully."

"Okay, Daddy. Bye."

Roberta Geller gathered up her purse and her courage and got into her rented car. If she hurried, she could get to the house before it got too dark.

Three men in a van watched her get into the car. They made a quick cell-phone call, and fell into traffic behind her.

"Hi, sweetheart!" Geller held the door open for his daughter, ushering her quickly through the blood-streaked hallway. Roberta felt her stomach tighten up, and tried not to look.

Geller had done a quick clean-up of his disheveled male lair, and Roberta looked around with approval.

"Well, at least you haven't gone to seed here."

"Roberta! What am I, an animal?"

She sat in the living room, facing away from the entrance. Geller fussed around her.

"Can I get you something? Wine? Vodka? Do you want to head right out for dinner?"

"You know, Daddy, I came down with a headache driving out here. Some old guy in a camper shlepping along at twenty miles an hour. It took miles before I could get around him. I'd love a drink, maybe a white wine?"

Geller nodded.

"And then maybe you can get some take-out?"

"I've been going to this new barbecue joint down the road. Great ribs."

"Daddy! A rabbi eating pork?"

Geller shrugged. "I'm already going to hell. I might as well enjoy it."

"Okay." She laughed. She missed her father, who could only sometimes be seen through the crust of the man who stood before her. "I'll join you in hell. Ribs it is."

"I'll call ahead. It won't take long."

"You know what? I'll lay down for a while in my old room, just until you get back."

"Deal."

When Geller left for the food, Roberta rose from among the stuffed animals on her bed in her old room. She looked at the posters of '70s and '80s rock bands and shook her head.

"A Flock of Seagulls? What was I thinking?" she said aloud.

Making her way downstairs, she slipped into her father's office. The real mess was in here, but her own office at home wasn't much better. Her husband had bought her one of those gag plaques reading, "A Clean Desk Is a Sign of a Sick Mind."

She snapped on the desk light and did a quick eyeball check of the piles of detritus. No obvious sign of a red leather appointment book. She began opening drawers. The bottom right drawer held a pile of the books.

Notable by its absence was the book for the year her mother was killed.

Roberta looked around. A file cabinet was unlocked, but no book was concealed there.

I probably wouldn't have kept the book for that year myself, she thought. But I also would have cleaned up the blood.

As she looked around, she spotted the liquor cabinet. She shrugged, and opened it up. There were bottles of expensive vodka, three or four different brands, some single-malt scotch, some Jack Daniel's and Wild Turkey, and various other bottles of liquor.

In the back corner was a fancy presentation box for some kind of brandy. Roberta reached into the cabinet and lifted the box, which seemed light for a bottle. She opened the box, and found the red leather appointment book.

Hearing her father's car come into the drive, she closed the cabinet, dashed over to the desk and turned off the light. Panicky, she ran to the living room and stuffed the book into her purse moments before her father opened the door.

"Hey, kiddo, you're up." He looked at her, concern in his eyes. "You're all flushed. You sure you're okay?"

"Yes, Daddy. I'll be fine. Can I get that glass of wine now?"

After a pleasant evening of catching up with his daughter, Rabbi Geller bid her good night, and decided to have a nightcap before bed. "A bit of frozen vodka," he said aloud. He headed to the refrigerator and opened the freezer.

There was just enough left in the bottle for a good jolt, which he poured and drank off. Time for a visit to the liquor stash, he thought.

Geller was not very fastidious about most things, but his liquor cabinet was in perfect order. "That's funny," he said aloud. The bottles were out of line, as though they had been moved around. The brandy box was not firmly against the back corner.

Geller lifted the box and shook it. "Goddamn it!" he yelled.

He opened the box to find it empty. "That bitch! I'll kill her!"

Malheur County, Oregon, 1968

Bobby Geller awoke to the sounds of birds. As summer approached, his sleeping bag was beginning to be too warm at night. His breath no longer froze into a coating on the inner surface of the teepee. And the snowfall was no longer a regular event out here in Malheur County.

It was still chilly enough for him to break out in goose bumps when he pulled his jeans on and stuffed his feet into his boots. Grabbing a towel and his toilet kit, he headed for the main house.

The dawn sky show was just about over. Steen's Mountain brooded in the near distance, and deer and antelope fed out on the horizon. Bobby approached the nineteenth-century ranch house, which was surrounded by almost thirty teepees, several camp tents, and a couple of yurts.

Jollity Farm was named after a song by a goofy English rock band. Owned by an eccentric with a history as a Wobbly, the one-time cattle ranch had become a haven for itinerant hippies, draft resisters, and AWOL soldiers. Bobby had cast up there after a couple of years of drifting around North America. A few months in Baja, a few weeks in Toronto, almost a year in San Francisco.

He was on his way to Canada to avoid the draft, when he realized that his injuries might exempt him. He gave Mildred a call, endured her pleadings to come back to New Jersey, and asked that she send him copies of his medical records. He reported to a draft board in Medford, Oregon, showed them the documents, and soon received a 1-Y deferment.

Another vagabond told him about Jollity Farm, and he had been there ever since. For a minimum of physical labor—he was not capable of real hard work since his beating—and a few regular household chores, he got three meals and a teepee.

Regular deliveries of superior marijuana, and the psychedelic mushrooms that grew wild in the cattle pastures, kept him and his fellow inhabitants mellow. The Grateful Dead dropped by from time to time on their way to or from a gig, and the party never stopped as long as they were there. The rest of the time there was plenty of music from his neighbors.

Bobby Geller was happy for the first time in his

life since Lindy Peress had died and he'd fled New Jersey and his mother, happy being a relative term. He was adrift in the flow of the hippie culture and had no plans and, alas, no dreams. But the gnawing anxiety that had defined his life was gone.

As Bobby entered the big ranch house, he got a chorus of hellos from the other early risers. A girl put a mug of coffee in his hand and gave him a big kiss.

"I'm going off to the shower. Later."

"Hey, Geller!" someone shouted. "Your mom called again."

Bobby grimaced. Mildred had actually hired a private detective to find him. It was the only disadvantage to staying put for so long.

"Yeah, okay."

After his shower, and a big breakfast, he washed up most of the dishes, passing the chore on to the next person. He went outside for a smoke.

The porch ran for more than a hundred feet across the front and down one side of the house. A small group was gathered at the feet of a guitarist singing Beatles songs. Others read or talked. Some dozed in sleeping bags on the porch floor.

It was going to be a beautiful day of blue skies and open spaces. Bobby pulled a pouch of Bugler and a pack of cigarette papers out of his jeans. He rolled the tobacco into a lumpy cylinder, and searched his pockets for a match.

"Need a light?"

Bobby jumped. He turned to see a tall, rangy, middle-aged man, long curly hair in a puffy cloud around his head. The man wore wire-rim glasses on the bridge of his nose, blue eyes magnified by the lenses. He sported a walrus mustache. There was a gold hoop in the lobe of his left ear. Bobby had never seen a man with an earring outside of a pirate movie.

"Jeez, you scared me."

"Sorry. I guess I tread lightly. Need a match?" His accent sounded like Boston.

"Yeah, sure."

The man snapped a kitchen match to life with a thumbnail. Bobby lit his handmade, and the man lit a pipe, sucking deep.

"What are you smoking?" Bobby asked.

"Moroccan hash," the man replied in a strangulated voice. "Want some?"

"Nah, too early. I don't get high during the day, just in case there's something I need to do. My name's Bobby Geller." He held out his hand.

"Marv Kronstein." He grabbed Bobby's hand in the hippie grip.

"Been at Jollity long, Marv?"

"Nope, just got here yesterday. I've taken a leave of absence for a few months. Gotta get out and touch the real world every now and then. I've never been here before. It's pretty far out."

"What do you do?" Bobby was making polite conversation while he smoked.

"I'm a rabbi."

Bobby's eyes bugged out. "You're fulla crap!"

Kronstein laughed. "You're not the first one to tell me that."

"Look, I'm sorry. That was rude. You, uh, you're really a rabbi? Never saw one like you."

"Too true. Wanna sit down?"

They walked over to an empty porch swing. Bobby still had an incredulous look. Kronstein sucked down hashish through a grin.

"So, you do, like bar mitzvahs and stuff like that?"

"Yeah, although we do the same thing for girls now, too."

"I know about that. Back in Jersey that was catching on when I left. It's cool. Did you get any grief when you decided to include girls?"

"Not me. My congregation is . . . unusual, I guess."

"How?"

"We're not orthodox, conservative, or reform. We kind of make it up as we go along. The conservative Jews won't talk to us, the reform ones are scared of us. The orthodox won't even acknowledge that we're Jews."

Bobby thought a second. "Well, look, I'm no scholar, but what do you believe that's so dangerous?"

Kronstein exhaled through his nose. "Wow, I'm pretty loaded." He gazed into the distance, then snapped his head around.

"What did you ask?"

Bobby laughed. A stoned rabbi. "Why are you so dangerous?"

"Oh, yeah. Well, we don't eat kosher food unless we want to. We take a pass on a lot of that angry Yahweh stuff in the bible. We take homosexuals, unmarried couples, black people, non-Jews, whoever. If they want to convert, cool. If not . . ." he shrugged. "It's like do-your-own-thing Judaism. Very upsetting, especially for the reform Jews. You kind of expect it from the others, but the reform seem to be the most threatened."

"Maybe because you're doing what they claim to believe."

"Right on." The rabbi coughed a discreet cough.

"So, like, what do you actually believe?"

"Glad you asked, my son." The rabbi laughed at his own witticism.

For the next hour, Kronstein rambled on about so-called Free Judaism. It was a hodge-podge of Zen, hippie doctrine, acid-head insights, and standard Jewish ritual. Bobby was fascinated. It reinforced and gave legitimacy to a lot of what he believed about brotherhood ("and sisterhood," the rabbi added), race relations, war and peace, the golden rule.

"Where's your temple?"

"Storefront in Eugene, not far from the university. You should come some time."

"Yeah, maybe I will. Give me the address."

For the next few days, Bobby and the rabbi hung out. It came out in conversation that Kronstein really was an ordained rabbi, from a liberal seminary in Vancouver, British Columbia. The night before the rabbi left, he and Bobby ate magic mushrooms and shared a profound experience of the kind unique to the times. Bobby was certain, in the light of a new day, that he had been called.

Bobby Kennedy was shot dead on June 4th, and Bobby Geller arrived in Eugene the next day.

The rains had not yet ceased in the Willamette Valley, and Geller had the foresight to purchase a rain poncho from an Army deserter for a harmonica and a half-ounce of weed just before he left Jollity Farm. It covered him and his backpack and kept off the slow, steady spring rains, and he had never learned to play the harmonica, anyway.

It hadn't taken long after Marv Kronstein departed the farm to return to Eugene for Bobby to follow him. Calm within, and with more perspective on his own life than ever before, he decided that life as a hippie rabbi would do him good, and fulfill his desire to serve people at the same time.

"Enlightened self-interest," as Mr. Peress used to call it. He wondered how those good folks were doing, and resolved to call them.

Bobby had hitchhiked from southeastern Oregon in only a couple days, lucking out on motorists willing to pick up a weirdo in a rain poncho. His last ride carried him to the edge of the University of Oregon campus, more sprawling now than it was in those days. The rain had let up, and the sun teased through breaks in the clouds, so he decided to walk around until he came upon the storefront synagogue.

Eugene did not seem that much different at first from Jollity Farm, other than that it was in a small city in a green valley, rather than out in the middle of the high-desert nowhere. And that there were far more people milling around.

It was finals week, and the students were blowing off steam and horsing around. Two guys with guitars became a party, and girls danced, often half-naked. Pipes and joints made the rounds, followed by bottles of cheap wine. If there were cops around, they were well hidden.

He stopped to listen to a fair rendition of "Journey to the Center of the Mind," when a girl came over and asked him to dance. She had tribal designs of some kind painted on her face, and her thin cotton shirt, wet with sweat, clung to her body. He was not in the mood, but didn't want to insult her.

"Whoa," he said, "cool out. I just got in from Malheur and I'm wiped out. Maybe next time."

She shrugged and started to dance away.

"Uh, just a second. Do you know where I can find a storefront Jewish . . ."

"Rabbi Marv's place? Far out!"

"Yeah, that's it. Do you go there?"

"Hey, I'm a Methodist, but everybody knows Marv. Cool guy. I'm Raindrop, by the way."

"Hi, Raindrop, I'm Bobby. Can you show me where it is?"

She took him by the hand and danced him a block west and a half block south. He laughed at her hippie enthusiasm. "Ta-da!" she trumpeted and indicated a store window reading, "Eytz Chaim Congregation. All Welcome. Price of Entry: Your Preconceptions."

Bobby laughed some more. "Yeah, that sounds like Marv. *Eytz chaim*, that means 'Tree of Life.'"

"Far out, man! Is that, like, Jewish or something?" Raindrop kept moving, arms swaying, hips rolling.

"Hebrew. I studied a little a long time ago. So, you've been here?"

"Oh yeah. They have food and music a couple of nights a week. Outta sight veggie food. I usually run out of money between checks from the parents, so I come here to cop eats."

"Well, thanks. I'm going in to see Marv. Wanna come?"

"No, man, I gotta get back to the party. And I might even study for my psych final."

"Later."

"Later, man." She boogied back toward the campus.

Bobby walked in and looked around. Ranks of folding chairs faced a low stage constructed of risers. There was a beat-up podium, a makeshift altar, and a plywood ark to hold the Torah. The curtain on the ark was hand-woven, with both traditional and mystical symbols, including the inevitable Sanskrit "Om."

Bobby smiled and shook his head. He found this very amusing, but not off-putting. It was cool, in a cockamamie kind of way.

A door opened at the left of the stage and a slender young woman walked out. Bobby's heart jumped in his chest. He was smitten at first glance.

She sized him up. Tall enough, slender, with a nice smile, but a haunted look in his eyes. She wondered what those eyes had seen. She liked his wild hair and beard, and the rough look to his hands, as though they had done hard work.

"Can I help you? " She was blue-eyed, with short, tousled light-brown hair. No makeup, peasant blouse and full skirt, barefoot with bells around her ankles. The top of her head came to Bobby's chin.

Boy, Bobby thought, you've already helped me just by showing up.

"Uh, yeah. Is Marv here?"

She smiled. Bobby's knees got weak.

"So, are you another one of Marv's foundlings?"

"Huh?"

"Marv is famous—notorious?—for gathering in drifters. They all show up here eventually."

Bobby grinned. "Well, guilty as charged. I met him out at Jollity Farm in Malheur County."

Her eyes lit up. "You're Bobby Geller, aren't you? Marv mentioned meeting you. Didn't take you long."

He shrugged. "I was ready, I guess. What's your name?"

She blushed. "Oh, sorry. Emily Levine. I work here."

"Are you and Marv . . ." he blurted, then regretted asking.

"Together? Nope. Whaddaya got in mind, big boy?" She threw a comic leer.

He laughed, relieved that she had a sense of humor. "Right now? Just finding Marv."

"Well, he's off scrounging food and furniture and money. Anything that he can find that's useful. He does this a lot. We're not exactly the synagogue of choice around here."

"So he said. What do you do?"

"Mostly cook, a little light housework. I'm a graduate student in social work, and I volunteer as much time as I can. Less and less as I head toward my master's."

Bobby wanted nothing more than to stand there and talk to this young woman, but he was tired and needed a place to stay. He looked over at the front door.

"Well, it's really been nice meeting you, but I gotta crash. I'm wiped out, and I have to find a place to stay."

Just then, Marv walked up to the front door carrying a big box. He kicked on the door to get their attention. Emily ran over to let him in.

"Thanks. I couldn't get the handle with this load in my arms." The rabbi put the box down and did a double take when he saw Bobby.

"Bobby Geller! Far out! When did you get here?" He walked over and hugged his friend.

Bobby hugged back, then stepped out of Marv's grip. "About half an hour ago. I went by the campus and Raindrop brought me here."

"Raindrop?" Mary looked puzzled.

"Francine Daytree," Emily explained. "She decided to adopt a new name after her last acid experience."

"Ah, yes." said Marv. "She sure likes your brown rice concoctions. Which reminds me."

The rabbi gestured at the box. "Check it out."

Emily opened the cardboard carton. "Oh, wow! There must be twenty pounds of brown rice in there."

"Fifty, actually, and my aching back will testify to that. Plus, split peas, lentils, and a bunch of onions under all the bags. We'll be in chow for a month, thanks to that commune out in the boonies."

"They grow rice?" Bobby asked.

"Nuh-uh," Emily replied. "They grow the onions, peas, and lentils, but they trade for the rice with a local grocery. The grocery gets fresh produce and the commune gets whatever it needs. Lot of barter arrangements around here."

"Man, we're changing the world," Bobby said.

"From your mouth to God's ears," the rabbi said. "But, hey, what's happening, Bobby?"

"Well, I need a place to stay. I'm beat, and I don't know a soul here."

"You can crash on the floor here, if you like," the rabbi offered. "I sleep on a cot in the back room, and maybe we can scare up another one for you tomorrow."

"Hey," said Emily, "I've got a couch at my apartment. I'll bet it's more comfortable than the floor."

Bobby's heart jumped a beat.

"Uh, well, I don't want to put you out."

"No biggie. It's not the Ritz, but I have a bathroom and a kitchen, and a stereo in the living room, and I can always hide away in the bedroom when I want to study."

"Thanks. That'd be outta sight."

"Well, okay," said the rabbi. "That's settled."

Emily looked at Bobby. "Do you want to go and crash? The place is only a few blocks away."

"Bobby, if you don't mind, can you give me a few minutes?" the rabbi asked.

"Marv, why don't you show him where my place is? I have to throw dinner together, and you guys can talk while I work."

"Good idea. Got any luggage?"

Bobby shrugged. "Just the backpack."

Emily gave them the key. "Be back by six and you'll get a home-cooked meal."

Bobby thanked her, and the two men left. A light rain accompanied them the short distance to the apartment building, an old structure long given over as part of the student ghetto near the campus. They climbed the stairs up the three flights to Emily's flat. Bobby fumbled with the door and got it open.

"Wow, not bad."

Plain, but comfortable. A couch, a chair, a cheap record player and a small TV in the living room, a Pullman kitchen, and a bathroom at the end of a short hallway. The door to the bedroom was open, and Bobby saw a mattress on the floor with an Indian throw covering it.

The walls sported several posters advertising rock shows at the Fillmore and Avalon in San Francisco: Jefferson Airplane, the Lovin' Spoonful, Buddy Guy, Steve Miller, the Dead. One poster made Bobby laugh out loud. It was a photo of John Lennon that someone had altered to make him look like a Hasidic Jew, with side curls and black hat.

"Rabbi John. What a riot!" Bobby shook his head and chuckled.

"Yeah. Amazing how easily Lennon assumes the new identity," the rabbi added. "It's like he was just waiting for the transformation. You should see what this kid did with Jimi Hendrix. Great imagination. The artist is in junior high."

Marv looked at Bobby. "Hey, I know you're tired, but I have to ask: Why are you here?"

Bobby put his backpack in a corner and sat on the couch. "You invited me. I needed a change from the farm."

The rabbi sat next to him. "Okay, sure. But is that the only reason?"

"Why do you ask?"

"I think you and I shared some kind of profound experience, and I believe it changed you. Am I wrong?"

Bobby puffed out his cheeks and exhaled. He decided to go for it.

"Okay, I feel like I want to do what you do. I want to be a rabbi."

Marv smiled and hugged himself. "Are you sure? I don't want to pressure you. I do want you to be sure."

Bobby nodded. "Yeah, I think I'm sure."

"Good. I can get you into my rabbinical college in Vancouver, but we have work to do. Can you read Hebrew?"

"I learned for my bar mitzvah. I can still read a little. I don't know any vocabulary or anything. I don't have much religious training."

"Okay, we can deal with that. I can give you an hour a day, maybe more from time to time. The rest is up to you."

Bobby Geller needed no time to think.

"Let's do it."

Later that afternoon, and mindful of the three-hour time difference, Bobby called the Peresses.

Mrs. Peress answered the phone.

"Bobby Geller! What in the world are you doing? We haven't heard from you in so long, since, uh . . ."

"Yes, since then. Before I say anything else, I want you to know how much I loved Lindy and how much I miss her."

"Thank you, Bobby. I know she felt the same."

He heard the catch in her voice, and it broke his heart.

"So, I'm in Eugene, Oregon. I thought I'd catch up with you and tell you what's new."

"Oregon? That's like the other side of the world. We've never been west of Cleveland, and that was for a wedding."

"I'm going to rabbinical school, in Canada."

"Oh, Bobby, that's wonderful! You have a beautiful soul, and you'll be a great rabbi. But, why Canada? You're not escaping the draft, are you?"

"No, just coincidence. I met a rabbi out here who attended, and he's helping me get in. My injuries from the, you know, the trip south got me a deferment."

"So, it wasn't a total loss," she said looking for something positive to focus on.

They spoke for a few minutes, she put her husband on, and he gave Bobby more encouragement. Bobby promised to keep in touch, they all cried a little, and he hung up.

He cranked up his courage, and called his mother.

"So, you're not dead, not that it matters to you if I fear the worst."

Good ol' Mom, he thought, as predictable as ever.

"No, Mom, I'm good. I'm in Eugene, Oregon."

"Hmph! The middle of nowhere. Are you still finding yourself?" Her voice was rank with sarcasm.

"Surprise, I think I've found me. I'm going to rabbinical school."

There was a silence at the end of the phone. It seemed to last for minutes.

"Mom? Are you there?"

"A rabbi. Perfect. You'll always be your father's son. You'll never make any money and you'll live with other people's *tsuris* the rest of your life. You could still get your CPA," she said, with a germ of hope.

"Thanks for the suggestion, but I've made up my mind. I feel this is the right thing for me. I was hoping you'd be happy for me."

"Happy? I've never had a happy moment since your father died. Look, you're a grown man and if you didn't listen to me when you were a kid, you're not gonna now. Live and be well, my son. Stay in touch."

She hung up.

Bobby made one last call, to Bill Goolsby, who

congratulated him and promised to cover his tuition and living expenses. Bobby thanked his benefactor for his support and financial help over the years.

It was six o'clock, he was hungry, and he wanted to see Emily again.

11. Hitting the Books

Hilda woke up with a smile on her face, rolled over in bed, and elbowed Lou, who was snoring.

"Hey, it's morning, and you're still sawing wood."

"Huh? Oh, yeah. Good morning." Lou stretched, and laid his arm over Hilda's face, prompting a brief and intense wrestling match which he allowed Hilda to win.

"Ha! Give up?" She straddled him, with a triumphant leer.

"Uncle! Or aunt, I guess."

"Such flashing wit, and half asleep at that. What's on your schedule today?" Hilda dismounted his chest and allowed him to think a second. She absently ran her fingers over the scar over his knee.

"Hmm. Oh, yeah. Today is the Biggs funeral. I think I want to go."

"Hell yeah," she agreed. "From what you say, so do I. Feel like putting me up back there in Stumptown?"

"Be my guest. But, what about Gar and Connie?"

"It'll take them a day or two to get that stuff together, but we can call them if you want."

"Okey-dokey. Last one in the shower is a rotten egg."

"Plenty of room for two, but let me start the coffee first."

In the few minutes that Hilda was gone, Lou thought about his conversation with Geller. "Hey!" he said aloud. He didn't recall Tom Knight mentioning that Grace Geller's purse was in the crime scene, or if it had been emptied. Otherwise, why a robbery motive? Maybe just an oversight, he thought, but worth a call.

Hilda ran back into the room and made for the bathroom. "Rotten egg!" she called out. Lou leaped out of bed and dashed after her.

The rabbi was not happy. He sat on his couch, paralyzed by loathing and vodka. There were two empty bottles, and the third had a serious dent in it. The large ashtray in front of him spilled over with cigarette butts and ashes.

He needed to use the bathroom, and had for a while. He was almost out of cigarettes and would have to make a tobacco run. He knew he'd have to get off the couch sooner or later.

But he needed more brooding time. He needed some kind of plan, maybe one that didn't include the kind of bumblers he had been stuck with of late.

Maybe it just came down to this, he thought. The

only one you can trust is yourself. Not Emily, not Grace, not Roberta, not even my goddamn mother.

"Why do they always betray me?" he asked out loud. Then, he asked why God hated him. Then he passed out.

Roberta Mendelson woke up in her hotel room with a sick feeling in her stomach. The trip back from the coast had been rainy and windy, but otherwise uneventful. Before she went to bed, she laid out the appointment book on the bureau, resolving to wait until morning to look at it.

The anticipation was causing her distress. That and the thought that she had betrayed her father.

She called room service for a light breakfast and took a quick shower. Wrapped in the hotel's plush bathrobe, and fortified with coffee and a soft-boiled egg, she sat at the small table and contemplated the red leather book.

I might as well get this over with, she thought. She began to leaf through the book, noting on a pad those appointments she found suspicious. These were different from the others in the notation. The large majority were complete with the name of the appointment, a brief description of the nature of the meeting, and a time, generally after lunch and before four o'clock.

The odd morning or evening meeting was written the same way. These conflicted with her father's regular hours and were always unusual circumstances, like emergencies or counseling. Roberta shuddered, noting several meetings with Larry Gottbaum, the confessed killer. They were characterized as "Addiction Counseling."

The ones that piqued her interest were all similar in that they were after four o'clock, and identified only by initials, with no purpose noted.

"March twelfth, CG; March fifteenth, AL; March twentieth, CG," she read aloud. Some initials would appear more than others for a length of time, then fade away. Some would appear once or twice a month over the months.

Toward the end of the year, and nearer to her mother's murder, the initials LL appeared more and more frequently, finally three or more times a week. Roberta picked up her cell phone and called her father's former temple.

"Temple B'nai Yisroel. May I help you?"

"Hello, can I speak with Jane Steinberg? Thanks."

A voice came on the line. "Temple office. Can I help you?"

"Jane? Roberta Mendelson. How are you?"

"Oh my God, Roberta? It's so good to hear from you."

Roberta shmoozed the temple secretary for a while, filling her in on those aspects of her life she didn't mind getting into the gossip stream.

Then, "Janie, can you do me a favor?"

"Of course."

"I need a membership roster for the last year my father was rabbi. Can you do that?"

"Yes, I think so. We've had very little in the way of

changes since then. A few new couples, a few deaths . . . Oh! I'm sorry!"

"No problem, sweetie. I've come to terms. Can you e-mail it to me?"

Roberta gave the woman her e-mail address, hung up, and got dressed. By the time she logged on to her computer and accessed her e-mail, the list was there. She poured herself another cup of coffee and called Lou Tedesco.

Lou and Hilda were just getting off the Sunset Highway in Portland when his cell phone rang. He took it out of his jacket pocket and handed it to Hilda.

"Could you answer this? I hate to drive and talk."

"Lou Tedesco's phone."

"Um, hello? Is Lou there? This is Roberta Mendelson."

"Just a sec. Lou? This is Roberta."

Lou pulled the car over to the curb. Hilda handed him the phone.

"Roberta. Is everything all right?"

"Yeah. Listen, I visited my father last night and I found something you might be interested in. A certain red leather book."

"You were out there the same time I was. I stayed at Hilda's."

"Was that Hilda who answered the phone?"

"Yes. She's my colleague, and, um . . ."

"Yeah, I get it. You stayed at her house. Can we get together? I'm at my hotel room."

"You bet. I'm back in Portland and on my way home. I'll call you, okay?"

"I'll be waiting." They rang off.

"Wow, she found her father's appointment book. This could be a break." Lou eased the car back into traffic.

"If we can use it to develop a list of possible candidates for Geller's extracurricular honeys, I'll get right on the interviews."

"Let's drop off this stuff, and I'll call her back."

They headed for the Broadway Bridge. Lou felt that something big was about to happen.

"Gary, it's Roberta."

"Hey, babe. Just a second." Roberta heard him talking to his associates. Some business thing.

"So," he returned to the phone, "when are you coming home? I miss you."

"I miss you, too. Maybe soon. I went to see my father last night."

Silence for a moment. "Was that a good idea? I kinda worry . . ."

"No, it went well. I did some snooping while he was out and found his appointment book from the year my mother died. It may help, one way or another."

"Hey, Nancy Drew, I'm not there to play Ned Nickerson. Be careful!"

"Ned was never much good for anything, anyway. How are you otherwise?"

"Oh, before I forget, Robbie called. I told him

where you were and what you were doing. He says he supports your efforts and to be careful."

"All you men worry about me. I can take care of myself."

"Don't get overconfident. Someone is capable of murder, and we're still not sure who that is."

"Point taken. By the way, I spoke to Stevie. Before you ask, yes, he's still angry. He hung up on me when I got another call."

"You know, I used to think my family was about as crazy as you can get, without being the Jukes or the Kallikaks. Now, I'm reevaluating. Look, my inept partner is calling me. I love you."

"I love you, too."

When Lou and Hilda got settled, they discussed plans.

"Lou, I think you should see Roberta alone. You have a relationship with her, and I'll just make her nervous."

Lou wiggled his eyebrows and did a Groucho Marx voice. "Well, you make me nervous. Are those my knees knocking, or are you playing castanets?"

Hilda smiled a wry smile. "Down, boy. I'll head up to the office and powwow with Blanche, maybe grab some lunch."

"Good idea, actually. When we get the book we can set up interviews with the women he saw. Maybe they'll be willing to talk by now."

"Assuming, of course, that there's anything there to hear. He may be slippery, but he might not be guilty of anything. Loose talk and all."

"Granted," Lou nodded. "Okay, see you later."

Hilda left for the *Oregon Weekly* office and Lou called Roberta.

"Hiya. How do you want to do this?" he asked her.

"Do you want to come over here? Or, should I take a ride over there?"

"Let me come and pick you up. We'll take the book over to the newspaper office, and you and I can go through it. Neutral territory, I guess."

Roberta explained the odd way her father noted certain appointments. Lou grumbled about nothing being easy.

"Aha," said Roberta. "I have a small surprise. I got a roster of the congregation, and we can compare the notations to the names."

"You're a regular Nancy Drew. Good work!"

"You know, you're the second person to tell me that. I'll wait for you in front of the hotel."

"Ten minutes. See ya."

Lou pulled up in front of the lobby entrance. He took a quick look around.

Nothing of immediate concern. A homeless woman pushing a supermarket cart, a white van across the street, mid-morning traffic on the street.

A moment later, Roberta emerged from the hotel. Lou gave a quick beep and she waved to him.

Lou got out to open the door for her. After they strapped in, he asked, "So, do you need to make any stops before we get to the office?"

"Nope. I expect you have coffee there?"

"Yes, and it's good, too."

He started the car and drove to the end of the hotel driveway, signaling and turning toward the office. He made small talk.

A block later, a white van cut them off and stopped in front of his car. Two men wearing ski masks and carrying baseball bats jumped out of the van's back doors.

"Open the goddamn doors! Now!"

"Oh my God, Lou. What'll we do?" Roberta had gone pale.

"We will do as they say," he told her. "Yeah, okay, okay," he yelled to the masked men.

Lou slowly opened his door, and nodded to Roberta, who followed. The two thugs, smacking the bats into gloved palms, backed up enough to let them out.

"Get the book!" a voice shouted from the driver's seat.

"Gimme the goddamn book!"

Roberta reached into her purse and took out the book. One of the men grabbed it and said, "Get into the truck," in a menacing voice.

"Do it," Lou said, and they clambered into the back of the van. The windows had been painted black, and there was a plywood partition separating them from the rest of the vehicle.

The doors were closed after them, plunging them into near-total darkness. The van started up and drove for a few minutes.

"Lou, what are we gonna do?" Roberta whispered.

"I guess we go where they're going, for now. We have to play this by ear. Do you have any idea who they could be?"

"Hell no. Do you?"

"Is your father capable of this?"

"Lou, I think he hired men to kill my mother. What do you think?"

"I guess he . . ."

There was a loud banging on the partition. "Shut the hell up, or we'll shut you up!"

Lou moved his hand toward where he heard Roberta's voice, and found her hand. He squeezed it to encourage her, although he didn't feel very courageous himself. He heard her begin to cry.

Then, they heard and felt a crash. The van lurched and stopped. Doors opened and voices cursed, there were muffled sounds of scuffling and shouts of pain. A few seconds later, it stopped.

"Lou," Roberta whispered, "what happened?"

"No idea," he whispered back.

They waited what seemed like hours. No noise whatever.

"What the hell," Lou said aloud, and felt around for a handle on the inside of the van doors. Finding one, he turned it, and the door swung open.

Nothing happened. He blinked in the light, and crawled to the door. He looked out, in every direction.

"I think it's okay," he said, and jumped out of the van. "There's no one here. Come on out."

Roberta joined him on the street, squinting in the light. Lou walked around the van. The doors were open, but there was no one there. The van had a huge dent in the driver's side, and the front tire was smashed off the rim.

"Okay," said Roberta, "I repeat. What happened?"

Lou scratched his head. "Roberta, a lot of strange things have happened to me in the last few years, but I think this is the top of the heap."

He looked in the van, back and front, opened the glove compartment, which contained fast-food wrappers and other trash. He took out his notebook and made a note of the license plate number, from Washington State across the river. The vehicle identification number was partially obliterated, but he took down what he could make out.

"Where are we?" Roberta asked.

"About four or five blocks from where we started, closer to the east side. Maybe that's where they were taking us. Let's walk back to the hotel."

"Are we gonna call the cops?"

"You know, I can't think of any reason to involve them at this point. Are you okay?"

"I suppose. Just shaken up. Are we gonna leave the van here?"

"You bet. This area is busy enough that someone else will eventually call this in. Let's see if we can find my car."

An hour later, Lou, Roberta, Hilda, and Blanche were holed up in Blanche's office. The women were sipping some expensive scotch Blanche kept for medicinal purposes, and Lou was drinking camomile tea.

"At times like this," he said, "I miss having a drink." His eyes stared into the distance.

"Never mind," Blanche said. "I remember you then. I like you better now. What's our next move?"

"I have an idea," said Roberta. "They got the book, but I still have the membership list for the congregation and my notes. We can start there."

"Yay, Roberta!" They clinked glasses.

She fished in her voluminous purse for her notes and the e-mail printout of the congregation. Then she laid them out on the table and they started comparing initials with names.

"We have CG," she said. "Carol Greenberg lost her husband. She might have come in for grief counseling."

Hilda wrote the name down.

"AL. Arlene Levenson. Her sister got arrested on a drug charge. She was pretty broken up about it. AL might be her. She's a looker, too."

They went through seven names, Hilda noting each one.

"This would be easier with the appointment book. We could look to see if there were legitimate earlier appointments that may have developed into . . . you know." Roberta frowned.

"This is very brave of you," Lou squeezed her shoulder, "and it's a place to start. What's left?"

"LL. I have no clue about LL. No one on the list, and no one I can recall. Who the hell could LL be?"

"Did your father have a secretary?" Blanche asked.

"No, but there was an office manager, Jane Steinberg. She's the one who got me this list. But, my father made all his own appointments."

"Did she announce the appointments?"

"Yes, yes she did. But, the suspicious ones all took place after her regular office hours. She may not ever have seen this LL."

Lou shrugged. "It's worth a call. Secretaries notice a lot."

"You bet, especially a yenta like Janie."

"If it weren't for yentas, I'd be out of business," Lou smiled. "Use the office phone."

Roberta got up and picked up the phone. She dialed the temple number and asked for Jane Steinberg.

"Janie? It's Roberta."

"So, we don't hear from you for a year, and now you call two days in a row?"

"This is important, and please keep it to yourself."

"Yes, of course." She spoke in a whisper.

"The last few months my father was there, did he have an appointment with anyone whose initials are LL? I can't think . . ."

"Oh, her!" Jane laughed.

"Who's 'her'?"

"Lois Lane."

"Lois Lane? Like from Superman?"

"That was the rabbi's little joke. It was a woman reporter, maybe from Portland. She was always pestering him while the investigation was going on. He started calling her Lois Lane, but not to her face. Her name was like an actress. Jenny, Julie . . ."

"Can you hold on?"

Roberta turned to the group. "LL was a reporter from Portland, with a name like an actress."

Lou riffled through his notes. "Jodie? Jodie Coram?"

Back to the phone. "Was it Jodie, like Jodie . . ."

"Yes!" cried Jane. "Like Jodie Foster. The rabbi told me she left town just before the trial."

"Thanks, Janie."

"Roberta, honey, can you tell me what this is about?"

"Sorry, not now. I promise you'll be the first to know when it's time."

Roberta made some small talk and hung up.

"Jodie Coram," said Lou, "was the original reporter on the case. She just quit, maybe went back to California where she was from. I need to read her stuff, and try to find her.

"And I need to call Gar and get him to trace that plate number on the van."

Vancouver, British Columbia, 1970

Emily tiptoed behind the scholar. Their flat in a semi-seedy part of Vancouver was small enough so that they could never be out of range of each other, unless in the bathroom. Bobby was reminded of the apartment he shared with his mother back in New Jersey, only the company was more simpatico.

Two years into his rabbinical training and he was tired, but righteous on many levels. Emily had found a little job in a restaurant, and her evening hours meshed nicely with his study requirements.

The couple had a small but interesting group of friends, including draft dodgers, refugees from southeast Asia, and native radicals trying to change Canada from its far west coast. Some of Bobby's classmates would pop over for discussions about Jewish law and custom, conducted in a haze of marijuana smoke and fueled by cheap wine.

They were very fulfilled, and Bobby thanked God every day for his good fortune. He loved Emily and she had been very good for him, encouraging, quick to support his dreams, loving. He tried hard not to take advantage of her good nature, not to take her for granted. He had never been in a relationship that called forth these altruistic feelings. Even with Lindy, she gave more than he did and he was too young and self-centered to know. Certainly he loved his mother, but the best he could do was tolerate her.

He loved Emily in every way possible.

"Okay, Rabbi, I'm off to work. I'll see you when I get home, unless the Talmud puts you under again. It's better than ether."

She planted a wet kiss on his lips and moved toward the door.

"Wake me up if you have to," he called. "I want to spend some time with you."

"Okay. TTFN." She was out the door.

Bobby had put on a little belly, from Emily's excellent cooking as much as from his sedentary schedule. "You must be happy," their friends said. And he was.

Someone was trying to interest him in going jogging, an exercise fad that was gaining popularity. It was sort of like the roadwork that boxers did for conditioning. He was considering it.

Like medical students daydreaming about where they would like to do their residencies, rabbinical students compared notes on where they would like to have a congregation. Most longed for a big-city billet, with lots of potential congregants, and things to do besides tending to souls. Some talked about taking the message to the boonies, where Jews would come from miles around to sit at their feet.

Bobby thought about what he wanted to do, but had come to no decision. So much of it depended on where rabbis were needed. It was often a long-term, if not lifetime, post. Like star baseball players, rabbis could be lured to larger, more prestigious synagogues for more money or perks. Absent the construction of a new temple, rabbis had to die or move on for an opening to appear.

It had been rumored that girls were entering seminaries, and that feminism had washed up on the shores of patriarchal Judaism. Bobby, known as "the hippie" to his more traditional classmates, was all for it, and there had been some spirited, not to say hostile, discussions.

"Geller," said one of his friendly adversaries, "you're gonna be the first Zen rabbi."

"Not the first," he replied, "Marv Kronstein has that distinction."

Kronstein kept in frequent contact with Bobby,

advising him, gently nudging him this way or that, picking up his spirits when things got to be too much. Bobby benefitted from his friend's advice and perspective.

"I'm a lucky man," he told people. And most people agreed that he was.

12. The Church of Your Choice

"Seagirt Police. May I help you?"

"Connie? This is Lou Tedesco." He was calling from his desk at work.

"Hi, Lou. We've got some stuff for you. Police reports, et cetera."

"Great. Can you fax it to the newspaper office?" He gave Connie the fax number.

"I have crime scene photos, but I don't think you want to see them."

"I'm with you on that. Hold on to them, just in case. Wait, is there a picture of the living room couch?"

He heard Connie shuffling papers. "Okay, I found the picture. What do you need?"

"Is there a woman's purse on the couch?"

"There is. It's open and some of the contents have spilled."

"Does the report mention anything missing?"

Connie started going through the documents. "Uh,

blah blah blah." Lou heard more paper shuffling. "Here it is. 'Victim's husband reports wallet missing from purse. Contains credit cards, unknown amount of cash.'"

"Anything about money missing besides the wallet?"

"Not that I can see."

Lou scribbled a note. "Connie, can we trust the cops who investigated?"

"Lou, this is a major crime squad. There would have been county and state detectives, possibly one or two down from Waldorf. These guys are the best."

"Good, okay. Please send me any photos that aren't related to the victim."

"When are you coming back here?"

"Well, maybe tomorrow. I have a wake, or memorial, or something, tonight. And it's been quite a day so far." Lou told Connie about the van incident.

"Did you say the men disappeared?"

"Like smoke in the wind," he answered. "I've never seen anything like it. Not only were the bad guys gone, but whoever routed them was gone, too. I don't know if they were captured or run off or what, or whom we have to thank for it."

"Lou, you've always been luckier than most people can hope for. It's saved your life at least twice by now."

Lou shuddered. "I haven't thought about what might have happened . . . Anyway, I have another favor . . ." His voice trailed off.

Connie heaved a theatrical sigh. "Okay, what now?"

"I have a license plate number and a partial VIN on that white van. Can you run them for me? It was a common Chevy van, maybe ten or twelve years old."

"Shoot."

Lou read the letters and numbers. He heard Connie entering them on a computer keyboard.

"Okay," she said, "Washington plate reported stolen last night from a parking lot in Jantzen Beach. The VIN, uh, still waiting. Yeah. There are still about thirty vans out there that have those numbers in the VIN. Here comes the list."

Lou fidgeted while he waited.

"Here we go. That's interesting."

"What?"

"One of the vans was reported stolen about ten years ago. The original owner was, get this, the Reverend Gale Malkin, First Church of Christ, Christian."

"Is that significant?"

"Oh, yeah, you haven't been here that long. I don't recall all the details, but basically they were a white supremacist group who were involved in the killing of a young African man in Portland. Hold on, let me bring this up." More keyboard clatter.

"Wow, I remember the incident. It made the national news." Lou waited.

"Holy cats!" exclaimed Connie. "I'm guessing you don't know this; I didn't. One of the people responsible for bringing them down was Rabbi Robert Geller."

Lou sat down. "Connie, can this get any stranger?"

"I wouldn't bet against it. I still can't get my head around a clergyman killing his wife. I'll get that stuff on the fax right away."

"Can you add the Malkin stuff?"

"You got it."

"What do you think?" Hilda, dressed in a slinky black dress, sashayed around for Lou's inspection.

"If I didn't know you already, I'd hit on you."

"Good answer. You look pretty good yourself."

"This old thing? Actually, I just bought this suit on sale and I've been looking for an excuse to wear it."

"Very spiffy. Nice tie. Is that new?"

"Nope, old. It belonged to my uncle. Hand-painted, 1940s vintage."

Hilda whistled through her teeth.

"I asked Blanche to come. She should be here soon. I can't wait until you two get a load of this house."

A short time later, Lou pulled up at the late Woody Biggs's house. There were cars parked up and down the long block on both sides of the street.

"Maybe I'll let you two off and try to find . . ."

A young black man came up to the car, and Lou lowered his window.

"Excuse me, sir. Are you Lou Tedesco?"

"Yes, I am."

"I've been instructed to watch for you. I can park your car for you out back."

"Thanks, that's great." Lou unbuckled his seat belt.

"Mr. Brown said you were an honored guest."

"Impressive," cooed Blanche, dressed in a vintage Mary Quant minidress and knee-high boots.

They exited the car and headed up toward the front door. The sound of raucous music reached them a good ten yards from the house.

"Nice little cave, no?" Lou grinned.

"Lou," Hilda said, "I want you to take notes. If I go before you, use this as a model for my wake."

"Jeez, me too," echoed Blanche.

"Unless I miss my guess, we ain't seen nothin' yet." Lou led them up the long stairs. A hand-lettered sign on the door read "Just Go In." So they did.

The grand foyer was mobbed with people. A riser under the windows held a band, roaring away on a groove. The parquet floor was covered with something to permit dancing while preventing damage. And there were dozens of people dancing.

Lou stared at the band. "Oh, my goodness."

Hilda and Blanche were overwhelmed, but Hilda managed, "What?"

"The band, Hilda. The players are famous, at least to music freaks. They come from the house bands at Motown and Atlantic Records. I didn't even know they were still alive, some of 'em. And the trumpet player . . ."

"All the way from New Orleans," said Blanche. "I have all his CDs, and his brothers' too."

Tables were set up around the room, laden with food of all kinds. What must have been twenty pounds of shrimp sat in a giant clam shell, a tub of cocktail sauce next to it. Then barbecued ribs, then fried chicken, then satay skewers, then potato salad . . .

"My God," Hilda said, "look at all the food."

"Forget the food," Lou whispered. "Check out the crowd."

There were people of every color and description, dressed in clothing from every era. Swing-era hipsters, beat cats and chicks, 1970s superfly soul brothers, rappers in baggy pants and chunky jewelry, beboppers—men and women of all ages in the clothing of their youth, or in costume.

The band mixed up '60s soul with '50s R & B, bebop, even a disco number. Anything to get people to move their feet.

"Look there," Lou gestured. In the center of everything, on a bier, sat an elaborate coffin.

"Let's go pay our respects."

They made their way, snaking among the dancers, eaters, and talkers up to the coffin.

Laid out in a gorgeous suit was Woodrow Wilson Biggs. He looked every inch the late king of his realm.

"I wish you two could have met him before he died. Quite the character."

"Lou!" All turned in the direction of the speaker, Herman Brown.

Brown shook Lou's hand, and Lou introduced his friends.

"Mighty fine to see such beautiful women, and call me 'Kid.' How do you like it so far?"

"Kid, this is amazing. I can't believe the band."

Brown nodded his head. "Boss loved his music. He

knew these guys from way back. Stick around, and you'll see some old heads from the Basie and Ellington bands, the later ones, you know."

"Kid," said Hilda, "Lou has told us a lot about Mr. Biggs and you. It's nice to meet you."

Brown got a mischievous glint in his eye. "Now, I'm guessing you might be that fine woman that Lou here claims for his own. I hope that don't prevent you from dancing with me."

"Not a chance."

"Kid," said Blanche, "how about I dance with you now?"

Brown bowed low. "Dear lady, it pains me to ask for a brief few minutes with Lou before I take you to the floor. I hope in the meantime you will try the food. Got a whole table of Chinese and Thai over there, unless the ribs and potato salad calls out to you. Please, take your pleasure. And," he pointed toward the far wall, where there was a bar and three white-coated bartenders, "tell those men at the bar that the Kid says you get into the private stock. I'll make this quick."

The women thanked him and made for the bar. Brown turned to Lou.

"Come with me, Lou. I got something for you."

Brown led Lou toward the back of the house, a section he had not seen before. Taking a key from his pocket, he opened a huge oak door and flipped on a light to reveal a two-story classic library with a staircase and catwalk for access to the upper shelves. Lou gasped.

"Blows your mind, don't it? To a book man like you, must be heaven."

Brown closed the door, and the noise of the wake was gone. This was a hermetic little world given over to the love of reading. He walked over to a desk and picked up a leather-bound book.

"Boss wanted you to have this." He handed it over. Lou opened it, and got lightheaded.

"Kid, I can't accept this. This is a first edition of *Huckleberry Finn* signed by Mark Twain. I . . ."

"Yeah, you can. Boss indicated this was for you. Maybe a few more yet. We donating this collection to a special room in the library, named for the Boss. Might be a few books light, though.

"Mr. Biggs wasn't no educated man, at least not by schooling. He read damn near half the books in this place, though. He lived long enough, he'd a' got through all of 'em."

"I'm overwhelmed."

"I got one more thing for you, then we can talk a bit, then I can dance with your women." Brown grinned. He picked up a brown paper bag and gave it to Lou.

"What's this?" Lou asked, as he opened the bag. "Where the hell did you get this?" It was Geller's appointment book.

"Long story, but for now, we been following Roberta around since she hit town. Geller family been under the Boss's protection for years. We ambushed those peckerwoods when they picked you up, got back the book."

"Where were your men? I didn't see anything."

"See that homeless woman? She called it in, and we weren't far away."

"She was working for you?"

Brown chuckled. "Lou, only thing more invisible than a black woman is a homeless black woman. We got a network around the city. That's all I can tell you. Grace Geller's work with the homeless brought them to our notice. The organization, what's left of it, found the alliance useful. Mind you, the Boss played his cards close to the vest. I just found this out by opening an envelope. All these years with Woody Biggs and I didn't know half of what was goin' on.

"Even now, curious as I am, I would no more think of just opening all the envelopes at one time than I would dance the Texas two-step. I still fear and respect the Boss."

Lou took a moment to process the information. "A couple of questions. First, what happened to the guys who attacked us? And why are you protecting the Gellers?"

Brown flashed a wicked grin. "Them boys will be wanderin' around in the deep woods with the rest of the animals for a while. They ain't hurt bad. They don't have no pants on, though.

"We protectin' that family for a couple reasons I know of. First, Bill Goolsby asked us to. Second, Rabbi Geller helped to find the killer of that African guy, back in the day. Might learn more in another envelope."

"Do you know what Geller did in that incident?"

"More or less. They was always suspectin' that

gang of white boys and that preacher that led them around. Geller saw them outside the courthouse one day and recognized a kid he knew. Worked that kid for a month before he got him to squeal on the rev. The boy didn't have to testify in court, because he told them where to find the weapons and such. Once they got some of them little weasels in custody, they sang like birds."

"That's a mixed metaphor, Kid."

"That the kind of thing you learn in them books? Long story short, the rabbi went out of his way to get involved, like Goolsby said he would. And, the boy served some time to protect him from his friends gettin' the wrong idea."

Lou shook his head. "How the hell does a guy like Geller get from hero to wife killer?"

Brown looked thoughtful. "It's a long road got no turnin', Lou. Now, we got to get back in there. Next time the band takes a break, we got some pretty-boy preacher to say some words over the Boss.

"The Boss never set foot in a church as long as I knew him, except maybe for a wedding or funeral. Told me he went to the Church of the Flatted Fifth." Brown chuckled, Lou smiled.

"But I open an envelope, and there it is. So the Boss gonna have some words said, get right with the man upstairs, and get a righteous planting."

"Well, thanks to you and the Boss, and let's get out there for the service."

Lou found Blanche and Hilda giddy and holding

drinks. He decided to wait to tell them the latest development in this strange case.

"Lou, this is vintage champagne, and a rare one at that," Blanche reported.

"And," said Hilda, "this sour-mash whiskey is made deep in the Tennessee hills in small batches. The label is handwritten, for Pete's sake."

"Lou," said Brown, "if you go over to the bar, they got iced tea made from special imported tea. The Boss loved it, and he would have been happy to share it with you."

"Thanks, Kid. Oh, it looks like the band is breaking."

"And here come the preacher man. Ain't he something?"

The preacher was resplendent in a gold silk brocade robe, walking toward the riser with a gospel choir in tow. The perfect setting for the marriage of religion and show business.

"Kid, it's just one thing after another."

Portland, Oregon, 1973

Rabbi Robert Geller sat on a park bench on the fringe of the Portland State campus and looked out on the scene with dismay. Young toughs circulating among the students and strollers in the spring sunshine. And he suspected he knew what they were about.

Oregon had a disgraceful history of racism, and more of it lingered than Geller found comfortable. In a state controlled by loggers, ranchers, and the remnants of a pioneer culture, the cities of the Willamette Valley were the exception, and even in Portland there was an uneasy relationship among the races.

Many blacks had come to work in the Kaiser shipyards of World War II and had been segregated into a community called Vanport, so-called because it was midway between Vancouver, Washington, and Portland, just across the Columbia River from one another.

That same river rose up past flood stage in 1948 and destroyed Vanport with great loss of life and property. Since then, the black community lived for the most part in north and northeast Portland, the local answer to the ghettos of the east.

Geller wondered how this kind of racism could develop in kids who lived in a city that was so white, with blacks segregated and so little daily contact between the races. In his current job as a youth coordinator for Temple Or H'Aviv, the position a "minor league for rabbis," he was told, he spoke often to others involved with young people.

None of them had any real ideas, except that working class kids felt the pressure on their parents as the traditional ways of working were disappearing. The forests were now more to be protected rather than harvested, the ranchers were under pressure from a small group of "malcontents" who claimed that cattle were destroying the ecology of the high desert. Lumber and cattle were still kings, but there was a new breeze blowing through their domains.

Geller assumed that things would be different out

here in the west. In the south there was the legacy of slavery, Jim Crow, long-held animosity. In the big cities of the north there was the de facto segregation and the ghettos and economic deprivation. But out here?

He remembered the assassinations of the '60s, the Kennedys, Malcolm X, Medgar Evers, Dr. King, and the explosions of rage that burned the cities. He had discussed them in depth with Emily, the thought of her causing him a pang of regret, and they had come to as much understanding as two white kids could glean from the events.

But out here?

The tough boys were passing out literature. He was undecided whether to go over to them and take some, just to see what they were saying, or to ignore them and hope they'd go away. The decision was made for him, as a pair of the boys headed over to him with handfuls of the stuff.

Geller took the offered pamphlet. The headline read, "Take Pride in the White Race!" A subhead mentioned the Jews aiming to own the world. The boys turned to go.

"Do you really think the Jews own everything?" Geller asked.

"Hell yeah. The newspapers, the banks, the TV stations."

"Can you name a bank the Jews own?"

The boy didn't hesitate. "All of 'em."

"The Lumbermen's Bank of Oregon is owned by the Barstow family, has been for a hundred years.

They're not Jewish. The TV stations in town are owned by corporations, and I don't think any of the officers are Jewish. The local paper isn't owned by Jews. Where do you get your information?"

The boy looked confused for a moment. "Uh, in there." He pointed to the pamphlet. "Dr. Malkin knows that stuff. Read it, you'll see."

"Dr. Malkin?"

"Yeah," the boy said, losing patience, "Gale Malkin. He's the smartest man in the world. He writes books."

"Really? Have you met him?"

"You bet." The boy swelled with pride. "He has these meetings once a month. I been to a bunch. Garth here, too."

His friend smiled and nodded.

"Have you read his books?" Geller asked.

The boy's face clouded. "Uh, I looked at 'em."

"When's the next meeting?"

The boy handed him a flyer. "Next Thursday, at the church out in Gresham. It's on the paper."

Geller looked down at the flyer. "Okay, thanks. Maybe I'll see you there."

"Cool, mister. White pride!"

They went off to find other prospects.

Geller thought he might just attend.

Rabbi Geller pulled his clunker into the parking lot of a strip mall in Gresham, a small town east of Portland. There was a hair salon, its sign reading, "Walk-in's Welcome!" He winced at the apostrophe in the plural.

There was a shop that seemed to have a little bit of everything, and nothing priced more than sixty-nine cents. There was a fix-it shop, and there was the First Church of Christ, Christian, Rev. Gale Malkin, Pastor.

He could see in through the storefront windows. The crowd was all white, mostly men, mostly young, with a few graybeards sprinkled in. The reverend—Geller guessed it was he because he wore a jacket and tie—looked to be about thirty-five or forty.

A modicum of research had turned up these facts: The Church of Christ, Christian believed that Jesus was not a Jew, that modern Jews bore no relation to the chosen people of the bible, and in fact were the spawn of Satan. The nonwhite races, or "mud people," were subhuman. The Church had alliances with the Klan, certain groups of separatists living in the wilds of Washington, Oregon, and Idaho, and with churches of similar name and doctrine in various parts of the country.

Reverend Malkin had been in jail on two separate occasions, for assault and forgery. He had also been suspected in desecrations of Jewish cemeteries, but nothing had been proved. There had been a rash of minority assaults and synagogue trashing following his speaking appearances around the country. He had circulated a petition to the Congress of the United States of America demanding a whites-only homeland in the Pacific Northwest, and claimed one hundred thousand signatures.

He had been suspected in two bank robberies, production and circulation of child pornography, and subornation of perjury, but nothing had been proved.

Geller wondered if he really wanted to go into the lion's den. He girded his loins, locked his tubercular Ford Maverick and decided that this would only be a fact-finding mission. He vowed to himself to keep his big mouth shut.

The air in the storefront church was thick with tobacco smoke from the social hour. Geller took a seat in the back. The crowd shuffled and murmured as Malkin walked to the front of the room. The reverend mounted the makeshift riser and arranged papers on the rickety music stand that was his pulpit.

Malkin raised his hands for quiet, and the room slid into silence. Sweat was already beading the rev's face, and Geller was feeling a bit warm himself.

"My children," Malkin began, "welcome to the Church of Christ, Christian. If this is your first time here, what kept you?"

Courtesy chuckles from the crowd.

"I am here, the church is here, to free you from the lies you have been force-fed since you were small. To free you from the slander that our Lord was a member of the Hebrew race. To free you from those selfsame greedy, conniving Hebrews, and from the criminal stench of the Negro."

"You tell 'em, Rev!" Applause.

Malkin graciously acknowledged the applause. He went on.

"The Jew, through the Elders of Zion, has plotted to take over the world since at least the Middle Ages.

While King Richard the Lionhearted was in the Holy Land trying to wrest the birthplace of Jesus from the heathen Mohammedan, the Jew was poisoning the wells of Europe with plague and creating their master plan.

"My children, they have been putting this plan into effect since then."

Nine hundred years and we're not there yet, thought Geller. Doesn't seem like much of a threat.

"The hidden Jew, Franklin Delano Rosenfeld, dragged us into a war against our Aryan brothers on the orders of the Elders of Zion. My children, we should have fought on the side of the Germans, not in alliance with the communist ape Joe Stalin, not to save the devil-spawn Jew!"

The crowd was warming to the overheated rhetoric. Shouts of "You said it!" and "Amen!" erupted. Geller's skin tingled. The rev smiled and gestured for silence.

"Right now, the president of the Zionist puppet government in Washington is taking orders from the Jew Kissinger." Boos and hisses. "We are wasting blood and treasure in a jungle war that we have no business fighting. If we want to kill communism, we should unleash our power on Moscow, not on jungle monkeys in Vietnam.

"If you kill the head, the body will die. Commies around the world will wither away and Russia can rot in a nuclear ash-heap!"

Geller noted that Malkin pronounced the word "nook-u-lar." This was another pet peeve with him.

The congregation was taking all this in like mother's milk.

"The Jew communists are out to destroy Christian civilization. The international Jew bankers are out to destroy the economic life of our country. In fact, they want to own everything they don't own now."

Geller thought, So we're both communists and bankers, and we own everything. I wonder when I get my first check from the bankers?

"The Jew banker is behind the ecology movement. They couldn't defeat us militarily, or compete economically, so they are subverting our livelihoods by killing our jobs!"

People in the crowd stood up and shouted.

"The mills are closing because we can't cut trees anymore. The loggers are starving, their children are losing a way of life centuries old. And all because of a Jew plot!"

Geller was really feeling creepy, and wanted to leave. He hadn't been this scared since that trip south in the '60s. He decided to stay, and shrunk down in his seat.

The Reverend Malkin went on for a while longer in the same way. Then, he reached some kind of climax.

"And so, my children, the Jew's frustration at his inability to bring the plot of his Elders to fruition has spawned a new tactic. The use of the Negro as his cat's paw. His tool.

"The destruction and burning of America's cities was not a spontaneous eruption, as the Jew media would have us believe. No. It was a carefully planned operation using the dumb Negro as shock troops, cannon fodder."

Here, Malkin reached out his arms to his audience. "Why, one might almost feel sorry for the Negro. Lacking human intelligence or feeling, the Negro has been victimized by the wily Jew, with the promise of 'equality.' Equality? Those monkeys aren't equal to my fine retriever, Rex. He is the smartest and best behaved of dogs, a joy as a companion, and a diligent hunter. He knows his place, doesn't soil the house, and is loyal to his master.

"Of course," the rev smirked, "he is also neutered. This may be one answer to the Negro problem." The congregation chuckled in appreciation of the rev's wit.

"In conclusion, whatever we think of the Negro, recall that they know not what they do. They are in thrall to the vilest race on earth, the Jew. The Jew, once his foul plan comes to pass, will not deal with the Negro as he has dealt with all others. He will not eliminate them by stealth and disease, but he will enslave them all.

"The Jew needs the blood of our children to produce his holiday foods, and the flesh of our virgin daughters to energize his flagging lust. Have you ever seen a Jew woman? Would you be tempted by her?" Shouts of "No," and "Ugh."

"And he will need the sweat of the Negro's brow to do his labor, for he labors not, but lives off the sweat of others. And where does that leave us, the white race? Expendable. Redundant. In the way. We are too smart to fool, too strong to dominate, too pure to corrupt. The Jew's plan for us is not a pleasant one.

"So what should our plan be? First, eliminate the Negro. Send the Negro back to Africa where he belongs. It will be an act of kindness, and we are nothing if we are not kind. We are Christians.

"Then, resist the Jew. In the back of the church is a table with literature, priced right for working people, explaining the battle to come. And for those with a few cents more to spare, copies of *The Protocols of the Elders of Zion*, the Jew master plan for world domination. Read them, my children, and weep for the world.

"And now, let us pray."

As Malkin and his flock bowed their heads, Geller rose and inched toward the door. Once outside, he found the young man who had invited him grabbing a smoke.

"Hey, mister, you made it. Cool!"

"Yeah, hi. Quite an experience."

"You should stick around for the fellowship meeting. That's where we learn the good stuff."

Geller took out a cigarette, and his new friend lit it with a Zippo lighter emblazoned with a curious logo.

"What do you mean, 'good stuff'?"

"The service is for everyone, but the fellowship meeting is for, uh, whaddaya call it? The chosen few."

"Chosen few?"

"Yeah, the ones who get to do the Lord's work. I'm gonna get my first assignment tonight." The boy's face clouded. "I probably shouldn't say no more."

Geller dragged and exhaled. "Well, I have to be on

my way. Just one thing. What does that emblem on your lighter stand for?"

The boy held it out for him. It was a red rectangle with a white circle in the center, and crossed lightning bolts in black.

"All us guys in the chosen few get one. It stands for 'God's Lightning.' The strong arm of the church."

Geller nodded, thinking what that might mean.

Someone called out from the church door, "Chauncey! It's time."

"Thanks. See you later." The boy turned and headed back into the church.

The rabbi got into his car and returned to Portland. He would not sleep much that night.

13. A New Beginning

Actual sunshine poured in the windows of Lou's loft. Free of a hangover, he sat in his kitchen reading the local paper and the *New York Times*, drinking coffee, and awaiting Hilda's emergence from the bedroom.

He heard the toilet flush and the sound of slippers shuffling on the floor. An apparition resembling his lady love entered the kitchen.

"Coffee," it croaked.

"Is this the vision of loveliness I danced with last night?"

"Lou, if you value your life, you will give me a cup of freakin' coffee and shut up."

He complied, gesturing toward the table. Hilda sat down.

Twenty minutes and two cups of coffee later, Hilda spoke. "What was I drinking last night?"

"As I recall, it was some kind of custom-made sour-mash whiskey, which you proclaimed as 'angel piss' at one point."

"Ugh." She nodded. "Yeah, right." Then, she groaned.

"Should I make some breakfast. I always . . ."

At the mention of food, Hilda took off in the direction of the bathroom. Lou sat back and opened the comics page.

"You lost the book, you goddamn idiot!"

"Easy, bubba. You got no call to talk to us like that. My boys and me just walked thirty miles to get home from the deep woods, and we was half naked. You ain't payin' us enough for that kind of abuse."

"What happened?"

"We got ambushed by a black gang, got the crap beat out of us and wound up in the middle of nowhere. We might not get our van back. You gonna replace that? Come to think of it, you still owe us for this job."

"Sue me, moron. I'll take care of this by myself." He hung up.

Chauncey stared mute at the dead phone. "Hey, boys," he yelled, "either of your cars workin'?"

Hilda managed to keep down some dry toast. She still looked like she'd been caught in a stampede. Lou determined to keep a smirk off his face and play nice.

"You should try to drink some juice, or even water. You're dehydrated, and . . ."

"I know what you're thinking. I can see it in your

blank expression. You're feeling superior to your friends, indifferent to our suffering." Hilda scowled.

"Hilda, why don't you go shower? It'll do you a world of good, and it might wash this ugly little mood away. Then we can get to work."

"Hmph!" she said, but rose from her chair in exaggerated slowness.

"I spent way too many mornings like this to feel superior. I'm serious about the juice."

"Later." She padded toward the bathroom.

Lou made a mental list of things to do: Call Lainie Reiter about Jodie Coram. Call Tom Knight about the robbery angle and Grace Geller's purse. He wondered if there were any point to talking with Gottbaum or Plisskin.

Taking the last of the coffee, he went over to his home office, a corner of the big room that comprised his loft flat. He called Knight's office in Waldorf. Miss Warden, aka "Old Ironpants," answered. The temperature dropped when she heard his name.

"The District Attorney is in court. I will give him your message."

He thanked her a bit too much, then dialed Reiter.

"Lainie Reiter."

"Hi, this is Lou Tedesco." They exchanged pleasantries.

"Lainie, I need to ask a favor."

"Ask away."

"You once told me that you might lay hands on Jodie Coram's current phone number. Can do?"

"Funny you should ask. I've been curious about this

myself. First, she left under something of a cloud. No idea why. No one else seems to know, other than to say that she needed to take some time off for personal reasons. Sounds like an official line.

"Second, I was told that this was a personnel action and that they can't legally say anything. At least, I can't get anyone to talk about it."

"Lainie, when I hear 'personnel action,' I understand 'got fired.'"

"Well, usually. It could be anything that violates policy. Sexual harassment, stealing, improper relations with the staff, or a source . . . Like I said, no idea what."

"Did you say 'improper relations with a source'?"

"Yeah. Do you know something here?" She sounded eager for gossip.

"Nothing, really. Just a hint of a possibility."

"Ooh," she squealed, "dirt. Come on, Lou, spill."

"Lainie, I promise you will be the second to know. It would be nice to go to the horse's mouth on this one. No doubts after that."

"I used to date someone from HR. I'll get him drunk."

Lou sighed. "Why has my universe become a sad vista of moral compromise?"

She laughed and snorted on the other end. "Oh, Lou, you crack me up!"

"Call me." He rang off.

He called Blanche at home, got her voice mail, and tried the office.

"Hey, Louie, great party! You know any other mob bosses on the verge of death?"

"Shame on you. You're not hungover?"

"I learned from the master about the evils of excess."

"That would be me, I suppose?"

"Go to the head of the class. After about three glasses of bubbly I switched to ginger ale. No one could tell the difference, and I was on a contact high anyway.

"It's hard to believe that the party just kept getting better. A twelve-piece big band playing Basie and Ellington tunes? Yowza." She made purring noises.

Lou filled her in on the latest, including the return of Geller's appointment book, and the role of Biggs's organization in its return.

"Damn, Lou, you never know what's going on right under your nose. An alliance between homeless people and African-American gangs? Who'd a' thunk it?"

"Reminds me of that movie, *M.* The Berlin underworld joins up to rid the streets of a child killer and take the heat off them. Beggars, pickpockets, prostitutes, the street people of the time."

"Think we can get a story on this? It'd make great copy."

Lou thought for a second. "I don't know. At this point, it would seem like betraying a confidence. Maybe after things cool down . . ."

"How's Hilda?"

"If you offered to shoot her, she'd buy the bullet."

"Oh, have you seen the morning paper? Check out

the Metro section. There's an article about the abandoned van and its, um, checkered history."

"Anything we don't know?"

"I doubt it. But, the reporter speculates a bit. Very amusing."

"Blanche, are you still friendly with that TV news editor?"

"Yeah, sure. He's got the hots for me, poor thing."

"Can you subtly ask him if he knows why Jodie Coram left town, and if he can track her down?" He explained the significance.

"Hey, if I agree to have dinner with him, he'll give me his safe deposit box key."

"I'll see you later."

Hilda walked in, freshly showered and looking a bit better. Her silver hair was still damp. She tossed her head, then crinkled her eyes as a twinge of pain hit her.

"Okay, the shower made me feel better, and I drank a whole glass of water, mostly to wash down the four aspirin."

Lou waited a beat. "Think you can have a light lunch?"

Her stomach growled, right on cue. "Maybe. What's going on?"

Lou boiled some eggs, and heated chicken broth. He filled her in, and she laughed at the story of the depantsed thugs. He found the article in the newspaper, and she read it aloud to him while he peeled eggs and gave her a mug of broth.

"The reporter thinks he discerns a gang war among black gangs," Hilda said.

"He smells a Pulitzer. More toast?"

"Yeah, okay."

The phone rang. Tom Knight calling back.

"Hi, Tom."

"Whaddaya need Lou? I gotta get back."

"Did you ever explore the robbery angle with the Geller murder?"

"Ah, let me see . . . Well, we were told that her wallet was missing, and we poked around but her cards were never used and the wallet never turned up. Then Gottbaum confessed and we kind of let it go."

"According to the trial accounts, Gottbaum claimed that he threw the murder weapon and the clothes they wore into a dumpster. Maybe the wallet went with them."

"Your speculation is as good as mine," Knight replied. "They became irrelevant after the confession."

"Did you learn whether Grace Geller brought home proceeds from the bakery that night?"

"No, like I said . . ."

"Gottbaum confessed and the focus shifted."

"Right. Lou, you're not making any judgments here, are you? We have limited resources, and . . ."

"No, no, not at all." Lou rolled his eyes. "Listen, get back to your case. I'll talk to you later."

"Wait a minute, Tedesco. Have you found something? I'll throw your ass in jail if you're withholding . . ."

"Relax, Tom. Nothing here yet. Maybe this is where I tell you that I can't compromise an ongoing investigation."

"Ha-ha, Lou," Knight said without humor.

"You'll be the first to know if we turn anything up." He was making similar promises a lot these days. They rang off.

"I feel better now." Hilda smiled a shaky smile.

"Good. Let's go to the office. We have work to do."

Portland, Oregon, 1975

It was just after the Sunday school class for children and Rabbi Alvin Tannenbaum, chief rabbi of Or H'Aviv, put his arm around Robert Geller's shoulder. "You asked to speak with me," he said.

"Yes, Rabbi. Can we go to your office?"

"Sure Rabbi. Follow me." Tannenbaum removed his prayer shawl, kissed it, and folded it neatly. He put it in his cubbyhole at the front of the classroom. They went upstairs to the main floor.

Indicating the open door, Tannenbaum showed Geller into his plainly furnished office. The modest appointments were part of the chief rabbi's personal philosophy, and looked good for the board at contract time.

"Close the door, Bobby, and we can have a smoke."

Geller shut the door, and reached for a cigarette. Tannenbaum opened a window, pulled out a pack of Winstons, and offered a light.

"So, what's on your mind, kiddo?" Tannenbaum sat, put his feet up on the desk and exhaled.

Leaning forward to tap his ashes into a soda can

there for the purpose, Geller collected his thoughts. He went for the main chance.

"Rabbi, I feel that I have to leave the congregation."

Tannenbaum's face darkened, and he nodded. "It's not like I wasn't expecting it, but I'm sorry to hear it. Is there anything I can do to convince you to stay? I can't promise you any more money, but perhaps some additional duties, some more bar mitzvahs . . ."

"Al," Geller interrupted, "how old are you?"

"Forty-five. Why?"

"You're about fifteen years older than me. You're healthy, you play racquetball, tennis . . . you're gonna live another forty years, easy. And I'm glad, you're a nice guy. What do I do in the meantime? If you die at eighty-five, or retire, I'm your seventy-year-old back-up.

"Forgive me, but I can't play second fiddle that long."

Tannenbaum sat up straight and crushed out his smoke.

"Like I said, I was expecting this. I was just hoping it wouldn't be so soon. You do great work with the kids, especially the teenagers. I just assumed that, some day, you would get your own congregation.

"There are more Jews moving out here all the time, and you have an inside track for a new temple. But you're right. It might take a while.

"Where are you planning on going? Seattle? California? Back east?"

"Uh-uh. Out to the coast." Geller took a last puff of his cigarette and put it out.

"Are you *meshugganeh?* There's nothing out there but trees and water."

Geller shook his head. "Not true. The congregation won't be a big one, but we'll be the only *shul* for miles. People won't have to shlep all the way to Waldorf. And I have a backer."

Tannenbaum's eyebrows went up. "Really? Who?"

"A developer, Mel Goldstein. He's building beach condos and an upscale hotel out there, north of Seagirt. He's observant, and it pains him when he can't get away to Waldorf or Portland for services. We've spoken, and he's made me an offer."

Tannenbaum whistled. "*Mazel tov*, Bobby. I'm happy for you, but sad you'll be leaving."

"Thanks. I've been happy here."

Tannenbaum leaned forward and spoke quietly. "May I ask a personal question?"

Geller shrugged.

"Tell me," Tannenbaum went on, "are you still hurting from Emily?"

"I think so," Geller sighed, "but it may never really go away."

Tannenbaum nodded.

Geller smiled a little smile. "Goldstein has a daughter, not married, about my age."

"Aha! Comes now the truth. You like her?"

"Not bad. She reminds me a bit of my mother."

"Oy! Is this a good thing?"

Geller laughed. "The jury's still out on that. She's very ambitious, a real go-getter just like her father."

"A baby doll, or a monkey?"

Geller laughed into a smoker's cough. "Well, she's no Natalie Wood, but hey, I'm no Paul Newman, either."

"Sounds good, Bobby. When will you be leaving us?"

"A couple of months, I guess. I'm going out for the groundbreaking next week, and I'll have to get the whole thing together so we can have a congregation when the place opens."

"You'll invite us? Betty would never forgive you if you didn't."

Geller forced a smile. "She's a good kid. She gave me plenty of trouble in youth group. Only a rabbi's daughter would know what buttons to push to piss me off, but it was never malicious."

He shuddered inside, remembering the nasty, over-sexed girl who had made a point of creating embarrassing situations with him to amuse her friends. Geller thought of her as Lolita, only scarier. He wouldn't miss her.

Tannenbaum chuckled. "Yeah, she's a pistol, all right. Look, I'll make an announcement to the congregation next Saturday night after services. We'll keep it upbeat and positive. How's that?"

Geller held out his hand. "Thanks, Al. You're the best."

Tannenbaum stood up and shook his hand, then hugged him in an awkward man-hug clinch with much hearty back-slapping.

Robert Geller left the synagogue, hoping he was doing the right thing.

14. Made in Heaven

That afternoon in her office, Blanche couldn't hide her amusement. "Poor Hilda. I heard you were, um, unwell this morning."

Hilda's eyes slitted. "Screw you, sadist. I heard you switched to soda pop. Moral cowardice if ever I saw it."

"Now, can't we all just get along?" Lou asked. "We have actual work to do. Blanche, did you call that TV guy?"

"Yup. Let's just say that he sounded eager. So, we meet tonight. I asked for Genoa, natch."

"Now I know you're a disturbed individual," Hilda sneered. "Not only are you seeing this poor schmuck just to pump him for information, but you're gonna pop him for seventy-five-dollar-a-head prix fixe. Oh, the humanity!"

"Wanna come along?"

"Can you swing it?" Hilda's eyes bugged out.

"I see how deep righteous outrage goes in this crowd," Lou interjected. "Perhaps you should vamp this guy one-on-one, Blanche. I'll take you both to Genoa if this pans out."

"Deal," said Hilda.

"You got it," agreed Blanche.

"Okay, let's go over this appointment book."

"Damn it, Roberta! Come home now!" Gary's anxiety seeped from the phone like a vapor.

"I love it when you get all macho and protective like that."

"This is not funny. You might have been badly hurt or, God forbid, killed. Haven't we had enough of that in this family?"

"Okay," Roberta sighed, "you're right that I shouldn't joke about it. If you had seen me last night you'd know that I'm not taking this lightly."

"Why didn't you call me?"

"Because I was afraid you'd react like this. I wasn't in any shape to argue with you."

"Oh, but you're fine with that now?"

"Well, yeah. We've made some real progress here. Lou Tedesco has resources a regular citizen finds hard to believe. And a great pot of dumb luck."

"I hope he has enough to rub off on you."

"So far, so good. I'm going to his newspaper office to work with him on the names in the appointment book. What else is new?"

"Your family is taking turns calling me to ask about

you. I'm not sure I can bring myself to tell them about this."

"Then don't. I'll do a conference call with all of them when I get back."

"And that will be exactly when, missy?"

Roberta laughed. "Soon. Anything from Stevie?"

"Only what I hear in random *kvetching* from your relatives. Apparently, he turns on his phone when he needs to make a call, turns it off otherwise, and ignores the messages everyone leaves. He seems to be keeping track of you thirdhand. He hasn't called me to ask about you."

"Nor has he called me. Look, I gotta go. I'm being picked up in about ten minutes."

"I hope Lou What's-his-face isn't picking you up."

"Tedesco. No, it's his girlfriend, Hilda. Different car, too. Just in case anyone is actually still watching us."

"Great. My wife thinks she's James Bond."

"The other day it was Nancy Drew. What's next?"

"I don't know," he sighed. "Amelia Earhart?"

"She was a pilot. What's that got to do with anything?"

"She's also the world's most famous missing person. Be careful. I love you."

"Gary, you are the best husband, and I don't want to lose you. I promise to be careful."

Chauncey Zerby winced as the rattletrap car came to a stop, the engine running for a moment after he turned off the ignition. It wheezed before it finally quit.

It was a blue 1970 Cougar, held together by unknown forces and racist bumper stickers. The radio didn't work very well, but a cassette player cranked out scratchy white power tunes with a jackhammer beat until he shut it off. Jeez, he thought, what I wouldn't give for some good ol' rock 'n' roll.

Zerby checked the address against a scrawled piece of paper. "This must be it," he said aloud. "Only damn house for miles." He got out of the car, walked up to the front door, and rang the bell.

Rabbi Geller opened the door and gawked. A middle-aged man with dark circles under his eyes stood before him. There was something familiar about him, his lumberjack clothing and his hangdog expression.

"Chauncey? Is that you?" He looked out at the car. "Nice bumper stickers."

"Yeah, well . . ." Zerby stared. Geller looked awful, and smelled bad. "Can I come in?"

"Sure, sure."

The house was dark. Zerby stepped carefully inside.

"Wait, let me turn on a light."

The light revealed squalor and neglect. Zerby decided that maybe his trashy double-wide wasn't so bad after all.

"Can I get you a drink? I was just about to pour myself one," the rabbi offered.

The floor was littered with fast-food trash. Several empty vodka bottles sat on the coffee table.

"No, no thanks. I don't drink anymore. A pop would be nice."

"Sit down. I'll be right back."

Geller disappeared for a couple of moments and returned with a bottle of 7-Up and a glass of iced vodka. Geller held up his glass.

"Cheers."

"Better days," Zerby replied.

They drank a sip and sat down. Geller stared at Zerby.

"It's been a long time, Chauncey. How are things?"

"Bobby, it's been better, but not much worse."

"I hear you." Geller gestured around. "You can see that I'm not at the top of my game."

"Sometimes I think that you're my only and last friend in the world."

"Right now, I feel the same. Just out of curiosity, why are you here?"

"I need a favor. I'm dead broke. No money for food, even. I was wondering if I could hit you up for a loan?"

Geller was silent for a minute. "Chauncey, I think we might be able to help each other."

Hilda sat back and stretched. Blanche stood up and walked around her office. Lou scribbled on a yellow pad, and Roberta sat and stared.

"Okay," Lou said, "I think we have it down. Hilda will talk to the women on the list, Blanche will seduce some info out of her dinner date, and I'll call Gar for some help. Is that it?"

Roberta snapped out of her trance. "Wait. Shouldn't I talk to the women? I know them."

"No," said Hilda. "Think about it. This is your father they would be discussing. They're not gonna talk about screwing him on his office couch to his daughter."

"Yeah, you're right. It's just that I feel a bit useless at this point."

"Honey, you have been amazing here. If I were you, I would've been on the first plane out of here after we got grabbed." Lou shook his head. "Maybe you should go home. Give us a chance to do some work, see your hubby. We'll keep you updated."

Roberta chewed her lip and thought a bit. "Okay. I'll get on a plane tomorrow."

"Meanwhile," Lou said, "Blanche has dinner plans tonight, but I think the rest of us should go out for Thai, or something."

They went out for a nice dinner, and Lou drove Roberta back to the hotel. As he and Hilda went back to his loft, they picked up a tail.

Waldorf, Oregon, 1976

The crowd was large and festive, overflowing the Columbia Room of the Beaver State Hotel. Champagne, hard liquor, and soda pop for the kiddies, a buffet of kosher food trucked in from Seattle, and an enormous cake in the likeness of the planned synagogue, now under construction between Waldorf and Seagirt.

The rabbi of the future B'nai Yisroel congregation, Robert Geller, was engaged to Grace Goldstein, and this was their party. Geller had never seen Grace look so good. She was radiant, and dressed in a custom-designed gown which emphasized her plump bosom while masking her full hips. The deep green color brought out her green eyes.

Her father Mel and her mother Shirley stood on either side of the couple. The crowd moved toward them, each one holding a glass for a toast. Mel raised his champagne.

"Family, friends, Governor, and all our guests, please drink a toast to the young couple, soon to be Rabbi and Mrs. Robert Geller. Mazel tov!"

"Mazel tov!" the crowd roared, and the band struck up a hora. Geller kissed his bride-to-be. Mel Goldstein took him aside as his wife dragged her reluctant daughter to the dance floor.

"Rabbi, you like the band?" Mel shouted over the music and noise. "I flew them in from New York. Can't find anything like this in the northwest."

"Great band, Mel. And call me Robert."

"Robert, Rabbi, what's the difference? The governor is here, the mayor, big shot businessmen from the whole state . . . of course, they're just here because they need to work with me. But still."

"Thanks, Mel. This really is a tribute to you."

"Baloney! It's a tribute to the free food and booze. But I'm looking toward the future, and you my boy are the future. I expect big things from you. My Gracie already has her own business, does charity work, a real chip off the old block! You'll be a great team."

Geller smiled at his future father-in-law and said a

prayer that he was right. "When do you think the temple will be ready?"

"Ah, this crappy rain. Pretty soon the rain will stop and they can really get busy. I love this place, but you can't get decent bagels and it rains all winter."

"Better than snow. You don't have to shovel rain, Mel."

Goldstein laughed a boozy laugh. "Go dance with the bride. I'm getting some more champagne before these locusts suck it all up."

Mel walked over to the buffet table and was swallowed up in a sea of glad-handers. Geller looked out to the dance floor and saw Grace dancing with a group of preteen children to "Proud Mary." Whatever else she has going for her, he thought, Grace Goldstein ain't got no rhythm.

He caught her eye and she held up a finger to indicate she would be a minute. When the song was over, Grace hugged all the kids and walked over.

"Hiya, big boy." Grace took Geller's hands in hers and put a light kiss on his lips.

"Happy?" he asked.

"For now. But we have to talk."

Something rolled unpleasantly in his stomach.

"What about?"

Grace laughed. "What a look! Don't worry, it's nice. I want to start a family right away. Maybe even before the wedding."

Geller's relief was not complete. He suspected that Grace would want children, but he feared that he did not know what a happy family was like. The Peresses were as close as he had ever come to one, and he was merely an observer. He had no idea what people did to make a family warm and loving.

He suppressed the darker thought that Grace might not be the woman with whom he wanted to share the rest of his days. He had lost two women who had claim to be the loves of his life, and Grace did not measure up.

"Grace," Geller cleared his throat, "don't you think it might look funny if the rabbi's bride is pregnant?"

"In this day and age? We could probably get away with living together. Don't be such a square."

Having lost the cultural high ground, Geller took another tack.

"It doesn't matter much what we think; it's the congregation. Why give them something to gossip about right off the bat?"

Grace made a face. "Yeah, you're right. Besides my mother would kill me, now that I think about it. But we start on the wedding night, right?"

Relieved, Geller answered, "Okay. Sure."

He looked around the room, hoping to find something to use to change the subject. His eyes fell on a boy, off in a corner of the room, fixing them with a baleful gaze. Geller was shocked at the open hostility in the look.

He leaned over and said in her ear, "Gracie, who's the kid with the poisonous face, over in the far corner?"

She looked around. "Oh! That's Stevie. I've seen that face before."

"Who's Stevie?"

"My baby brother. You haven't met the whole family, yet."

Geller was surprised. "Yeah, but another brother? No one has even mentioned him."

Grace sighed. "He's a bit of a problem. He's away at boarding school, one for troubled boys. When he comes home, he mostly stays in his room. I'm pretty much the only one he'll talk to. He seems more like my son sometimes than my kid brother. My mother has given up on him. A shame, really."

"How does he feel about your getting married?"

Grace laughed. "He wants to kill you."

Geller jumped. "Damn!"

"Don't sweat it. He wants everyone to die except him and me. He draws pictures of hideous accidents, catastrophes. Smoke, blood, people running . . . all made worse because he draws so well. The shrinks say it's worrisome, but the drawings help him vent it off."

"Grace, I've worked with some troubled kids. This sounds . . ."

She put a finger to his lips. "Shush. Forget it. This is a day to be happy, and Stevie is usually hundreds of miles away. Let's get some champagne. Or, maybe you need something stronger?"

She took him by the arm and led him to the buffet table, to be greeted by her mother and a gaggle of giggling aunts. Stevie watched, fingering the drawing in his pocket, and willing the picture to become real.

The Geller House, Oregon, 1991

"I hate you!" shrieked Roberta, running out of the living room in tears.

Grace Geller sighed and went into the kitchen to pour herself some water and take a couple of Advil. Once the pills went down, she called her husband at the temple.

"So, what couldn't wait until I got home?" he asked.

"Your daughter. She used to be such a sweet kid, like Robbie is, but now I know why mothers kill their children."

"Gracie, don't even say that! She's fourteen, and the hormones . . ."

"Don't give me 'hormones.' When I was her age I was working and helping to take care of my sick mother, not to mention my crazy kid brother. What she needs is for you to stop spoiling her. You give her whatever she asks for, and I'm the bitch."

Geller sighed. "Gracie, you're not a bitch."

"Oh no? Ask your daughter."

"Look, I have a light day today. Do you want me to come home?"

"Do what you like. I'm going to the bakery."

"You're going to leave the kids home alone?"

"Robbie is at soccer practice and has a ride home. She can set fire to the place for all I care."

"Gracie, please, she's a teenager. All this will blow over. In a year or two she'll be fine."

"Yeah, if I don't strangle her with my bare hands

before then. Okay," she puffed her cheeks and exhaled between her lips, "I'll stick around until you get here, but make it quick."

"Fix us both a drink. You can use it."

Geller hung up and looked up at the ceiling for a moment, didn't find anything there, then threw some papers in his attache case and headed out to his car. In a matter of minutes he was home.

"Roberta, your father wants to see you." Grace handed her husband a stiff Scotch and water. He hated Scotch but wasn't about to complain.

"Roberta, Goddamn it, didn't you hear me?"

Geller touched his wife's arm. "Easy. I'll go back and talk to her in her room."

"Good luck. I'll be back later." She finished her drink in a gulp, grabbed her purse and a sweater, and went out the door.

Roberta peeked around a doorway.

"Is Cruella gone yet?" she asked.

Geller tried not to smile, amused as he was by a fourteen-year-old's frame of reference.

"Now look, young lady . . ."

Roberta rolled her eyes, and Geller had to laugh.

"Seriously, come over and sit down, we have to talk."

Roberta slouched over to the couch and dropped on it like a sandbag. She had pimple cream smeared randomly on her face, her jeans were out at the knees, and her shirt would have fit a professional wrestler. Geller took her in.

"Tough being fourteen, ain't it?"

"Don't say 'ain't,' it makes you sound common," she replied in a fluting voice.

"Does your mom tell you that?"

"She tells me what's wrong. That's all she tells me. Day after day. Sometimes I want to kill her."

"Not nice. Listen to me. Your mom has a lot on her mind. She runs the business that helps put food in your belly and buys you your charming clothes."

Roberta flashed him a face and started to say something. Geller raised his hand in a conciliatory gesture.

"Okay, okay, just a little joke. She also has a bunch of other things she does to help poor people, blah blah blah. You've heard this before. But she also manages to get you off to school with breakfast and a lunch, and tolerates your, um, wardrobe. All she wants is a little respect and reasonable obedience."

"She's a bitch," Roberta mumbled.

"Don't call your mother that. I'm not kidding."

"She's the worst mother, really. No other girl has to put up . . ."

"You know what, I don't believe that. Most girls and boys have to deal with being a teenager, and most do it in the worst way. I don't want you to be a little Miss Perfect, but I do want you to get along with your mother. Let it roll off your back. If she's being unreasonable, try to understand. Come to me with whatever it is. You be the big one, here."

"You think that's easy?" She rolled her eyes once more.

"No. I know how hard it can be. My mother was, ah, difficult to get along with."

Roberta looked at her father. "How come you never talk about your parents?"

Geller took a drink.

"Can I taste that?" Roberta asked.

Geller hesitated, shrugged. "Yeah, okay, but just a sip."

Roberta sniffed the drink and made a face. Then she took a small sip.

"Eee-ew! Why do you drink that stuff? It tastes like medicine." She put the glass down, spilling some.

Geller laughed. "I don't like it that much myself. Your mom drinks Scotch." Roberta flashed an "it figures" look. "I'm more of a vodka man, myself, but you wouldn't like that any better."

She shook her head. "Grown-ups are weird. Tell me about your father."

"Barney? He was a good man, very calm and forgiving. He had a love for humanity, but he liked people, too."

She wrinkled her nose. "Is that a joke?"

"Unfortunately, no. I've met too many in my life who love people in the abstract, but don't get along very well with anyone on a personal level."

"I told you grown-ups were weird. What happened to him?"

Geller sighed. "He died way too young. My mother, who had a rough childhood, a Depression kid, she just saw it as another piece of bad luck."

"He died and she felt unlucky?"

Geller looked at his daughter. "That's a very good question. It tells you a lot about her."

"What was she like?"

"Tough, hard, always right. Cynical. You know what that means?"

"I think so."

"She never saw the good in anything, always expected the worst. She told me it was better than hoping and getting disappointed. She seemed to be happiest when she was destroying other people's dreams. A killjoy."

"Really?" Geller nodded. "Well, you turned out okay. How bad could she be?"

Geller chewed his lip. He had no answer to that. It was silent for a time.

"Is she dead?" Roberta asked.

"I don't know. We haven't spoken in years."

"I wish I could say the same . . ."

"Roberta! That's terrible."

"Oh, yeah? You don't know anything. You know what she says about you when you're not here?"

"Roberta, I won't have you telling tales on your mother . . ."

She stood up, clenched her fists, face going red.

"She says you have no ambition, that you don't care if we're stuck in this wilderness forever. She . . ."

"Stop that!"

"No, there's more. She told me that you didn't want me, that you fought when she told you she was pregnant, and that it happened again with Robbie. She told me . . ."

"Enough! Go to your room."

"You always take her side, but she doesn't love us!"

Geller grabbed his daughter, caught between slapping her face and hugging her. She threw herself into him and began to sob. He clutched her to himself and stroked her hair.

Geller whispered, "No, honey. I know you're hurt and angry, but she loves us, and she's doing the best she can, and all this will go away in a while."

He waited until she cried herself out, wondering if he believed what he just told her. He recalled, burning with guilt, the argument they'd had, standing in the newly built synagogue, when she said she was pregnant. He still felt ashamed of that, but knew that he had been crippled emotionally by his childhood, and didn't want to inflict that kind of thing on anyone else.

He just wished that Grace hadn't used that against him to get at the kids.

"Why don't you go to bed, baby. I'll come and tuck you in after you wash up."

"It's too early."

"You're right. Okay, wash up and we'll watch some TV and make popcorn."

She smiled at him, face runny with tears and zit cream, and went off to the bathroom. His shirt bore smears from Roberta's face. Geller wondered if vodka would react badly with Scotch, and headed for the bar.

A few hours later, Roberta and Robbie in bed after a cable movie and greasy popcorn, Grace walked in and found her husband on the couch, well into a bottle of vodka.

She dropped her purse and a stack of papers on the

coffee table. "Did you straighten that little snotnose out?" she asked.

"She's okay. You should cut her some slack."

"Slack!" Grace yelled.

Geller waved his hands. "Shh. They're both asleep. Please keep your voice down."

The rest of their discussion was hissed through clenched teeth.

"Don't give me 'cut her some slack.' She's a rotten and spoiled brat. If I talked that way to my mother, I would've gotten my head handed to me." She took the bottle of Scotch off the counter, and poured some for herself.

"Please realize that she is not you . . ."

"A damn shame."

". . . and she's just a kid awash in puberty. Get used to it, because Robbie is gonna go through some version of this in a short time."

"My God, if I ran my business like this house is run, we'd all starve to death." Grace took two pills from her purse and washed them down with the Scotch.

"This is not a business, this is your family, and you are supposed to know the difference. You can't fire your kids now, can you?" Geller allowed some sarcasm to slip into his speech.

"Another damn shame."

Geller sat back, and was quiet for a moment. "Did you tell Roberta that I had no ambition?"

Her eyes narrowed. "That little rat."

"I'll take that as a yes. What's wrong with our lives

here? My being the head rabbi of a congregation isn't good enough for you?"

"Do you think I wanna be stuck in this backwater my whole life? Life! Hah! This is some life. A pissant rabbi of a pissant temple in the middle of nowhere. Great."

"Allow me to remind you that your father built the *shul*, this house . . ."

"Without consulting anyone, surely not me. I thought I could hack it for a while, but I was always hoping to move on, Seattle, San Francisco . . . somewhere with something to do besides work and take care of kids."

"And who's the one who wanted those kids, nearly consummated the marriage on the floor of the engagement party?"

"This conversation is over. I work hard, and I'm going to bed."

"I have an idea. Why don't you give up some of your charity work and put some effort into being a mother and a rabbi's wife? It doesn't go unnoticed that you're seldom at any temple functions."

"And why don't you act like a man for a change."

Grace downed the Scotch and swept out of the room. Not for the last time, Geller slept on the couch.

15. Action and Reaction

"Okay," said Hilda, "let's get going. Do we have to drive Roberta to the airport?"

"Nope. She rented a car. I hope she's actually going home. She's nuttier than I am about her lack of concern for personal safety."

"Maybe you should call the Kid and arrange for protection."

Lou scoffed. "Are you joking? Do you expect those guys to try anything after a beating and a long walk in the woods? We don't even know if they made it home yet. Maybe they were eaten by cougars."

Hilda sniffed and gathered her overnight bag and a stack of papers with notes on the women she wanted to talk to. "I'm ready if you are."

"Yup. Just let me get my papers together."

"Hey, wait. Call Blanche, at least to find out how the meal was."

"Oh, yeah." He picked up the phone. Blanche answered, and they greeted each other.

"Well, Louie, aside from the dinner, it wasn't much of a success. Especially for him."

"No hope for the boy, you say? What about the Coram thing?"

Blanche sighed. "He doesn't know, and never heard any scuttlebutt. Apparently, she was a bit mysterious about everything at the end. He did promise to make subtle inquiries."

"Thanks for taking one for the team, gorgeous."

"Seven courses of delicious food is hardly a problem."

"Okay, we're off to the coast."

Five minutes later, they stood in front of Lou's building. His neighborhood was industrial and commercial buildings on both sides of a wide street. His building housed four floors of lofts, three artist's studios, and his flat. Lou's car was down the block in front of a warehouse. There were several trucks parked and double-parked around it.

"Damn! I'll have to go talk to the warehouse guy. We may be stuck for a few minutes until the deliveries, or whatever, are finished." Lou set down his bags.

"Well, this is what you get for living in an industrial district. I never have any parking problems out in Seagirt." Hilda made a smug face.

"Yeah, and no hidden agenda in that observation, either. I'll be right back."

Lou walked down to the warehouse, which handled imported household goods from Asia and distributed them to various specialty stores in the city. The owner, an Iranian man named Nasser, was friendly and accommodating. They had shared lunches before.

Nasser was standing with a clipboard, deep into a discussion with a truck driver. Lou waited a short distance away.

After signing the driver's papers, Nasser said, "Mr. Louie. How are you today?"

"Oh, pretty good, Nasser. Listen, that's my car behind those trucks. Any chance I can move it out?"

Nasser looked around. "Good chance, Mr. Louie. This man is now leaving, and the one in front is loaded up. Driver is using my bathroom. Can you get it out when that moves?"

Lou nodded. "Yeah, I think so. It's pretty tight, but yeah."

"Good, good. I just got in some hand-woven baskets from Malaysia. You are interested?"

Lou watched the driver get into his truck and start the engine.

"Maybe, Nasser. Can I look another time? I'm kind of anxious to . . . Hey, that truck is a bit close to my car."

Lou ran toward the truck. "Hey, watch it there on your right!"

Nasser was yelling at the driver and waving his arms. When the truck's bumper caught the back of Lou's car, the car lurched and exploded in a ball of flame. The noise reverberated in among the buildings.

"Jesus!" the driver squawked, and dove out of his truck.

Lou yelled over his shoulder, "Nasser, call 911,"

and took off toward the truck while Nasser reached for his cell phone. "Yo, driver, you better move that thing. It may go up."

"I'm outta here." The driver ran up the street.

Lou jumped in the truck cab, his metal knee unhappy with the effort. He jammed down the clutch and wrenched the gear shift into what he hoped was a low forward gear. Easing up on the clutch, he turned the wheel away from his burning car.

"Lou!" He heard Hilda scream. "Get out of that thing. It's gonna blow!"

The truck lurched forward, but Lou kept it from stalling, and drove it across the street, and out of contact with the flames. Then, the car's gas tank exploded.

Hours later, after the fire and police personnel had finished securing the area and Lou and the other witnesses had been questioned by the investigators, he and Hilda sat in the newspaper office with shell-shocked expressions on their faces. Blanche had been plying them with tea or liquor, according to their preferences.

The whole office staff had not gone home, even though it was past normal business hours. Two *Weekly* reporters were out beating the bushes for any information they could get, and Lou expected another visit from the police any moment.

Patti ran in, all flushed and out of breath. She had been out of the office.

"Hey! Are you okay? Oh my God!"

Blanche held up her hands to calm Patti down.

"Whoa, catch your breath. No one was hurt badly, a couple of burns and some temporary ear damage." She turned to Lou. "I swear I heard that all the way from here."

"Not much fire damage either, considering," said Lou. "And besides, that car was on its last legs."

"Maybe that's because you always buy a cheap used jalopy," Hilda said between sips of scotch. "You can afford a new one, for Pete's sake."

"Imagine how bad I would feel if that were a new car."

Hilda nodded, raised her glass in salute, and took another sip.

"Louie, who would do this to you?" Patti stroked Lou's shoulder.

Lou shook his head. "Patti, the cops asked me that, and I gave them the runaround. There's no one I would mention to the cops, because it's all speculation anyway.

"But I've been asking myself that for hours. Geller is mad at me, and he's certainly capable of doing this, or at least hiring someone to do it. The men who tried to grab us that day, they might have done this. They probably know where I live.

"Bottom line, no prime suspects. It might even have been unrelated to this case. Hell, it might have been meant for someone at the warehouses."

"Okay, you two are staying with me tonight," Blanche ordered. "And if you feel up to it, you can rent a car and leave for the coast tomorrow."

"Are you sure you want to have us over?" Hilda asked. "It's a little like painting a target on your back."

"I'll take the chance. If you like, you can hide on the floor in the back of the car on the way home."

"Like movie stars avoiding the paparazzi," Patti chirped.

"Blanche, we have to get moving on this and, frankly, I'm not hurt as much as terrified, and even that's fading. I can't let this scare me."

"Yeah, I guess I feel the same," added Hilda, "but I reserve the right to be scared out of my mind."

Gary Mendelson picked up his wife at the airport. The gray mood of Oregon was behind her, and the semitropical San Diego environment lifted Roberta's mood. She was happy to see her husband. They drove to their home in Point Loma.

"Honey," he offered, "why don't I fix you a drink? You can tell me about the last few days, or you can just chill out. I'll be happy to sit with you either way."

"Good idea. Can you take my case to the bedroom? I'm going to the patio."

A few minutes later, under the blue dome of the southern California sky, Roberta and Gary clinked their martini glasses and tasted the ice-cold cocktails.

"Funny," she said, "my father didn't drink much when I was a kid. Or, at least he kept it under control. You know, some wine with his friends at dinner, or maybe a few shots at a wedding or bar mitzvah. Just enough to get, what's that old word, tipsy?

"Since I was in high school, I've noticed that he's

drinking more, and getting more sullen about it. Not for giggles, but for, I don't know, medication, anaesthesia, escape. Whatever. And it ain't pretty."

Gary nodded and sipped his drink. "Oh," he said, "Stevie called. He needs to talk to you. He left his cell number, in case you didn't have it."

"Hmph! I hope it's an apology. The little bastard hasn't improved with age. He's still as angry as he was as a kid."

"You know, it seems to me that some people are just bitter. It's almost as if whatever happens to them in life, the attitude never changes. This kid has a good job, he's making money, but he has no friends and no companionship of the romantic kind."

Roberta shook her head. "When I was a teenager, I had some problems with my mom. You know, just my hormones asserting themselves or something. But it got nasty for a while. My dad, and he was still my dad in those days, sat me down and talked me through one of my snits.

"He told me that Mom worked hard and expected the same kind of effort from everyone, including him. She didn't have time to deal with the kind of problems I was giving her. He asked me to let it go if she pissed me off and come to him."

"Well, he's a rabbi. It's part of his job." Gary sipped his martini.

Roberta shook her head. "No, it was more than that. He never talked much about his life before he met Mom, but he opened up a bit then. He told me that his mother had been soured by her childhood in the Depression, and that she had never been able to enjoy her life, that her only joy seemed to be in spoiling things for others."

Gary whistled. "Whoa. What was he trying to say, do you think? That your mother was like his?"

"I'm not exactly sure, even now, but it made me think about a lot of things. I got through that rough patch in about a year, my mom started to soften a bit toward me, and he began to get more distant. From everyone, even Robbie, who he doted over."

"I wish I could peer into your father's brain. I'd really like to know what makes him tick."

"How'd you like to take me upstairs and make me tick?" Roberta arched an eyebrow.

Gary grinned and put down his drink. The phone rang, and he groaned.

"Don't answer it."

"I've got to. It might be Stevie."

Gary groaned louder. Roberta picked up the phone.

"Roberta?"

"Hello? Blanche?" She felt a chill. "Is something wrong?"

Blanche asked if she was all right, then filled her in on the car bomb.

"Oh my God! You sure everyone's okay?"

"Well, so far. I'm worried that Lou will experience some kind of post-traumatic thing. Hilda just got shook up, but she went with it and it passed. Lou, you know, he was the rock."

Roberta indicated to Gary to bring her drink over. "What did the cops say?"

"Not much. They took a bunch of information at the scene, but Lou wouldn't cough up any names. He just led them to believe that it could've been anyone he annoyed in the past few years. But the lead detective came back later."

"So?"

Blanche sighed. "The preliminary report on the bomb was that it was crude, but obviously effective. The forensic guys suspect a mercury switch, one that would make the thing go off when it hit a hill. Around here, that could be anywhere. But when the truck made the car lurch, it made contact in the switch and went off."

"So what's happening?"

"Lou is determined to go out to Seagirt tomorrow and start doing some serious investigating. He says he's been too distracted to do a decent job so far."

"Distracted?" Roberta screamed. "Distracted my tush! He's nearly been killed twice. We have no idea what would have happened to us if we hadn't been rescued. I'm ready to call the whole thing off. It's not worth it."

"Well, forget that. It's become a bit of a crusade with him. They'll probably call you tomorrow for more information on the women in the appointment book. Will you be around?"

"Damn right, I will. In fact, I'm coming back up there as soon as I can get things in order down here."

"Lou said you would say that."

"I'll see you soon." They hung up.

"So," said Gary. "I'm guessing our little afternoon delight is postponed?"

"Make me a fresh drink. I'll get that call to Stevie out of the way, and then we can discuss that."

"First," he replied, "tell me about the car bomb."

Chauncey Zerby drove back to his lair in the shadow of Mount Hood. His two young henchmen greeted his return.

"Hey, Chaunce, we got a job?"

Zerby stopped, looked up at the patches of blue among the clouds, and thought for a moment.

"I don't know, yet. Meanwhile, I got some money for groceries. You two go get some grub, and go easy on the beer. I'm gonna go lie down."

Zerby tried to doze off, but his mind reeled, going in unknown directions. He felt things that he never felt before, or at least things he never gave any room to grow. Every time he thought of Bobby Geller, it gave him a chill.

It was hours later that exhaustion forced him into a troubled sleep.

Late that night, the phone rang at the Mendelson house. Gary grumbled, but Roberta wasn't asleep and she grabbed the receiver.

"Hello?"

"I bet that'll stop him."

"Stevie? Where the hell are you? I called your house and got voice mail, I called your office and they said you were taking time off, I called your cell . . ."

"That reporter? The one you were working with? His car got bombed."

"I know. Thank heaven he wasn't in it at the time."

There was a moment's silence. "What?"

"Lou wasn't in the car. The bomb got set off by a passing truck."

Stevie swore. "Are you sure? I heard about the explosion on the news."

"Yes, I'm sure." Her tone hardened. "Steven, do you know something about this?"

Gary was awake by this time and listened to the conversation. Stevie was talking loud enough for him to hear both sides.

Stevie's voice took on a sweet tone. "Now, how would your Uncle Stevie know about this? All I know is what I see on CNN."

"Stevie, one more time. Where are you?"

"You know, home."

"I don't believe you. Are you in Portland?"

"What if I am? And I'm not saying that. So what?"

"Stevie, I need to see you. If you are home, I'll fly up there tomorrow. We need to talk."

"I gotta go." He hung up.

"Gary," Roberta sighed, "I have to get back to Portland. I think Lou, and maybe even my father, is in danger."

"Okay, I'll go with you." She started to object. "Nope, not listening. If you're gonna go up in flames, I'll be there with you."

16. Legwork

"Lou? Are you up yet? You have a visitor."

"Huh?" Lou looked around, bewildered, then recalled that he was in Blanche's bedroom. Blanche insisted that Hilda and he take the bed, while she spent the night on her foldout couch.

"A visitor? What are you talking about?"

"Throw on a robe or something and get out here."

"Hilda? Are you awake?"

"I am now. Someone is here to see you?"

"I guess. You don't have to get up."

"Are you kidding?" she laughed. "This I gotta see. Who even knew we were here?"

When they finally made it out to the living room, they saw Herman Brown drinking a cup of coffee.

"Kid. Good to see you. What's up?"

"This girl makes some good coffee." He turned toward Blanche. "You married?"

"Is this where I giggle and blush?" she asked.

Brown smiled. "Okay, time to get serious. I heard about your, uh, exciting day yesterday. I think we got to cover you twenty-four/seven. People out to kill you, Lou."

Lou sighed. Blanche handed coffee to her friends.

"Yeah, it seems that way. No idea who did it, either."

"Well, I know it ain't that white trash we played with the other day. We'll check this out, see what's shakin'."

"Good coffee. We're off to the coast as soon as we get ourselves together and rent a car. I'll check back with you."

"No need to check back. We all over that. Also, no need to rent a car. Boss left a fund to pay you for the book. I made an executive decision to release some funds for this."

Brown held out a set of keys with a Cadillac logo prominent on them. "This car got that GPS thing, all that smart stuff to tell you where you are, and an emergency system that call for help." He grinned. "Also, my man rigged another button that light up in our office if you need us. One on the dash, one on the remote. Very cool. I got one my own self."

"Kid, I can't . . ."

Brown held up his hand. "Don't even annoy me with this. We got a deal on it, and the thing is yours. Use it in good health."

Lou smiled. "My mother always said that when she gave a gift."

"They all go to the same school. Now, you get

ready and I'll show you the car. Meanwhile, I will talk to this fine woman here."

"Oh, Mr. Brown!" Blanche batted her eyelashes.

Lou stood there with a stunned expression on his face. Hilda grabbed his arm.

"At least they jump up and down on *The Price Is Right*. Say thank you."

"Thanks, Kid."

"The Boss says you're welcome."

A few hours later, Lou drove the big SUV into Hilda's driveway.

"You know," she said, "I could get used to this level of luxury."

"Please. I am so embarrassed. I was thinking of buying one of those hybrids. The Kid didn't say how I was gonna pay for gas for this hog."

"Yeah, well, get over it. We have work to do."

The weather was starting to show the effects of the oncoming summer. The episodes of sunshine lasted longer, and the rainfall was less driving. The air smelled magnificent, clean and fresh.

"Okay," Hilda said after they got organized, "you call Gar on the landline, and I'll make some calls on the cell."

Lou picked up the phone and got a stuttering tone. "You've got messages."

Hilda punched in her codes and listened. "It's Roberta. Here." She thrust the phone at him and he listened to her message, holding the receiver so Hilda could hear.

"Hi. Listen, Gary and I will be flying up there as soon as we can get on a plane. I spoke to Stevie. He may be responsible for the car bomb, and I think he's still in Oregon. Please be careful. He may be after both you and my father. I've called my dad and left a message. Can you go by his house sometime? See you soon." Click.

"Well, isn't that nice? Not only do we have persons unknown after you, we now may have persons known." Hilda made a face.

Lou rubbed his new knee, which was registering changes in the atmospheric pressure.

"I'm gonna call Geller."

The phone rang. "Yeah?"

"Rabbi? It's Lou Tedesco."

"I gotta get caller ID, so I can avoid talking to you."

"Have you listened to your messages?"

"What? You mean that paranoid rant my ungrateful child left for me? Yeah, I heard it. What about it?"

"There may be something to it. My car . . ."

"She mentioned it. Wow, lucky you weren't in it." His voice dripped sarcasm.

"Look, I know there's no love lost here, but I don't want to see you dead."

"Ah, one of an ever-diminishing list. Listen, did you know that my daughter came into my house on false pretenses and stole my personal property? What's that line about sharper than a serpent's tooth? Of course you know about this. I'll bet you have it."

"Have what?" Lou put on his innocent voice.

"Don't BS me, *putz*. I'll thank you to return it."

"I can't return what I don't have."

"Okay, play dumb. It won't help you or Roberta in this vendetta. I'll see you both rue the day you messed with me." He hung up.

"That went well," Lou sighed. "I'll call Gar, now."

"At least your greeting will be better."

Lou dialed. "Connie? Lou. Is Gar there?"

"He is. But it's not like you not to make small talk before business. Something wrong?"

"Why is it that I'm an open book to every woman in the world?"

Connie laughed. "Relax. It's part of your charm. Now, what's up?"

Lou told her about the recent events.

"Lou, have you ever considered a safer line of work, like nitroglycerine driver?"

"Every day. I did get a big new car for my troubles. Not one I would have chosen . . ."

"I'll put Gar on."

"Howdy, Lou. I'm guessing that you have some questions for me."

"Brilliant deduction, Chief Loober. I need to know a few things. Tom Knight told me that they stopped caring about any robbery motive when Gottbaum confessed. I'm not so sure they didn't miss something. For instance, can we find out if Grace Geller's bakery account showed a deposit the day she died?"

"This is a tough one, Lou. I need a court order, and I have no jurisdiction here, nor any probable cause. It would be seen as a classic fishing expedition. My advice is to go to the bakery and ask them to see their records. If you tell them why, they'll probably cooperate."

"Good advice. Next, can you trace someone for me?"

"Google won't do on this one?"

"Actually, I've already tried that. No dice."

"Who are we looking for?"

"A woman named Jodie Coram, former crime reporter. She covered the Geller case for a while, then took off for parts unknown."

"Nothing except her name? No Social Security or anything?"

"Nope. I'll spell the name for you." He did.

"Okay, give me some time on this."

"Thanks, Gar."

Lou hung up and looked over at Hilda, who was deep into a conversation. She threw Lou a look, rolled her eyes, and went back to the phone.

He checked his notes for a phone number for Gottbaum's lawyer. He dialed.

"Weinstein and Gabler."

"May I speak to Mr. Weinstein? This is Lou Tedesco from the *Oregon Weekly*. I'm working on the Geller case."

A moment later, "Dave Weinstein. Is this Tedesco?"

"Yes, sir."

"What's your interest in this matter?"

"I'm just doing a follow-up on the Geller case, you know, a kind of wrap-up," Lou fibbed. "I thought it might be a good idea to speak with your client."

"Mr. Gottbaum is not available for interviews, at his request. I'll be happy to answer what I can."

"Has he ever recanted the jailhouse confession exonerating Rabbi Geller?"

"As a matter of fact, yes. But, let's say his credibility was not at a high level at that particular time."

"So, his position now is that he was hired by the rabbi to kill Grace Geller?"

"Yes."

A lawyer of few words, Lou thought.

"Your client claims that Rabbi Geller stiffed him on the fee. True?"

"Yes. I took this case more or less pro bono."

"Gottbaum had no money to pay you?"

"Damn little. He made a few bucks as a private eye, but his bank account wasn't exactly flush."

"Do you know what his wife and children are doing?"

"Last I heard, they had moved and cut ties with him. He's pretty much alone and friendless."

"Do you know where they moved to?"

"They won't talk to you, more than likely. His wife was fed up with him before the murder occurred."

"Still, do you know where they are?"

"Maybe in Waldorf."

Lou made a note. "Any idea what was causing the problems between them?"

"Besides chronic financial and substance abuse issues? He told me she couldn't trust him anymore. She even suspected him of cheating on her."

"Any truth to that?"

"He denies it. She followed him once and saw him with a woman. He said it was an innocent relationship. She didn't buy it."

Lou wondered about Gottbaum's partner. "Do you think I could talk with Plisskin?"

"Well, you'd have to ask his lawyer, but that really won't do you any good. The guy is at the gibbering and drooling stage, completely gaga. He never was very stable."

"Thank you, counselor." He hung up.

"So," Hilda asked, "what have you got?"

"Gar is working on Jodie Coram, Gottbaum's lawyer says he won't talk to me . . ."

"The lawyer or Gottbaum?"

"Gottbaum. The lawyer told me that Gottbaum's wife suspected he was having an affair, and was ready to split before the murder. You?"

"Well, I called four women on the list. Two hung up on me right away. A third cried for a minute, apologized, and then hung up. But, the fourth . . ." Her eyes lit up. "I have an appointment with Arlene Levenson this afternoon. At the Dunes Café, of all places."

"Ah, the scene of old triumphs."

"And old frustrations. I'll work on the crier if I don't get anything from Arlene. She seemed like she might have some remorse."

"Okay."

Hilda's phone rang. She answered it. "Roberta? Where are you?"

"I'm in Portland. Gary and I just flew in. What's going on?"

Hilda filled her in with the occasional comment from Lou.

"Let me speak with her," he asked. Hilda handed him the phone.

"Hi. Say, what do you know about Gottbaum's wife?"

"Pearl? Not much. A real sad sack. The Yiddish word is 'nebbish.' Practically a foregone conclusion, she being married to a loser like Larry."

"Do you know where she is now?"

"No," Roberta laughed, "but I'll bet my favorite yenta could tell us."

"That would be the temple secretary?"

"None other. If Janie doesn't know, she'll find out."

"Give her a call, if you don't mind. What's next for you?"

"We'll come out there. I guess it's where the action is."

"Be careful." He turned to Hilda. "She and Gary are coming out here."

"Tell them they can stay here," said Hilda, "we have plenty of room."

Lou relayed the message.

"We'll see. I don't want to put anybody out," Roberta said.

"Hey, this place used to be a boardinghouse for loggers. Room we got. See you later."

"I'm off to town," Hilda announced. "I'll drop in at the office before I meet Ms. Levenson."

"Okay, I'm off to the Geller bakery. Meet you back here?"

"How about at the Dunes? I'm sure the girls would love to see you."

"I don't want to cramp your style, or scare her off."

"No worries. She doesn't know you. If you see me in a tête-à-tête with her, just go to the counter and have a cup of coffee."

"Deal."

The bakery was called Angel Food, and Lou could smell the luscious aromas before he got near the door. It smelled like bread and cookies and other good things.

The place was set up with a U-shaped counter. Breads, rolls, and bagels on one side, cookies and pastries in the center, and cakes on the other side. The staff was young, high-school girls. He caught one's eye and walked over.

"Can I help you, sir?"

"Well, I'd love to buy something, but, uh, could I speak to the manager first?"

Her face darkened. "Is there a problem?"

"Oh, no! I'm a reporter, and I'd . . ."

She nodded. "I understand. I'll get Marty."

A minute or so later, she emerged from the office with a large man. His face was scarred, and a patch covered one eye.

"Can I help you?" he asked.

"My name is Lou Tedesco. I'm doing some investigative work on Grace Geller's murder."

He nodded. "Yeah. Come in." He gestured toward the office.

The office was neat and orderly, with two desks supporting late-model desktop computers. File cabinets and shelves of business books filled one wall.

Marty offered Lou a chair, and sat down at a desk.

"I'm with the *Oregon Weekly* . . ."

"I know who you are. You have a good rep in this town. I used to be homeless, and Nutty Bud was my friend. When he got himself together and became Jim Twitchell again, he and Grace helped get a lot of people off the street and into a real life. I was one of the first."

"You've done well by yourself."

Marty shifted in his seat. "I promise you that without Grace Geller I had more than a fifty-fifty chance of winding up back in the old life. She made sure I learned the bakery business, made sure I had a clean place to live . . ." His voice trailed off.

Lou nodded. "I wonder if you can tell me whether Grace Geller took home any bakery money the night she died?"

"Well, she did the books in those days, and I kind of shut down for a while after her killing. She used to take home the weekly proceeds, and sometimes they accumulated for a few weeks before she did. She made the deposits herself."

"Are those old books handy?"

"You bet." He rose and walked over to a file cabinet. He rummaged through a drawer and came up with a computer disk. "Let's take a look."

He inserted the disk into a computer and brought up the spreadsheet.

"Okay, this is the last of her entries. It looks like . . ." He squinted at the screen. "It looks like she had about twelve thousand dollars ready to be deposited that night. It was so miserable out, I'm sure she went right home. Probably planned to deposit it the next day."

"Was the deposit ever made?"

Marty sat back in his chair. "I don't know. Let me pull the bank records."

Back to the file cabinet. He pulled out a manila folder with the month and year of her murder written on it in red.

"Let's look." He leafed through bank statements. "Nope. I don't see it."

"Wouldn't anybody have noticed that?" asked Lou.

"Well, not necessarily. Grace ran this place, and she often used cash proceeds for her own purposes. As long as we could make payroll and pay our suppliers, the profits were all hers. Plus, we were all in a bit of a state after she was killed. Then I took over. Truly, I could have missed a lot back then."

"Did the rabbi have much to do with this place?"

Marty shook his head. "Uh-uh. After Grace died, he basically gave this place to us and became a silent partner. He shares in the profits, but doesn't make any decisions."

"So, twelve thousand dollars is unaccounted for?"

"Bottom line."

"Thanks. That's all I needed to know."

"Uh, Mr. . . ."

"Lou. Call me Lou."

"I don't know how to ask this. Are you thinking that Grace's murder isn't a settled matter?"

"Marty, all I'm doing so far is rechecking the facts of the case. I may decide that everything is as it should be."

"And if not?"

Lou shrugged. "What's the cliche? It remains to be seen."

Marty smiled. "Want some bagels? On the house."

Hilda walked into the Dunes Café. Ronnie was at her post at the counter. Phyllis sat at the counter having coffee.

"Ladies," Hilda greeted them.

"Hey, Hilda," Ronnie waved her over. "Say good-bye to the short-timer." Phyllis bowed.

"Don't tell me you're retiring. I'm shocked."

Phyllis grinned. "Honey, these old bones are tired of chasing up and down this place. I'm gonna spend the rest of my life drinking margaritas and reading romance novels."

Hilda sat on a stool. "I'll bet you'll go nuts after a few weeks. You can't stay away . . ."

"From all this excitement? Watch me."

"Well, good luck. I mean that. I'd love to see you relax, after all these years."

"Yeah. When I do come back in here, I'm gonna sit around and change my order constantly, then leave a lousy tip."

"Horse hockey," said Ronnie, "you'll grab an apron just out of habit."

"How about a cup of coffee?" Hilda asked.

Ronnie grabbed a cup and the fresh pot. "Where's your sweetie?"

"Lou? He'll be along later. I'm supposed to meet someone here. A woman . . ."

The door opened and an attractive, well-dressed woman walked in. She walked up to the counter. She seemed nervous, furtive.

"Is there a Hilda Truax here?"

"*C'est moi*. Ms. Levenson, I presume?"

"Yes."

"Ronnie," Hilda turned toward the counter, "another cup, I think."

"Maybe some tea?" asked the woman.

"Camomile? Green?" asked Ronnie.

"Green. Perfect," she said.

Carrying their cups, the two women went to a back table.

"Ms. Levenson . . ."

"Please call me Arlene."

"Arlene, are you comfortable talking here? Someplace more private, perhaps?"

She shook her head. "No, this is good. Not crowded, and no one knows me here."

"Do you know what I'm going to ask?"

"I have a good idea. First, I want you to know that what I tell you I can still hardly believe myself. It's not, um, I don't . . ."

Hilda reached across the table and gripped her hand. "Arlene, I need to know this because it may have life-and-death consequences. It's not for titillation or gossip. I will make every effort to keep your name out of it, and will kill the story rather than embarrass you. Okay?"

Arlene nodded.

"So, let's cut to the chase. Did you have an affair with Rabbi Geller?"

She colored, and nodded. "Yes, I did. I came to him for counseling after my kid sister was arrested for dealing cocaine. She was, is, a stupid kid. We all smoked a little pot, some of us ate mushrooms, but we generally grew out of it after college. Gaby didn't. She got involved with, what? The wrong crowd? She started to sell to cover her habit." Arlene began to cry.

"Listen, I know this story. Some part of it is my story, too. No judgments, here."

Arlene sniffed, dabbed her eyes with a tissue, and went on.

"So, her crummy boyfriend gets busted and turns her in to reduce his charges. She's in prison for a few more months. First offense, but it was a big quantity. She had to do some time.

"I have to explain all this to my widowed mother, for whom drugs are from another universe. It took a lot out of me. Still does."

"So you went to see Geller?"

"Sure. I figured, he's my rabbi, this is what he does. We have three-four sessions, all is going well, but I'm thinking, this is certainly taking longer than it needs to.

"Then, he asks me to come in at five o'clock, later

than usual. I guessed, you know, he's got a full schedule and has to see me after hours."

"It didn't seem unusual?" Hilda asked.

"Not really. Like I said, full schedule. Well, I get
there and he lets me in because the doors are locked.
He takes me into his office, and tells me a tale about a
girlfriend of his who had the same problem with coke,
and how she ran off with a dealer and left him flat. He
gets real emotional, starts crying . . ."

"He started to cry?"

"Yeah!" Arlene was warming to the topic. "He's all
weepy and the next thing I know, I've got him in my
arms and I'm comforting him!"

"Don't tell me," Hilda sighed. "One thing led to another."

"Bingo." Arlene sat back and sipped her tea.

"How many times?"

"Four in all. I finally got my head on straight and
broke it off."

"What was his reaction?"

She shrugged. "Took it like a man. He called me,
apologized for the affair, said it was his fault, and
would I please not say anything, as his marriage was
shaky as it was. That was okay with me."

"Did the cops ask you about this?"

"Not the cops, the assistant DA, some woman. I
lied, because, you know."

"You weren't worried about lying to the DA?"

"Not really. I knew Rabbi Geller wasn't going to
say anything, and he swore that I was the only woman

he had done this with. I believed him. I mean, he's a rabbi, right?"

"Right. Why are you telling me this now?"

Arlene sighed. "Guilt, I guess, and the uneasy feeling that what happened between us may have had something to do with Gracie's death. It's time."

"Arlene, do you know Carol Greenberg or Rebecca Fenster?" Hilda asked.

"Sure. They're in the congregation. Why?"

"I have good reason to believe that they had affairs with Rabbi Geller as well. There are others. Quite a few, we think."

Arlene went pale. "Oh. My. God."

"Could I get you to talk with them about this?"

She started. "Not a chance! I'm humiliated enough as it is."

"Okay, never mind. It's not important. Thanks so much for talking with me."

Arlene leaped out of her seat and was out the door quickly. Hilda looked surprised.

Ronnie came over. "The drinks are on us. Your friend sure left in a hurry. Something you said?"

"It wasn't me she was running from. Lou should be here soon. I'll come back to the counter."

Stevie Goldstein sat brooding in a cheap motel room in the distant western outskirts of the Portland area, almost halfway to the coast. Brooding was his natural state of being, when he wasn't plain miserable. The TV set was turned to a basketball game, the sound just loud enough to be a murmur. But he wasn't paying attention.

He looked at the array of electronic gear in front of him and wished he had paid better attention in his community-college electronics courses. It was clear to him that his designs were flawed. The diagrams were crude and incomplete, guesswork, and the margins were filled with his drawings of hideous death.

He paced around the cramped, dirty little room and tapped his forehead between sips of a caffeine-spiked soft drink. His mind raced, as much from frantic thought as chemical stimulation.

"Maybe," he said aloud. "The old-fashioned way works best."

He took another long pull of the energy drink, belched, and picked up a blasting cap.

The Geller House, Oregon, 2000

Geller dragged himself up the front steps of his house, worn out after a day of fighting the temple board bureaucracy and his own staff and listening to the problems of his congregants. He wanted a stiff drink and a light supper.

He knew he was in trouble when he walked in the front door and saw Gracie's face. She was on the couch, a glass in front of her, and might have been a bit drunk.

"Where the hell have you been?" she demanded.

Caught between responding with sarcasm, which

would only make things worse, and capitulation—bad enough—he chose to try to avoid trouble.

"At the temple, as you well know. I had the meeting with the board, then . . ."

"Don't lie to me."

"What are you talking about?" He put down his coat and briefcase. "You know very well that this meeting was happening. It's a regular . . ."

"That was hours ago. Where have you been since then?"

"I had a small rebellion with the office staff, and then . . ."

"I repeat: That was hours ago."

"Actually, Gracie, it was an hour and a half ago. Then I had to deal with Larry Gottbaum, some nutcase with a family problem owing to his alcohol and drug habits. He'd been waiting for hours. I couldn't throw the guy out the door, could I?"

"I called your office. You didn't answer."

"We went outside for a smoke."

She snorted. "Boy, you've got an answer for everything."

He sat heavily on a facing chair. "Did it ever occur to you that it might be because there really is a logical answer for everything? What's this all about, anyway?"

"I ran into Sookie Goldsmith in the market. She couldn't even look me in the eye. I think you're having an affair with her."

Now Geller was truly shocked. "I've been in love with three women in my whole life, including you, and

I've never betrayed any of you. One actually carried on a flagrant affair with a drug dealer before leaving me. I was the last to know, because I trusted her.

"And, besides, what do you base this on? A nonlook on Sookie's face?"

"Don't get smart with me." Grace wagged her finger, a gesture Geller despised. "I see the way she looks at you. And she's not the only one. Don't tell me you don't see that."

"Grace," he sighed, "I'm a rabbi. Some women develop crushes on their doctors or their psychologists, or even their rabbis. Sookie is a shy and mousy . . ."

"Just the way you like 'em."

"Oh? Does that describe you in any way? I married you, didn't I?"

Grace rose up from the couch. "And I bet you regret it every day. I've always been too much for you . . ."

"Except in the sack, Grace. Maybe if you took care of business there . . ." He let his voice trail off.

"Drop dead!" She stormed off toward the bedroom.

Geller sighed. No longer interested in anything like food, he went right for the bottle of vodka in the freezer. He poured a generous drink and took a big sip.

So, he thought, she believes I'm unfaithful. And with Sookie? The poor girl would probably faint at the sight of a naked man. She can't look Grace in the eye because she's frightened of her. Who isn't? Even the people she helps are scared of her.

Geller took another pull on the iced vodka and thought some more.

She's away from home more than I am, especially

since the kids are grown. Maybe she's the one whose needs are being looked after elsewhere. Maybe what's good for the goose is good for the gander.

Maybe . . .

17. Come Together

"Lou? It's Lainie Reiter."

Lou was sitting in Hilda's office.

"Must be ESP," he replied, "I was just going to call you. Do you have anything on Jodie Coram"

"Yeah," she coughed.

"You have a cold or something?"

"No, just smoker's cough. One of these days I'm going to quit. And stop drinking so much. Oh yeah, and lose twenty pounds. But enough about me. This Coram thing is starting to interest me. Curiouser and curiouser."

"Okay, I'll tell you what," Lou decided to strike a bargain, "if this lead pans out, I get to break the story, but you get next exclusive."

"Lou, as a deal that sucks. I could call her now and pump her, give her the old rah-rah about loyalty to her old newspaper, and likely get the whole story. I'm very persuasive. I know it has something to do with the Geller case, because that's why you called me.

"Now, you can tell me what this is all about, get credit in my story, and get an 'atta boy' from your editor. Then you can do your own story."

"Jeez, you drive a hard bargain. Give me one more little goodie. Hold your story until the *Weekly* comes out, and we publish on the same day."

Silence on the other end of the phone, then a small cough. "Deal. Now, what's this all about?"

"Truthfully, I'm not sure, but here's what I suspect. Geller may have had an affair with her. He was quite a lothario, from what I can infer. I know of at least one woman he seduced, but her name has to be kept out of this. We're working on her to speak with others who might have done the same. You know, sisters in, uh . . ."

"Horizontal togetherness. Whatever. Okay, I have a phone number that at least used to be good. The HR guy really felt sorry for her, but he's a bleeding heart anyway. Works for us in this case."

"Why did he give it up?"

She laughed. "I'm such a stinker. I told him that I read her stuff on the Geller murder and was so moved I wanted to talk with her. Have you read it?"

"Never got a chance to hit the microfilm. I was, uh, overtaken by events."

"Yeah, I heard. Wow, no one ever cared enough about me to blow me up. Anyway, it was real sob-sister stuff. Somewhere along the line, she lost her, what, reportorial distance from the case? Got mawkish, yucky. Maybe now I know why."

"Tell me about the status of the case while she was covering it." Lou grabbed a pen and his notebook.

"She covered it before it went to trial. As you may know, the DA was having trouble putting together a case. Then out of the blue, Gottbaum confesses to killing the vic. He said he couldn't look his wife and kids in the face, couldn't handle the guilt, yada, yada, yada. So he implicates Geller, and the indictment comes down like gentle rain. After the trial starts, Gottbaum drops his little bombshell, and there's a mistrial. But you know that."

"What's the time frame on this?" Lou asked.

"Uh, let me see." Lou hears notebook pages rustling. "Here it is."

Lou noted the dates. "Hold on a second." He opened Geller's appointment book and cross-checked the dates. "These dates coincide with the beginning of the affair. Very interesting."

"What are you looking at?" Lainie asked, with a suspicious edge.

"Oh, just my time line that I created out of pure speculation." Lou felt bad about lying, but not for long.

"So what's next?"

"Should I call the number you got, or do you want to do it?"

"Let me think for a minute," she said. "It might actually be better if you do it. She obviously wanted some distance from her old newspaper. Then, after you soften her up, maybe we can do a conference call."

"Yeah, okay. What's the number?"

Lainie read it off.

"This is an Oregon area code."

"Yeah, but it might be a cell. No telling where she is."

"Thanks. I'll get back to you."

Lou hung up. He picked up the phone to call the number she gave him, and heard the stuttering tone. He punched in the code for voice mail. Gar Loober had left a message, and Lou dialed the police station.

"Gar! What's up?"

"I think I found your girl. She's working in a hospice in Ashland. I found her through payroll records, and this whole thing is dancing on legal thin ice."

"You love it, don't you?"

"Officially? It's appalling and unethical. But, yeah. It's fun. I have an office number. Will that do?"

"It will do nicely, my friend. I can't thank you enough."

"I wish I could get in on the collar, but it's out of my jurisdiction."

Just then, Hilda walked in. Lou waved her over.

"Gar, Hilda needs me. Thanks again." He hung up.

"Are we making any progress?" she asked.

"Are you kidding? This whole thing is starting to jell. Maybe. I got two phone numbers for Jodie Coram. One of 'em must be good."

"Okay, so we have one woman who had a thing

with Geller, and now maybe two. What does this do for us?"

Lou thought for a second. "Good question. If we know that he was fooling around, he's a liar, on the record. But so what? Even if we come up with a few more women, that just makes him a disgraceful person and a morally deficient rabbi. Does it make him a killer?"

"Doesn't it go toward motive?"

"Well, his official position is that he could have divorced his wife, and outside of a little gossip, no problem."

Hilda sat down. "Really? No problem? If he has an affair with a woman and gets a divorce, then marries the other woman, well, the heart has a mind of its own, as the country song goes. Her daddy's money goes away, but he'll likely survive in his job.

"But, if his wife finds out he's doing the nasty with a small harem, big scandal, who knows what?"

Lou nodded. "Yes, I see that. But, we still have only one, and she feels as responsible as Geller."

Hilda made a sour face. "Don't you hate it when women participate in their own humiliation?"

"Oh, yes. You bet." Lou nodded vigorously.

Stevie sat in his car across the coast road from Hilda's house. He peered at the house with binoculars from time to time. He noted the new SUV with dealer's plates, which inspired a self-satisfied giggle, and another more modest car in the driveway, and wrote down the license numbers.

Then he took a bite of his cold cheeseburger. He had to go to the bathroom from his intake of caffeinated drinks, but he felt that this phase of his plan was complete. He knew where they lived, he knew what their cars looked like, and time was on his side.

He liked his revenge served cold.

"Lou? It's Roberta."

"Hi. Where are you?"

"In downtown Seagirt. I'm not sure where Hilda lives."

"Do you know where the *Oregon Weekly* office is?"

"Sure. I went on a class trip there when it was still the *North Coast Clarion*. Cool place. I met her father."

"Well, just drive over there. She's taking care of some newspaper business, but she'll be glad to see you, and she can fill you in on the latest. I'm expecting a call back from Tom Knight."

"Okay, I'll get off the phone."

"Wait. Before you hang up, did you ever speak to the temple secretary?"

"Yup. Janie says that Pearl and the kids moved up to Waldorf, and that she was filing for divorce."

"Any idea what she's living on? Gottbaum's lawyer told me he worked the case nearly pro bono."

"Janie didn't say anything about that. Wait. She did mention that Pearl left here driving a new car. Should I call her back?"

"May not be necessary."

"Okay. See you later."

Lou decided to give Knight what he knew about the

missing $12,000. It never got deposited in the bakery's account, and he wondered where it went. Even in these inflated times, it wasn't chump change.

The phone rang. It was Knight.

"So, Lou, what can I do for you, now?"

"Tom, maybe we can help each other. Can you pull financial records for Geller?"

"We may have some already, but they'd date to the pretrial investigation. Why?"

"The night Grace Geller was killed, she came home with twelve thousand dollars in cash. Did Geller ever report it stolen?"

"No. Just the wallet, which we never found."

"The bakery told me that that money was never deposited in the bakery account. Grace often used cash profits for her good works, but I'm guessing that you won't find it at the homeless shelter either. Or, for that matter, in Geller's personal account."

"Lou, what are you suggesting?"

"Just speculating at this point. But Gottbaum alleged that Geller stiffed him, the lawyer worked virtually for nothing, and when Gottbaum's wife left him, she was driving a new car."

"Are you saying that Gottbaum lied about the payoff? That in fact Geller gave the money to the wife?"

"Tom, what I'm saying is that it looks like it should be investigated. Geller receives twenty-five percent of the bakery's profits, and can collect the money in cash if he wants. Someone needs to compare the bakery's books with Geller's bank records to see if any of that money is deposited, and whether some part of it is regularly missing. Then, you know, check on Pearl Gottbaum."

"I'll get a court order. I know a judge who'll buy this. Hell, I'm buying it. Anything else?"

"Nothing I'm prepared to go out on a limb with."

"Thanks for this. Keep in touch." He hung up.

Lou dialed the number Lainie gave him for Jodie Coram. It was disconnected. Then he called the hospice in Ashland.

"Hello, is there a Jodie Coram working there?"

"I'm sorry, who wants to know?"

Lou thought a second. "I'm calling from Portland. I used to be her landlord, and she has a refund coming from her security deposit."

"Well, we have a Jodie Carson here. Could that be her?"

"Gee, I hope so. We've had a heck of a time finding her."

"I'll put her on. One moment, please."

"Hello, Jodie here."

"Jodie, my name is Lou Tedesco . . ."

"The reporter? How the hell did you find me? Oh, jeez . . ."

"Please, I need to talk with you. It may be a matter of life and death."

"You don't know the half of it. Oh, hell. Look. I can't talk here. Call me at home." She gave a number.

"Okay, thanks. I'll talk to you later."

Just to make sure, Lou dialed the number.

"Mabel's Mansion, rooms to let." It was a boardinghouse.

"Is there a Jodie Carson there?"

"Why, yes, but she's at work. May I take a message?"

"Oh, just tell her that Lou called. I'll try again later."

He rang off and dialed Hilda.

"Hilda, I have to go to Ashland."

"Hey, the Shakespeare festival doesn't start . . ."

"No, no. I found Jodie Coram, and I'm afraid she's gonna rabbit on me."

"You've been watching too many cop shows. You're starting to talk like Detective Fontana. But yeah, do it. Stay in that cute downtown hotel near the theater, so I'll know where to find you."

"Done. Is Roberta there?"

"Yup. We'll go out to dinner here in town. Sorry you'll miss meeting Gary."

"It'll have to be tomorrow. It's gonna take me at least six hours to get there. I'm outta here."

"Watch your step, pal."

"And you say I sound like a TV detective? Later."

In twenty minutes, Lou packed a bag and took off for Ashland.

18. Road Trip

It was nearly seven o'clock when Lou drove into the southern Oregon city. He drove directly to Mabel's Mansion from the gas station where he got directions.

It was a big, old Victorian pile, creatively painted in several colors. Like Hilda's house, it was likely once housing for loggers.

He unfolded himself from the car, wondering if he had started to take root in the seat. As he walked up to the house, a young woman flew out the door lugging suitcases and boxes. She was tall and attractive, but harried-looking and seemed to be behind in her sleep. There were dark circles under her eyes.

"Jodie Coram, I presume."

She swore. "Not fast enough, I guess." Sighing, she dropped her burden.

"If you want to go back and reregister, I'll help you with your stuff."

She threw him a frustrated look. "Don't rub it in."

"No, I'm serious. You're a reporter, you know what my job is. I'm not trying to hurt you."

"I don't know. Maybe I've had enough of this place anyway." She sounded resigned.

"I'm starving. Let me buy you dinner, and you can do some soul-searching tomorrow. What's one more night? Besides, if I had this much trouble finding you, I don't think you're in any immediate danger."

She considered the offer. "Deal. Here, you can carry this suitcase."

A half hour later, they were seated in a little café with an all-organic menu, down to the coffee and beer. Lou drank the coffee, Jodie the beer. They were waiting for veggie sandwiches on seven-grain bread, with a side of onion rings.

"Jodie, what are you running from? Why are you so scared?"

"Look, since I was a little girl, all I wanted was to be a newspaper reporter. When I was eight, I started a newspaper on my block, typed and photocopied at the local office supply store. It went great until I reported that one of my neighbors was receiving company while her husband was at work.

"My mom decided it was time for me to cease publication at that point. I didn't understand what I had done, not until years later. I guess that I'm not any smarter, even all these years later. Please believe that I didn't think about any of this while it was going on. Not in any intelligent, critical way. In some ways, I'm still eight years old."

"Did you have an affair with Geller?"

She nodded.

"Well, you know, he's an opportunistic seducer, a predator. You're not the only one he victimized."

She looked up at him. "So you don't know?"

"Don't know what?"

"You don't know the whole story. If it were just that Bobby . . ."

"Bobby? You called him 'Bobby'?"

"He insisted. Apparently, it's the name he likes best."

"Wow, he doesn't strike me as the Bobby type."

"Yeah, not at first. But, he can be so charming and boyish . . . It just seems right after a while."

Lou took out his notebook, and Jodie flushed.

"Time to get down to business, huh?" she asked. Lou nodded. "Okay, then.

"At first it was purely professional, adversarial, even. Then, the give-and-take became banter. Soon, he was pouring us drinks from a bottle in his desk. Not too long after, he was all over me like a wet sheet. And . . . well, I was amused and flattered, and a bit lonely."

"I'm guessing," Lou said, "that his, uh, attention, softened you up so that he began to ask you for favors?"

"Is my life that much of a cliche? Yes, you're right. At first, even though that little voice in my head was like, 'No no no,' I wasn't too worried. He'd ask me to hold off writing about certain things, nothing I considered any great compromise with my journalistic integrity."

Lou looked her in the eye. "Then things got gradually more serious?"

"Gradually, hell! He hit me with a sledgehammer."

The freckled college-kid waitress walked over with three plates and a bottle of organic ketchup. She made small talk with them and left.

"Eat something," Lou said. "I know I'm starving. I was in Seagirt this morning."

They ate and talked about how the food was good, if not quite what they expected. After the last onion ring was dragged through the last glob of ketchup, Lou went back to the main event.

"Tell me about the sledgehammer."

"He had already been indicted, after Gottbaum named him as the one who hired him to kill Mrs. Geller. The trial was scheduled to begin. I had already been removed from the story for getting involved. Lainie Reiter took it over. Have you talked to her?"

"Several times."

"Yeah," Jodie smiled, "she's a piece of work. I wish I was more like her. Anyway, Bobby calls me and asks for a meeting. By this time, I'm ashamed and a bit depressed but, I don't know, I kinda liked his attention."

"Weren't you concerned that he was a dangerous man?"

"You would think so, wouldn't you? The innocent eight-year-old is never far from me. He swore to me that Gottbaum was a liar, and that he was trying to clear his name, but that he was afraid that the outcome was inevitable. And, now that his wife was gone, he had no one to talk to, to care about. God, I can't believe I fell for this." She began to cry.

Lou waited for a few minutes while she gathered herself together.

"I'm sorry." She sniffled.

"No apology necessary. Remember, you're the victim, here."

"Oh yeah? See how you feel after I tell you this. The sledgehammer? He wanted me to develop a relationship with Gottbaum, see him in jail, and talk with him. I was supposed to be doing one of those backgrounder pieces on the major figures in the trial. All this was Bobby's idea."

"Clever fellow."

"Well, yeah! So, I do this, but I'm not sure what he has in mind. I figured that he was trying to get Gottbaum to trust me so that I could extract some gem of information that would exonerate him.

"After a few sessions, poor, dumb, trusting Larry Gottbaum is pouring out his black little heart to me. I'm starting to get nervous and uncomfortable. So, I go to Bobby and I say, 'Enough. What do you want from me?'

"He says, 'I want you to convince Gottbaum to admit that I had nothing to do with this, that it was all his idea.'

"So I'm, like, amazed. But he says, 'Convince him to say that he did it because we used to be real pals, and I'd been giving him the cold shoulder, so he implicated me to get even.'

" 'Look,' I said, 'this is what's known as suborning perjury. We could go away for a few years behind this.' He says, 'Don't worry. I've got this all figured out.' "

Lou looked up from his notes. "Are you telling me that Gottbaum's dramatic jailhouse announcement was orchestrated by Geller?"

Jodie nodded. "Like he was Edgar Bergen. You know who that is?"

Lou laughed. "Yeah. I'm surprised that you do."

"I saw him and Charlie McCarthy in old movies. In some way, we were all dummies for Bobby Geller, and he worked us like Bergen. Had his hand up my clothes more than once, too."

Lou shook his head. "Something tells me this confession is good for you. Your native cynicism is returning. By the way, what the hell was Gottbaum supposed to get out of this?"

"Oh, jeez. I knew you were going to ask that. Here's where I get depressed again."

"No sense stopping now."

She shrugged. "I told him that Geller would take care of his family if he did that."

Lou started to speak.

"No, wait, it gets worse. I was, uh, I led Gottbaum to believe that I was romantically interested in him. He thought that I would be there for him when he got out.

"You can just kill me now." Jodie hung her head.

"Jodie, did Geller tell you to say that he would take care of Gottbaum's family?"

"Oh, you bet."

"Well, that much seems to be true."

"You must think I'm awful."

"I think you are another of Geller's victims. And I think we can do something about it. I want you to drive up to Waldorf. Do you have a car?"

"Yeah, and it runs good. Why Waldorf?"

"Because I want you to go to Tom Knight and tell him what you told me."

Her eyebrows shot up. "What? Are you nuts? I was thinking of Costa Rica."

"You have to trust me on this. He'll be so glad to have this information that he'll be inclined to cut you a deal. You may not have to serve any time. You'll be a hero, even."

Her eyes slitted. "You're full of crap. This is a trick."

"Do yo have a cell phone?"

She nodded.

"May I?" He took her phone and dialed Knight's home number.

"Tom? Lou. I'm in Ashland."

"It better be good. You're interrupting my bridge night."

"How would you like to trump Geller's ace? I have someone here I want you to speak with. And I want you to cut her a deal."

"Who is she?"

"Never mind that now. Listen to what she says, make her an offer, or she's on a plane to South Africa tomorrow." He winked at Jodie, who grinned.

"This better be good. Put her on."

He handed the phone to her, and she repeated the story, minus emotional pauses and comic references to dead ventriloquists. She listened for a while, then handed the phone back.

"So, what's the story?"

"Lou, not only won't she do any time, I'll get her a medal. Thanks. I'm going to swear out an arrest warrant for the rabbi."

"See you soon." He hung up.

"So? Happy?"

Her eyes glistened. "Yeah, I'm happy. I can't thank you enough. I thought this was gonna mess up the rest of my life." She sighed. "I'll probably never work as a reporter again, but . . ."

"I'll tell you what. When all this is over, call Blanche Perry at the *Weekly*. She may give you a try. Go back and get some sleep, and take off for Waldorf in the morning. I'll get back to Seagirt and watch this go down."

A few miles outside of Seagirt, as the mists rose up from the Pacific, Rabbi Geller heard a knock on his door. He put down his drink, lurched up off the couch, and shambled over to open it.

"Stevie! What the hell . . ."

Stevie raised his arm. He was holding a .25 caliber pistol, and pointing it at the rabbi's face. It looked like a cannon to Geller.

"Put some shoes on, Bobby. We're going for a little ride."

The next morning, Lou Tedesco was so happy that he didn't even mind the cold snap. The Rogue River valley was good for sudden and capricious changes in weather. He had breakfast in the hotel restaurant, quite respectable, and went to settle his bill.

"There was a call for you while you were at breakfast, sir." The fresh-faced kid at the desk could have been the sister of last night's waitress. Plenty of young people in a college town/ski resort.

"Thanks." It was from Hilda, and marked Urgent! "Is there a pay phone?"

The clerk pointed across the lobby.

Lou punched in his credit card number, and waited for the ring. "Hilda?"

"Lou! All hell is breaking loose, and Connie tells me you might be responsible."

"Man, word sure gets around. Did you hear about Jodie Coram?"

"Yowza, but I'll bet you don't know what happened this morning."

"What?"

"The state boys came down to serve an arrest warrant on one Rabbi Robert Geller, but he wasn't home. His car was there, his wallet was on the kitchen table . . . he, well you're guess is as good as anyone's."

"Damn! Think he flew the coop?"

"How would he have known about Jodie? You don't think she called him?"

"Not a chance. She wouldn't cross the street to spit on him if he was on fire. What a puzzlement."

"One more thing. Roberta was looking through the

appointment book and found a notation to call a Marv Kronstein out in Malheur County."

"Who's he?"

"Seems that he was Geller's reason for becoming a rabbi. He's one himself, and he met Geller back in the day. Knew him when, and all that. Roberta thinks he may be dying."

"So?"

"Well, you are halfway to Malheur County. Maybe Geller copped a run-out to see his old friend."

"Hilda, that's another seven-eight hours of driving. It'll take me two days to get back to Seagirt."

"Isn't it fortunate that you have such a nice, new car?"

"Is this really necessary? Won't a call do?"

"What would you tell me?"

He sighed. "Okay, what's the address?"

"Somewhere outside of Frenchglen."

"Outside of nowhere, you mean. Let me get a pencil. And a phone number."

Lou drove his car carefully on the dirt road and turned onto the gravel drive, which was in pretty good shape. The large ranch house and outbuildings glowed in the bright sunlight.

Once a working ranch, then several iterations of hippie commune, the Farm was now a haven for the indigent and infirm, funded by an endowment and the contributions of interested people. Much of the help was volunteer, and there was a small paid staff. Room and board was free, or whatever one could pay.

This was where Rabbi Marvin Kronstein was living out his days.

Lou walked to the reception area and asked to see Kronstein.

"Is he expecting you?" a fresh-faced young woman asked him. Her name tag read "Skye."

"Yes. I called him to make sure he was up to this."

"Well, okay then. Follow me."

She led Lou to a long, low building just out the back of the main house. The white paint seemed freshly applied.

"He's in this room, number twenty-three," Skye indicated the door. "Please check out with us after your visit."

"Sure. Thanks." Lou knocked on the door.

"Yeah? Who's there?" a voice from within wheezed.

"It's Lou Tedesco, Rabbi."

"Come on in."

Lou opened the door on a clean, comfortable, but spare room. There was a kitchen sink and a small refrigerator. A bathroom was visible toward the back of the room. Also, a bed, a night stand, a small table with four chairs, a bookcase with a radio on the top shelf, and a lounger-type chair occupied by a wraith-thin man with long iron-gray hair and beard. He was wearing sweats and a robe, slippers on his feet, an afghan over his legs. It was not cold in the room.

On the floor next to the chair was an oxygen tank, feeding a tube under the man's nose. Rabbi Marvin Kronstein waved Lou over to one of the chairs.

"Sit down," he said, a hollow liquid sound in his voice. "It's good to have the company. Most of us around here are tired of listening to one another."

He took several deep breaths, as though speaking the sentence had winded him. Every intake of air wheezed and gurgled.

"Rabbi," Lou opened, "do you remember why I'm here?"

"Bobby Geller, right? Can I call you Lou? Call me Marv. My brain still works. It's my lungs that are the problem."

"No offense meant." Lou smiled. "How long have you known Geller?"

"Since 1968, met him right here. It used to be called Jollity Farm. Sort of a refuge for hippie weirdos. We spent a couple weeks here, then he rambled over to Eugene where I had my storefront synagogue."

"Jollity Farm? Like the Bonzo Dog Band song?"

Kronstein's face lit up. "Whoa, I'm impressed. Not too many people know that."

Lou shrugged. "A testament to my wasted youth. I spent a lot of time in my room playing air guitar to rock 'n' roll. I liked the pop music, but my passion was seeking out weird stuff. The Bonzos qualified."

"Did they ever!" Kronstein laughed, starting a coughing fit. Lou started toward him, but the rabbi waved him off. Lou thought that Lainie Reiter might benefit from seeing this.

When the coughing waned, he said, "Damn cigarette habit. Also, lots of weed and hash, and, alas, freebase for a while. Totally screwed me up. Despite how

I look, I'm not that old. Not the years, but the mileage."

"I understand. I once had a drinking problem. Haven't touched it in, wow, twenty years or more."

"Good for you. AA?"

Lou shook his head. "No. Uh-uh. I couldn't deal with the higher power thing. Mostly just toughing it out with a lot of help from my friends."

"Not religious?"

"Not much. My parents didn't seem to have any religion at all. No Christmas or Easter, no Jewish holidays . . . I don't know what we were. It's not that I'm an atheist . . ."

"You have an interesting name, Tedesco."

"It's Italian." Lou shrugged.

"Yeah, but it means 'German' in Italian. More than a few Jews escaped oppression by the Lutherans and Catholics in Germany and wound up in Italy. You could be descended from those refugees."

He stopped to take some breaths.

"I've never thought much about it. My parents told me nothing."

"Pretty common among hidden Jews. Let me ask, did your mother light candles on Friday night?"

Lou's head swam. "Yes! How did you know?"

Kronstein smiled. "It's rare that nothing survived from the old life. Candle lighting is very common among conversos and hidden Jews. Conversos were outwardly converted, but kept Sabbath and other rituals.

"But you came here to talk about Bobby, right?"

Lou was still mulling the candle ritual. "I'm going to have to think about this." Lou's eyes glazed over.

"Are your parents still alive?"

"Huh? No, but I have an aunt, my mother's youngest sister. I'm gonna call her . . ."

"Bobby Geller? Great kid. Kind, sensitive, funny. Had that haunted poetic look, real attractive to certain kinds of women. He really was haunted, though."

"How so?"

Kronstein told Lou about Geller's family life, Lindy Peress, and the trip south, stopping from time to time to catch his breath.

"This was all before you met him?"

The rabbi nodded. "When he showed up in Eugene he took up with a girl named Emily. May I say that these two were perfect together? Two sweet, loving kids who found each other. Her life had been no picnic, either. I began to think that maybe there was some justice in this world."

"But Geller married Grace Goldstein. What happened?"

A tear rolled from Kronstein's eye. He dabbed at it with the sleeve of his robe, sniffed, and went on.

"Sorry. They moved to Vancouver, BC, so Bobby could attend rabbinical school. Things were working very well, until . . ." He took a deep breath, and continued.

"Until Emily discovered cocaine. I never saw such a complete personality change in such a short time."

"Cocaine? When was this?"

"Oh, 1971, or so. Coke had slowly been making

inroads into the hippie pharmacopeia for years. Nothing like the 1980s epidemic, but it was there. Bobby didn't like it, mostly because they couldn't afford it. Emily liked it a lot, and began sleeping with the dealer to defray costs. Before long, she and the dealer were gone, allegedly to Hawaii. I don't know for sure.

"That was the worst blow Bobby ever suffered, worse than Lindy's death, because he loved her so, and it was so easy for her to throw it all away."

Lou had been listening, rapt. "So this was the thing that made Geller what he is today?"

Kronstein shook his head. "Not right away. I flew up to Vancouver from Eugene, and Bobby had many friends to comfort him. Several girls were quite willing to step into Emily's shoes. He was cute and well-liked, and considered a catch.

"But he threw himself into his studies, accepted invitations from his friends for movies and concerts. Oh, he had a girlfriend or two. But he wasn't the same. And he was like that guy in the comic strips with the rain cloud over his head all the time. He seemed to recover, eventually, but . . . the old Bobby was gone."

The rabbi started to cough again.

"Can I get you something?" Lou asked.

"Yeah, there's some sodas in the fridge. Get yourself one if you want."

After he drank a bit, Kronstein asked, "What was Grace like?"

"I never met her. My impression was one of a

strong-headed, very together woman. Independent, competent, tough, demanding, maybe not very demonstrative in her affection. Their marriage was not a love match, I'm told."

"Mildred."

"Excuse me?"

"Bobby's mother. Bitter, cold, self-centered. A widow who blamed her dead husband for their dire circumstances, when she wasn't blaming life itself. Never gave Bobby much emotional support. He had to arrange his own bar mitzvah. She didn't even attend."

"Rabbi, are you saying that Geller was symbolically killing his mother, or that it was justified by his unhappy childhood?"

"No, Lou. Murder is never justified, especially as callous a one as this. But sometimes it can be explained."

"Rabbi, I have to ask you this. Have you heard from Geller recently? Do you know where he is?"

Kronstein shook his head. "No to both. We've kept in touch, but only once in a while. Truthfully, I'd love to see him get help. Somewhere inside of that man is the old Bobby."

Lou nodded. "Thanks, Rabbi. Can I do anything for you before I go?"

"Not unless you've got a pack of Camels in your pocket."

Lou gawked.

"Easy, boy. Just kidding. Even I'm not that crazy."

"Thanks. I think I may keep in touch."

"Yeah, do that. Let me know if you're a member of the tribe."

When Lou went back to the desk, Skye asked, "How'd he seem?"

"Well, not bad, considering the circumstances."

"Did he ask you for cigarettes?"

"Yeah, a real joker."

"Seriously, does he need anything?"

Lou thought for a second. "Maybe some company from time to time."

Skye smiled. "That sounds like Marv. We try to keep him amused. He may not live out the month. His lungs are, like, gone."

"Damn shame. He's quite a guy. Oh, if I may, do you know his friend, Rabbi Geller?"

"Yes, sir, but only by phone. He's called here several times, but never visited, as far as I know. Why?"

"He's missing. This is as good a place as any for him to come."

Skye looked concerned. "Is he in some kind of trouble?"

"He may be in danger. Will you call me if you hear from him?"

"Gosh, I don't know if this is ethical . . ."

"I understand. I'll leave a card, and you can decide what to do if and when it becomes necessary."

"Okay. I guess that's okay." The concerned look went away, and she smiled. "Come again."

"I may do that."

Lou went out to his big, new car. Okay, he thought,

do I do this in one trip, or do I stop for an overnight? After a moment, he decided to do the whole trip and stop if he was getting tired.

Lou wished he had a Bonzo Dog Band CD for the ride home.

19. All Together Now

After twelve hours driving, with stops only for food, gas, and visits to the bathroom, Lou pulled up to Hilda's house in Seagirt. It was three in the morning. He was ready for a shower and a night's sleep.

I wonder if Jodie made it to Waldorf, he thought, or bailed out from panic. He shrugged and decided it could keep until he woke up. He opened the car door, and heard the night sounds of the Oregon coast. Frogs, gulls, the sound of the surf bashing itself against the rocky shore.

Then he noticed that there were lights on in Hilda's house. She was not prone to late hours, so he thought something might be wrong. There were two strange cars in the drive. One, a white Ford, was likely a rental. Roberta and Gary. The other was a beat-up Volvo with California plates. No idea who that might be.

He thought of driving right to the police station,

then decided he was being silly. Hilda probably just got into a social mood with Roberta, who also liked her little drinky.

He pressed the remote and locked the car. When the car chirped, the lights went out in the house. Now, he was concerned. He hit the red panic button on the remote. Herman Brown was almost a hundred miles away in Portland, but it made him feel better to do it.

Girding himself, he went up to the door and let himself in.

In the faint light coming in through the windows from the distant streetlight, he began to discern people sitting in the parlor.

"Why doesn't somebody turn on a light?" he asked "What is this, a surprise party?"

A light went on, blinding him, and he felt something against his head. "Surprise, asshole."

His eyes adjusted. Seated in the parlor were Hilda, Roberta and a man he took to be Gary, and Geller. All had strain and fear in their faces.

"And who might you be?" Lou asked the voice behind what he assumed was a gun. In answer, he was pushed away. He turned to see a short, slender young man with dark, beetling eyebrows and a sallow, unshaven face.

"'And who might you be?'" Stevie mocked him. "Mr. Big-shot Reporter. So, did you find what you wanted to get Bobby off the hook? Did he pay you enough to do it, or are you gonna hit him up for some more?"

"Let me guess. Stevie? Are you aware that the cops

have a warrant out for Geller's arrest? You probably snatched him before they got to his house."

"Save your breath, Lou. We've been trying to tell him that for hours," Hilda said.

Stevie swung the gun around toward her. "Shut up, bitch! I'm tired of lies."

Lou noticed that Stevie had several sticks of dynamite strapped to his waist, with wires leading into his pants pocket. Now he was getting worried.

"Stevie," Lou said in a soothing tone, "all you need to do is call the cops and ask."

"What do you think I am, an idiot? I call the cops and you all start screaming."

"Use the phone in the hallway," Hilda said. "It's private."

"You do think I'm an idiot! I go to the hallway and you all run out the door."

"Steven, not only are you an idiot," the rabbi sneered, "you're a goddamn nutcase. You always were. It's over. I'm going to jail for the rest of my life. Why don't you let these people go?"

"Shut up, Rabbi!" Stevie shrieked. He was red-faced, coming unglued. "You killed Gracie, the only one who ever loved me. I thought Roberta loved me, but she sold me out, just like everyone else. She wanted Mr. Big-shot to get you off. If that goddamn bomb had done its job, we wouldn't even be here. I could have come after you any time."

Geller stood up. "What do you know about betrayal, you little *putz*? I've been betrayed my whole life by everyone I ever loved. The most painful was my own daughter. She didn't go to Tedesco to get me off. She wants me in jail, or with a lethal injection in my arm. If you weren't such a stupid psycho, you could see that."

Geller looked at his daughter. "You never knew half the stuff that went on between me and your mother. If you did, you might not be so quick to condemn me.

"How do you know she wasn't carrying on the same way? Saint Gracie, ha!"

Roberta hung her head and started crying. Stevie sneered and reached into his pocket. He pulled out a box, wired to the dynamite with a button at the top, and thumbed the button.

Roberta gasped. "Steven, don't! I didn't expect my father to get off. I always believed he was responsible. I couldn't go on living not knowing the real truth. That's why I came to Lou."

"It's true," Lou said. "Roberta told me to let the evidence speak for itself. I've found someone to testify against him. Geller made her convince Gottbaum to lie about hiring him to kill your sister. She's in Waldorf right now talking to the DA."

"Shut up! She lies and you swear to it." Stevie wiped his nose with his gun hand. Lou started to evaluate the possibility of catching him off guard.

"You found Jodie?" Geller asked. Lou nodded. "You're better at your job than I thought." He turned to Stevie. "Steven, it's all over for me. I'm toast. Let these people go."

"The only thing keeping him from the cops is you," Roberta said. "You have to think about this. If you let us go, you can get help. Stevie, honey, you need help. You know that."

"Don't tell me what to do. My mother always did, everybody did. Only Gracie let me alone. She loved me no matter what." He started crying. "I'm so sick and tired of this life. Nobody's innocent. I'm gonna take us all out of it. Whaddaya say, Rabbi? Put in a good word for us?"

"My influence may not be what it used to be," Geller said. He sounded weary and resigned. "You may want to consider that you're no better than a suicide bomber. Only, no virgins for you in paradise. Seems like a no-win situation."

"Oh, yeah?" Stevie snarled. "Taking you out will probably get me into heaven, you miserable . . ." He raised the button.

"Stevie, no!" Roberta screamed.

He pushed the button. Nothing happened. He mashed it repeatedly. Nothing.

Geller hit the floor laughing. "Oh, this is too much!" he roared. "You are such a freakin' nebbish. You wired it wrong. Oh, jeez, this almost makes all this worthwhile." He dissolved into giggles.

"You asshole! This gun works. Wanna see?" He swung the gun around and aimed it at the rabbi. Lou jumped and hit Stevie with a shoulder, sending the gun flying, and then the door burst open, smashed in by two huge men. Lou recognized Marty from the bakery.

They grabbed Stevie, kicked the gun across the room, and tied him up. Everyone seemed to be in motion. After a few minutes of pandemonium, things settled down.

"Marty," Lou asked, "how the hell did you get here?"

"Got a call from Portland that you were in trouble. They zeroed in on you with GPS, and we came right over."

"Portland? Do you know Herman Brown?"

"The Kid? Sure. He got in touch with us after Woody Biggs died. Biggs and us, we'd been in contact for a long time. Homeless people get around, you know, so there was a regular traffic from Portland to the coast. Up to Waldorf, too. It's been useful."

Lou laughed. "It's certainly been useful to me. When did you get here?"

"Actually, a few minutes ago. We peeked in the window and saw the dynamite." He grinned. "We waited to see if it was going off."

"Very wise." Lou thought a second. "I wonder why this one didn't go off? The other one worked fine. Stevie, what went wrong?"

Stevie grumbled. "Come on," Lou said, "it can't make much difference, now."

"I bought it," he mumbled.

"What?" asked Roberta. "You bought it? Who the hell would sell a bomb?"

"One of the kids I work with." He looked at Lou with defiance. "He makes computers and stuff, wires car stereos. He did it for an ounce of weed and a new video game. I wish I'd had him make two."

"Yeah, I'll bet you do." Lou couldn't squelch a chuckle.

While they spoke, Geller was inching over toward the gun, and Roberta saw him. He lunged toward it, but before he could pick it up, she yelled, "Daddy, no!"

Marty's friend, who looked like a Hells Angel in extra large, was there in two strides, and grabbed the rabbi by the collar. Geller slumped in final defeat.

"Rabbi Geller, I believe that we'll take you directly to the police station," Lou said. "I'm gonna wake up my friend Gar Loober. He might like to make the official arrest."

"Screw you, Tedesco. I don't have to be nice to anyone anymore. Not to my daughter, no one."

"You know, I saw Marv Kronstein just a few hours ago. He told me that he believed that a remnant of the old Bobby Geller might still be there inside of you. You didn't have to try to bargain for our lives, but you did." Lou shook his head. "I know about Mississippi, about Lindy, and about Emily, too. I know that you were once a decent and honorable man. Almost as bad as your wife's death is the death of Bobby Geller. We could use more like him.

"You, the current version? I've seen too many like you the last few years. I have no love for the death penalty, but I know that Tom Knight will push for it. I hope he fails. Maybe the old Bobby will re-emerge and your prison time will be useful."

Geller spat. "Sanctimonious bastard!"

Lou shrugged. "Stick and stones, Geller. Now, I'm calling Chief Loober."

Two days later, things had settled down. Geller was in custody in Waldorf. Jodie Coram was still talking to the DA's office up there, getting the story down. And Lou Tedesco had finally caught up on some sleep.

Roberta and Gary had come to terms with the unspeakable facts. A mother murdered. A philandering father responsible for her death. A family in emotional agony, and the prospect of another relative incarcerated. Stevie was being evaluated by state psychiatrists, and he was assumed to be criminally insane. He was also being interviewed by the FBI and Homeland Security, who were very interested in his bomb-making accomplice.

The group was sitting in the Dunes having a late breakfast. Roberta, Gary, Lou, Hilda, and Connie. No matter what subject came up, the conversation drifted back to recent events.

"Lou," Roberta said, "I think it's time for me and Gary to go home. I can't get any distance from this here."

"Will you come back for your father's trial?"

Her eyes glistened. "He's my father."

They all nodded.

"Did you hear, by the way," Lou asked, "that Lainie Reiter reneged on her agreement with me and ran the story today?"

Connie grimaced. "No honor among thieves, Lou?"

"Thieves, maybe. Reporters? Nah."

Hilda started another thread of conversation, but was interrupted by the appearance of a man dressed in work clothes. He approached the table.

"One of you Lou?"

"I am."

"My name is Chauncey Zerby."

The name rattled around in Lou's mind. "From the white supremacist case, years ago?"

"Yeah. Can we talk?"

Lou looked around. "Pull up a chair. Want some coffee?"

"You sure? In front of everybody?"

"I'm sure." Zerby shrugged, pulled up a chair. Lou signaled for another cup.

"Lou, Bobby Geller wanted me to kill you. He tried to hire me to do it."

Roberta gasped. Everyone froze. Lou cleared his throat. "And?"

"I never answered him. We go back, me and him, you know?"

"I know. What stopped you?" Lou leaned over. "I mean, you're not gonna do it, are you?"

Zerby smiled a wry smile. "No, sir, I'm not. I'll tell you why not. Bobby was once a great man. He changed my mind about a lot of things. Not everything. I'm still strugglin' with a lot.

"But when he asked me to kill you, I knew that we had passed each other goin' in opposite directions. I needed to get this off my chest, that he felt I was capable of this. I done things I'm not proud of, but I ain't that man anymore.

"I didn't really know it until now. I'm free at last."

Phyllis brought over a cup, and Lou filled it.

"Mr. Zerby, I don't know how to thank you. Not only for not taking the job," he grinned at Zerby, "but for having the guts to tell me. Now, you must have seen that an officer of the law is at this table"—Connie started to say something, but Lou kicked her under the table—"and you may need to accompany her back to the station to give her a statement. Is that okay?"

"Yes, sir. In for a penny, in for a pound. The Boss used to say that."

Lou's eyebrows shot up. "The Boss?" He couldn't be talking about Biggs.

"Yeah, the Reverend Malkin. He just may be Bobby's cell-mate up to the prison."

"Did you own a van . . ."

Zerby blushed deeply. "Yeah, that was us." He looked over at Roberta. "I'm sorry I scared you, ma'am, you too, Lou. If we wasn't strapped for money . . . We wasn't gonna hurt you. Just get the book and drive you out to the woods. It's not what we were hired to do, but I couldn't do . . ."

"Do you know who hired you?" Roberta asked.

"I only met the man once, ma'am. Wormy little guy with a Volvo, California plates."

Roberta laughed. Zerby looked puzzled. "Um, somethin' funny, ma' am?"

"Mr. Zerby. I couldn't begin to explain."

"One more thing, if I may?" Lou asked.

"Yes, sir," Zerby replied.

"Why have you decided to come clean now? You didn't have to do this."

"Someone once told me: Sometimes you have to stand up and be counted, and there may be a price for it. I'm paying that price now, I guess."

Connie stood up. "Are you ready to go with me, sir?"

"Yes." He looked at Lou. "I'm sorry." To Roberta. "I'm sorry, ma'am." Connie led him out.

"Hilda," Lou asked, "can this case get any stranger?"

Hours later, in Hilda's big bed, Lou lay with his arms around her. Silvery light broke in through the window as the moon escaped a cloud.

"You awake?" he asked.

"Mmm," she said.

"Hilda, why would a man like Bobby Geller turn out the way he did? A guy who was once willing to risk his life for what was right?"

She made an "I don't know" noise.

"It makes me think that we could all be capable of something like that."

She made a disgusted noise.

Lou was quiet for a while, then, "Hilda?"

"Mmm?"

"Do I look Jewish to you?"

Penguin Group (USA) Online

What will you be reading tomorrow?

Tom Clancy, Patricia Cornwell, W.E.B. Griffin,
Nora Roberts, William Gibson, Robin Cook,
Brian Jacques, Catherine Coulter, Stephen King,
Dean Koontz, Ken Follett, Clive Cussler,
Eric Jerome Dickey, John Sandford,
Terry McMillan, Sue Monk Kidd, Amy Tan,
John Berendt...

You'll find them all at
penguin.com

*Read excerpts and newsletters,
find tour schedules and reading group guides,
and enter contests.*

Subscribe to Penguin Group (USA) newsletters
and get an exclusive inside look
at exciting new titles and the authors you love
long before everyone else does.

PENGUIN GROUP (USA)
us.penguingroup.com